TEMPEST

INFINITY ENGINES BOOK VII

ANDREW HASTIE

This edition published by Here be Dragons Limited 2024

ISBN: 978-1-0683098-0-9

6.2 HB

Dec 2024

To K, A and E. All my love x

We are such stuff
As dreams are made on…

…O brave new world,
That has such people in't.

Other books in the Infinity Engines universe.

The Infinity Engines

1. Anachronist

2. Maelstrom

3. Eschaton

4. Aeons

5. Tesseract

6. Contagion

7. Tempest

Infinity Engines Origins

Chimæra

Changeling

Infinity Engines Missions

1776

1888

Victoria Rex

1

MOCTEZUMA

Mexico Valley. 1519

On an island in the middle of Lake Texcoco stood the city of Tenochtitlán. With over two hundred thousand inhabitants it was one of the largest cities in the world, being nearly five times the size of Henry VIII's London.

The city was the epicentre of the Aztec Empire, which had expanded to an estimated population of over five million in the last hundred years.

At its heart was the palace of Moctezuma II, a grand building containing two zoos, an aquarium and a botanical garden.

In one of its many richly decorated rooms stood the throne of the fire serpent. Fashioned from volcanic stone, the surfaces carved with reliefs of terrifying gods and rituals of human sacrifice.

Moctezuma, a stern-faced man in his mid-forties, sat proudly upon his throne, his leather-brown chest proudly bearing the fine scars of old blood rituals. Around his neck he wore a dazzling golden collar embedded with turquoise and other precious stones. His head dress and cloak were made from brightly coloured quetzal feathers, and the fingers of both hands were adorned with finely crafted gold rings.

He looked every inch the ninth Emperor of the Aztec Empire.

Moctezuma's hooded eyes barely blinked as the captive was ushered into the chamber by an entourage of heavily-tattooed warriors, each carrying a club fletched with obsidian.

The nobles and priests of his court gaped in amazement at the prisoner's white skin and blond hair; this was the first westerner they had ever seen.

They called him *Tlācatēcuhiti*, or "one who comes from across the sea." although no one had actually seen him arrive by boat, nor were there any reports of him travelling through their kingdom.

The stranger was a giant, taller than most of his men by nearly a head. He was dressed in a long leather coat and breeches, with black boots that finished just below the knee. His fair complexion showed hardly any sign of being touched by the sun, not an easy thing to avoid when travelling the long, arduous journey from the coast.

'My Lord,' the stranger addressed him fluently in their native tongue. 'I come before you with the deepest respect and humility.' He bowed his head and knelt before the Emperor.

Moctezuma slowly raised one hand to the guards, who were poised to strike the prostrate man down for his impertinence.

The courtiers whispered amongst themselves, obviously astonished at his ability to speak their language so eloquently.

Keeping one wary eye on the guards, the stranger drew a long silver blade with an ornately woven metal hilt and held it out to the King.

'My name is Silas Wormwood, and I bring you this gift as a tribute and a token of friendship,' he continued, using the reverential dialect of a nobleman. 'It is forged from Toledo steel, the hardest and most deadly of all metals.'

Silas slowed his breathing, this was the moment of truth. Bowing his head, he closed his eyes and reached out with his mind, feeling for the consciousness of the Emperor.

For as long as he could remember, Silas had always been able to 'push' people, a subtle adjustment of their mental state to tip things in his favour. It was a rare talent, but one that had saved his life on more than one occasion.

The Aztec leader was no different from any of his other marks. His interest was already piqued by the beautiful weapon, reinforcing the fascination was simple, like turning up the dial on a stereo.

Silas opened his eyes and smiled. *Got you.*

Moctezuma paused, a moment of confusion crossing his face, then nodded to one of his advisers who stepped forward and took the sword from Silas's hands.

Examining the blade, the emperor's dark eyes widened as he tested the keenness of its edge with his thumb. His court gasped at the sight of blood that ran down the shining side of the sword.

Moctezuma stood, shrugging off his cloak while his minions attended to the head dress. There was a considered grace to his movements as he stepped down from the dais and motioned to one of the guards to come forward.

The room fell silent as the brute of a man approached and knelt before his master, his face upturned.

The emperor raised the sword and took off his head with one scything arc.

Everyone in the chamber cried out in astonishment when

the man's corpse fell to the floor and then clapped eagerly at their leader's prowess at mastering the weapon.

As the body was dragged away, Silas began to wonder if he would be next.

'You have more of these?' Moctezuma said, levelling the sword at him.

'No my Lord, but I can teach you how to make them,' Silas replied quickly, his eyes focused on the unwavering tip of the blade. The shock of the execution was making it hard to think clearly. Silas never liked the sight of blood, and there was a large pool of it gathering around his knees.

The Aztec leader nodded his head slowly. 'My scouts tell me there are others coming. Red-haired men from great wooden ships, with many of these.'

Silas knew that Hernán Cortés and his conquistadors had already landed on the Yucatán Peninsula with an expeditionary force of approximately six hundred men. According to his research, it would be less than seven months before they would arrive in the Capital.

'They are coming my King, with other, more deadly weapons.'

'We have much to discuss,' Moctezuma replied, motioning to Silas to stand. 'Come, let us eat.'

The banqueting hall of the palace looked out over the lake and the lush valley beyond. It was an idyllic location and an impressive city.

Silas studied the correspondence between Cortés and the King of Spain in preparation for this mission. The conquistador was clearly impressed by the sophistication of the city's infrastructure; describing intricate causeways and aqueducts that carried fresh water into the city.

More importantly, the Spanish chroniclers had drawn maps of the city, adding detail on the most significant buildings, including the massive temple complex dedicated to the Aztec god *Huitzilopochtli,* which housed the most precious of ancient artefacts and the one that his client was keen to possess: The Skull of Doom.

Huitzilopochtli was the god of war, believed to imbue their warriors with strength and courage, but also one that required human sacrifice.

Silas knew this would be a dangerous assignment; the kind that would require his specialist skills. The risk came at a premium, no one came to him unless they could afford it.

He was an Acquirer, a freelance agent, working for discerning collectors willing to pay for the most rare and in many cases, sinister artefacts, more commonly referred to as "Dark Relics".

The Skull of Doom was carved from a single piece of quartz crystal, and was said to have been a centre piece to the ritual slaughter of thousands of Aztec sacrifices. It was believed to absorb the souls of the victims, something his client was particularly interested in.

Silas never concerned himself with the provenance of a relic, except when it increased its value.

What was more distracting was the gold that hung around the necks of Moctezuma and his courtiers. As they dined on the lavish banquet of tortillas, tamales, avocado, fish and tropical fruits, Silas's keen mind couldn't help but estimate the accumulated wealth of each of the guests.

'So, what is it that you require in return for this knowledge?' the King finally asked, holding up a golden goblet for a serving girl to refill.

'I merely wish to serve you,' Silas lied, raising a silver cup which was still half full of Atole that had been flavoured with vanilla.

'These men who come from the East, what do they seek?'

The King spoke quickly and his words were hard to translate, Silas had only intuited the lexicon of *Nahuatl* twelve hours ago and it was still bedding in.

'Conquistadors. From a land across the great ocean. They seek wealth and land,' Silas said, nodding towards the King's necklace. 'And gold.'

'They are conquerors?'

Silas nodded. 'With very advanced weapons,' he replied, struggling to find the nearest equivalent term.

The history books described the conquest of the Aztecs by the Spanish as a clash of the modern world against the Bronze Age. Moctezuma's people had not yet developed the skills needed to make steel, and certainly never fought against an army armed with muskets or cannons.

There was a certain satisfaction in giving them the technology they needed to defend themselves. Even though it was forbidden under the directives of the Oblivion Order, Silas didn't care, he had never been in favour of the Copernican's constant fiddling with history for the greater good of mankind. As far as he was concerned, it was a dog-eat-dog world, and he tended to favour the underdog every time.

He smiled inwardly at the thought of all the years of unravelling that Professor Eddington and his actuaries would face from this one simple change.

In the original timeline, six hundred conquistadors marched into the Mexico valley with a superior military advantage and wiped out a civilisation – but that was all about to change.

Once Moctezuma had successfully repelled the invaders, Silas would be able to ask for anything he wanted in return.

The Skull would be a suitable reward, and he was pretty sure he could find a buyer for that necklace too.

Map Room, Copernican HQ, 1688

'Sir, I think I've located the change agent,' said Sim, his face illuminated by lines of scrolling glyphs as he stared down into the view-screen of his holoscope.

The Map Room was packed with actuaries all studying various parts of the continuum. Professor Eddington stood in the centre of the space studying the ever-changing map of the last twelve thousand years that revolved around him.

'You think!' the professor snapped, his hands a blur as he manipulated the hologram. 'Have you forgotten the first principle Master Simeon?'

Assess the probability, Sim reminded himself, knowing how much Eddington hated uncertainty. He narrowed his eyes, adjusting the dials on the side of his scope and the symbols slowed until the lines of probability converged on one date.

'There is a ninety point five per cent possibility that he's currently located at 11.519-04.' As he read off the holocene date, Sim's mind was already processing the most significant events of that year.

Eddington's arms moved with the grace of an orchestral conductor, finding the point in the four-dimensional model with relative ease. 'Location?'

Sim paused, looking up from his screen, unsure of how his master would take the information – he knew it had potentially serious consequences.

'Mexico, Tenochtitlán.'

The professor froze, his eyes glaring at Sim over dark-rimmed spectacles. Worry lines furrowed his forehead and his voice faltered slightly when he spoke.

'Cortés?'

'No sir, Moctezuma II, seven months before Hernan Cortés arrives. From the nature of the bifurcation there is a seventy-four per cent probability the agent is trading knowledge related to weapons. It's highly likely the conquistadors will now lose the military advantage against the Aztec.'

'Highly likely!' the professor exclaimed. His sudden outburst causing the other actuaries to look up from their work. 'Be precise Master Simeon. What is the statistical probability?'

Sim tried to hide his blushes, looking down at the screen. 'There is a ninety-six point two probability that the Spanish expedition will fail.'

Eddington nodded, his expression hardening as he turned back to the model and focused on the point in time. Numerous lines of possibility were branching out from it and none of them seemed to lighten his mood.

'Notify the Protectorate that we have a confirmed breach of the Prime Directive. Have them assign an investigator immediately and inform them that we will monitor the situation from here.'

Sim did as instructed, trying to control the shaking of his hand as he wrote the message into his almanac. This was the first time he had been involved in an actual criminal investigation. The older actuaries would discuss them in hushed tones in the canteen. The involvement of the temporal police was not something to be wished on your worst enemy, not that Sim had any. The Protectorate suspected everyone and were generally despised by the other guilds.

During the formation of their Order, there were some factions who refused to join, who saw the Prime Directive as an infringement of their civil rights. Others were mavericks, selfish renegades with a talent to travel through time and no interest in preserving the past for the greater good of the continuum. They treated the past as their personal treasure trove, plundering it for their own gain.

They had numerous names: Outlaws, Rogues, Dark Dealers or Acquirers, and there was even rumoured to be a

Dark Guild, called the Syndicate, but no one really spoke about them and Sim wasn't sure whether they really existed.

Except now he had actually located one of their kind, and was about to assist in his capture. He took a deep breath. This was shaping up to be one of the most exciting days of his career.

Seconds later a response from the Protectorate dispatcher arrived in an elegant copperplate, if not a little terse:

OFFICER 29109 ALLOCATED.

Maastricht, Netherlands. 1673.

It was the height of summer and the heat inside the city walls was becoming unbearable. Inspector Sabien stood on the battlements above the Tongeren Gate, casually swatting away the mosquitoes as he watched the French army dig a series of parallel trenches and embankments in front of the walls.

It was an impressive sight. According to the notes in his almanac, the siege was being overseen by the famous French engineer Sébastien Le Prestre de Vauban and personally by King Louis XIV.

The Siege of Maastricht would last fifteen days, but that was not why he was here. Somewhere behind him, in the walled city, the Prince-Bishop of Liège, Maximilian Henry of Bavaria, was about to be murdered – a contract killing by a notorious assassin from the Syndicate, known only as L'Oscurità, or "The Darkness".

Sabien had been shadowing the Prince-Bishop for the last four weeks, watching his timeline for any sign of the elusive hit-man who managed to avoid all the usual traps he laid out for him.

Rumour was that the Habsburgs had ordered his assassination. It was supposed to occur during a secret meeting that Maximilian was attending inside the city – some political shenanigans to do with the succession of the Holy Roman Empire.

The information had come from a suspect Sabien arrested three months earlier for memory trading. The man was only too willing to give up L'Oscurità in exchange for his freedom. The assassin was on the Protectorate's most wanted list and information leading to his arrest was worthy of a plea bargain.

Although Sabien was beginning to believe the man was pulling his leg.

Memory trading was deeply frowned upon by the Order. Taking memories without consent was a first degree crime and came with a heavy sentence.

It was a lucrative business on the black market, especially the memories of notorious figures from history or witnesses to terrible events. In most cases the victims of these crimes suffered permanent mental health issues, since the practitioners were not expert redactors.

He would get twenty years in the Château and another ten for wasting police time.

Sabien's tachyon began to vibrate, signalling the arrival of a priority message from dispatch. He took out his almanac and read the note. It was from headquarters, the incident was categorised as a 25-10: "The transfer of future knowledge to a primitive civilisation."

The temporal location was only a hundred and fifty years from his current era, making him the nearest available officer. Tagged as urgent, which meant it overrode the current investigation he was working on, Sabien acknowledged receipt of the message and put away his almanac. He knew better than to challenge a priority directive, even though a twenty-five-ten was not usually rated above a homicide.

The selling of future knowledge was one of the more common offences amongst the lower ranks of the Syndicate. Known as "Chroniclers", the perpetrator required nothing more than the ability to memorise a certain amount of information.

There were those who became specialists, some of his previous cases included offenders who could recite entire technical manuals after one read. These were naturally gifted savants with photographic memories, but there were also drugs that could help – which were also illegal. Their street name was 'Recall', and while it did temporarily increase the user's ability to retain a colossal amount of data, the long term effects led to dementia and in some cases complete memory loss.

Giving a primitive civilisation advanced knowledge was a dangerous game, one that caused the Copernicans no end of problems, but that was their concern; all Sabien had to do was catch them.

Something that he was very good at.

He adjusted the dials of his tachyon to the temporal coordinates in the message and felt the time-lines unravel around him.

Temple of Huitzilopochtli, Tenochtitlán. 1519

The towering temple to the god of war dominated the city, casting long shadows over the bustling streets below. It was one of two vast stepped pyramids, each an awe-inspiring monument to their patron god and a testament to the unyielding power of their capital—where life and death were intertwined.

Walking in procession, Silas followed Moctezuma and his

feather-cloaked priests as they mounted the steep steps towards the temple at its apex.

The sun was setting over lake Texcoco, turning it a shimmering amber. The last of the fisherman were paddling their way back in canoes filled with fish. It was a breathtaking sight, one that Silas knew would end tragically in less than a year once the Spanish arrived.

After the banquet, Moctezuma had invited him to witness a sacrifice. The Emperor declared that it was necessary to celebrate their new alliance.

Apparently it was a great honour, one that could not be refused. Although, it wasn't something that Silas envisaged in his original plan, he was obviously relieved not to be the offering.

An hour later, he found himself inside a ritual slaughterhouse.

The crystal skull rested in a recess on a carved stone altar. Like many of the other carvings that decorated the walls of the pyramid, it appeared to depict various gods devouring parts of their human sacrifices.

Silas was beginning to regret eating so much at the banquet. Exotic herbs were burning in clay dishes around the edges of the temple, but the smoke failed to mask the lingering scent of death.

His stomach began to churn.

An old priest smiled, noticing the colour draining out of the stranger's face. He handed him a small piece of resin and motioned him to chew on it.

Silas did as he was told, surprised to find the taste was refreshing and the texture similar to chewing gum. The nausea passed quickly and he felt the colour returning to his cheeks.

It was only then that he remembered about their use of psychoactive drugs like mescaline and discreetly spat it out.

As Moctezuma and his priests gathered around the altar, one of his unfortunate prisoners was brought out by the guards and stretched prostrate over the stone.

From the frantic pleading of the victim, Silas gathered he was from a neighbouring tribe known as the Tlaxcalans. Long-time rivals of the Aztecs, they would eventually form an alliance with Cortés in an attempt to overthrow their enemies, but that was yet to come.

The head priest was accusing him of aiding the Spanish, which the prisoner fiercely denied. The man wore a silver crucifix around his neck which he claimed he'd taken from a conquistador he killed.

One of the men produced an obsidian blade and passed it to the priest. Holding it aloft, the holy man recited an ancient rite, bowing his head towards the crystal skull, before passing it to his king.

As Moctezuma leaned over the prone body of his victim, Silas felt a cold shiver run down his spine. Not from the fear of what he was about to witness, but the all-too-familiar precursor to a temporal shift somewhere close by.

It was something he could sense since he was a child; an ability that his family had used to their advantage – they used to call him "the canary".

Sure enough it was only a matter of seconds before the Protectorate officer appeared in the doorway of the temple.

His survival instincts kicked in. Rushing forwards, Silas grabbed the skull from the altar and as Moctezuma's guards raised their weapons, he ripped the crucifix from the prisoner's neck and opened its timeline, disappearing into thin air.

. . .

In the midst of the chaos, Sabien calmly retreated into the shadows and opened an audio channel on his tachyon.

'Officer 29109 requesting immediate trace on Silas Wormwood, last known location 11-519-04.'

'Patching you through,' came the calm voice of the Protectorate dispatcher.

There were a series of whirrs and clicks as the temporal communications network redirected the call to the Copernican monitoring station.

'This is Actuary Simeon De Freis, Inspector. I have a lead on the suspect, sending you the coordinates now.'

Medellín, Spain. 1485

Silas appeared inside the dusty courtyard of a medieval castle. Falling to his knees, he could feel his heart hammering in his chest and it took several deep breaths to calm himself. The drugs the priest gave him were making it hard to think straight and he needed every neuron to be firing right now.

In his haste, Silas had followed the timeline of the crucifix. It was instinctive, not the carefully prepared escape route that years of experience had taught him to plan for. The patronising voice of his father echoed in his head. 'Never enter a room you can't get out of boy. Always have an exit strategy,' he could still hear the words so clearly. 'Never enter a room without knowing two ways to leave it.'

It was advice the man neglected to take himself on the day he was captured.

Opening his fist, he studied the silver cross. Briefly scanning the lines of its past, he quickly realised it had led him to the birthplace of Hernán Cortés. Whoever the sacrifice had stolen it from was obviously a close friend of the leader of the Spanish expedition.

It was a valuable gift. One that Silas knew would have some worth on the Dark Market, should he make it out of here in one piece.

This was the closest he had come to being caught since his parents were arrested. Whoever was tracking him was good, to appear less than ten feet away took real skill and there were few Crows who could pull it off. That was the name they gave the Protectorate, mainly because of their black uniforms. If the copper was that clever he was going to need to put more distance between them.

Silas placed the crucifix in one of his many pockets and got to his feet. Orientating himself, he looked around the courtyard for something of suitable age to make his next jump, but there was nothing except farm equipment, a few chickens and pigs.

He spotted a leather gamekeeper's satchel hanging on a rack of rabbits drying in the sun, placed the skull carefully inside the bag and moved quickly into the shadows.

It must have been an impressive fortress in its heyday. With thick, sturdy walls, tall towers and battlements that had clearly seen their fair share of action.

Silas ran his fingers over the crumbling stone. Natural materials were notoriously difficult to read, but amongst the fragmented moments he learned that it was a defensive outpost reaching all the way back to the Roman occupation of these lands.

Lifting his hand from the wall, he felt the cold prickling sensation on the back of his neck once more and ran towards the main gate.

Inspector Sabien took off his glove as he knelt down and touched the footprints in the sand. The traces of the suspect's timeline were nothing more than a faint echo, but it was enough to confirm he had been here seconds before. Getting to his feet, he let the grains slip through his fingers, and brushed the dust off his palm. There was too little to work with, even for him.

'Subject is two hundred yards south of your location,' came the voice of the actuary in his earpiece.

'Understood,' replied Sabien, turning towards the main gate.

The Castillo de Medellín stood on a hill overlooking the Guadiana River. Silas careened down the dusty track towards the town. It was a hot day, and sweat ran down into his eyes as he negotiated the steep slope. He could hear the boots of the officer a few hundred yards behind him, but didn't dare look back.

Spotting the ruins of an old amphitheatre carved into the side of the hill, Silas left the path and scrambled down the bank towards it.

Sabien saw the man disappear below the edge of the track and stepped up his pace.

'Suspect has entered a Roman ruin. Do you have any details?' he asked, climbing over the rocks to get a better view.

'The amphitheater dates back to the first century AD, during the Roman occupation of the Iberian Peninsula. It was likely constructed during the reign of Emperor Augustus,' came the response.

Silas was nearing the bottom of the rows of stone benches when he saw the officer appear above him. He recognised him immediately.

'Sabien,' he cursed under his breath. 'Of course, it would have to be you.'

This was not their first chase, although it was a few years since they last crossed paths. The Protectorate Inspector was one of the best. The Syndicate had a name for him, "Thief-taker General". It was a mark of respect to acknowledge his existence at all, and to give him an honorific was reserved for the elite, bestowed on those responsible for putting many of their Guild behind bars.

Reaching the floor of the auditorium, Silas found it over-grown with brambles and bushes. Realising there was no easy way out, he frantically searched for the floor for anything that might have a timeline. It wouldn't take much, he'd once used the head of Cleopatra's hairpin to make his escape.

Closing his eyes, Silas calmed his breathing and cleared his mind which was still clouded with the after-effects of the drugs.

He opened himself to the surroundings. It was one of the first games his mother taught him as a child – a way to find lost things; "skimming" she called it – little did he know that the coins and rings he found in the drains and gutters were not hers.

His heightened senses allowed him to visualise the temporal vibrations of the world around him. Tiny pinpricks of colour appeared inside his mind like a thermal imaging camera. He quickly picked up something lying on the floor under a rotting timber. Sliding his fingers under the worm-ridden wood, he found a tarnished old belt buckle. Brushing away the dirt Silas felt the bronze warm to his touch, and there it was, a beautiful line weaving back over a thousand years.

· · ·

'This is getting us nowhere,' Sabien said to himself, stepping down into the arena. He opened a channel to the Copernicans once more. 'Can't you estimate where he'll be next? I need to get ahead of him.'

Battle of Sucro, Hispania 75BC.

Silas found himself in the midst of a pitched battle on the banks of a wide river. Confusingly, both armies seemed to consist of Roman Legionnaires and an assortment of what he assumed were local Celtic tribes.

The sound of metal clashing against metal drowned out the cries of the injured and dying as the opposing forces slaughtered each other in the cloying mud.

Trying not to retch at the sight of so much blood and gore, he made his way through the melée towards higher ground. The smell of sweat and death was overpowering.

Silas had never liked violence, there had been too much of it in his house growing up. His father was quick-tempered and a mean drunk. They all bore the scars. Being this close to so much brutality brought it all back. He could see the same wild look in the eyes of the men around them, they were like rabid animals filled with insane rage.

There was always a danger with rapid jumps that things could go wrong. There was no time for the usual safety protocols, the ones that ensured you didn't find yourself inside an active volcano or a heaving mass of what appeared to be two rival Roman armies – one of which was being assisted by a horde of blue-faced berserkers.

Dodging various sword strikes and spear thrusts, Silas wove between the warriors. The conflict was clearly escalating and neither side seemed to be gaining any ground.

A spear point burst through the chest of a legionnaire

directly in front of him and the man fell to the ground. Without a second thought, Silas knelt down and took hold of the soldier's sword, feeling for a path into its history, and shifted further back in time.

Rome. 42 BC.

Inspector Sabien waited patiently in the cool shadows of the Temple of Saturn. It was late morning and the sun shone down from a cloudless sky, painting the streets of Rome in a warm golden light. The Senate were slowly making their way across the square towards the Forum. Watching from between the massive columns of the grand temple, Sabien followed the slow progress of the elderly senators as their entourage wove through the bustling marketplace.

'Are you sure he's coming here?' he whispered.

'Yes, there's a ninety-three per cent probability he will appear in the next five minutes,' replied the actuary through his earpiece.

Sim was being cautious, in truth it was actually slightly higher, but he knew better than to use the upper ranges in his temporal calculations – fate always tended to favour the worst case scenario.

'He used a buckle of a centurion in the amphitheatre to shift back to the Sertorian War. The war began when General Quintus Sertorius was exiled from Rome after his opposition to the dictator Sulla and went to Hispania to join the forces of Gaius Marius.'

'So how do you know he's not still there?'

'Your suspect miscalculated his entry vector and landed in the middle of heavy fighting. There was a high probability he would take the first opportunity to leave that encounter and the most likely escape route would be via the equipment of a fallen soldier. The Senate sent General Lucullus to Hispania to suppress the Sertorian rebellion, his forces took the heaviest casualties. Statistically it is more likely that your suspect would follow it back to Rome.'

Sabien was not convinced. He hated pursuits like this, even with the help of the Copernicans they were generally hopeless tasks. There were too many blind alleys and forgotten paths, with every jump it became harder to follow.

He walked around to the Basilica Julia and sat down at the top of the steps, adjusting his cloak to conceal his uniform. It was an unnecessary gesture, the passing citizens and their slaves ignored him, the temporal shielding of his armour made it difficult for casual observers to focus on his appearance – their eyes would simply slide away.

The sudden clatter of shields and the sound of marching announced the arrival of the Praetorian guard. Parting the crowds, an elite unit of soldiers escorted two of the most powerful leaders of the Roman Empire, Octavian and Mark Antony, on their way to the House of the Senate.

'Octavian was the adopted son of Julius Caesar, who would one day become the first Roman Emperor, Augustus, but at this point in time he was part of the second triumvirate, with Mark Antony and Lepidus. It was a power sharing partnership put in place after the assassination of Caesar,' continued Sim.

This was a tumultuous time in Rome's history, the rivalry between the powerful members of the triumvirate would eventually lead to civil war and the end of the Roman Republic.

Sabien rose to his feet, one hand instinctively going to his tachyon as a voice chimed in his ear.

'He's here, look to your left.'

The inspector moved his head slowly until he glimpsed the figure moving through the crowd, unaware of his presence.

He followed the man until they were clear of the main square and then quickened his pace.

The snap of the temporal handcuffs was a satisfying sound as he closed it around the man's wrist.

'Silas Wormwood, you're under arrest.'

2

SHADOW REALM

Founder's study. 1688

The Grand Seer appeared to be having an argument with himself as he sat across the mahogany table from Professor Eddington and Lord Dee. Both were waiting patiently for him to resolve whatever it was that was bothering him. Oblivious to their impatience Kelly continued to leaf through one of Lyra's journals, muttering over notes and illustrations like a drunk struggling to remember a half-forgotten conversation.

Eddington cleared his throat, clearly irritated by the Grand Seer's indifference to their presence.

'As I was saying my Lord. There is no actual evidence of a "Wanderer" nor any reports of unusual activity in the early twentieth century. Especially no mention of demons.' He emphasised the last word with something of a sneer.

The founder nodded, sitting forward and pouring himself another glass of wine. 'Edward, I have to agree with Arthur. I've been aware of this so-called "Shadow Realm" for some time, but mainly due to the work of Emily Williams. I assumed it was nothing more than an enclave, one of

Belsarus's so-called "mirror dimensions". Not the breeding ground for a malevolent host of wraiths and Demi-gods.'

'Nor did I until I saw it with my own eyes,' Kelly said, picking up the book entitled "The Wanderer, by E.M.Williams", and began to read aloud from the frontispiece.

'In the dusky corners of existence, where time's hand wavers and shadows dance, lies a realm veiled from mortal sight.' Kelly swept his hand theatrically through the air as if conjuring a spirit. 'Therein, mysteries unsolved and truths untold whisper softly, beckoning daring souls to tread where light fears to reach. Yet, beware the allure of such realms, for in their depths, time's tapestry frays and the echoes of forgotten whispers may ensnare the unwary traveller in a web of unending night.'

The founder sat back in his chair and sighed. 'Dear Emily was quite the poet, may she rest in peace, but that leaves us no clearer on the origins of the realm, nor this so-called "Wanderer".'

The Grand Seer closed the book and placed it on the table. 'The Old King's paths wind further back than the days of man.'

'And Lyra De Freis has travelled many of them, or so we've been led to believe,' Eddington added, steepling his long fingers. 'Did you not think it would have been pertinent to bring her to this meeting?'

Kelly shrugged. 'She is but a heartbeat away.'

He clicked his fingers and seconds later Lyra stepped out from a long mirror at the back of the room. The young seer looked frail, her face pale and her eyes darkly circled. She was hugging a small satchel.

The founder rose to his feet. 'Lyra, my dear, how good it is to see you. How are you?'

'A little cloudy, my Lord,' she replied, performing the smallest of curtseys and going to sit beside the Grand Seer.

The founder struggled to think of a suitable response. 'Oh,

well, yes. Anyway, we've been discussing your report,' he continued, retaking his seat. 'This outbreak of demonic activity in 1914, you believe it originates from the Shadow Realm and not from the Maelstrom?'

Lyra nodded and cleared her throat. 'I do. I've checked with my brother, Simeon,' she glanced towards Eddington who narrowed his eyes slightly at the mention of his actuary. 'There are no reports of any breaches during that period. The Old King, Abandon, took possession of a man before my very eyes. I was able to send him back, but he was clearly not of this continuum nor the chaos realm.'

Professor Eddington huffed and crossed his arms.

The founder ignored him. 'So it seems.' He turned to another page in her report. 'And this so-called "Department of Psychical Research", can you tell us more of this group?'

Lyra took a deep breath and explained how she came to meet King George's extraordinary gentleman. How they rescued her from drowning in Loch Ness and captured the Spirit Dragon, Shenlong, the war room under the Tower of London and their ongoing battle with the demonic forces around the world.

The others listened intently, but it was clear from the deep furrowing of the professor's brow that he had never heard of them.

'And you say they've been fighting this war for some time?' asked the founder.

Lyra nodded. 'For over a hundred years.'

'A vampire, a werewolf and a dragon?' Eddington said, unable to hide his disbelief from his voice. 'Whatever next? Unicorns?'

'There are more things in Heaven and Earth, Horatio,' quoted the Grand Seer.

'There are many stranger things in the Shadow Realm,' added Lyra, producing a stack of her journals from her leather satchel and placing them in a neat pile on the table.

'The Grand Seer told us you've been following in the steps of Ms Williams, trying to map the paths,' the founder continued, picking up one of the books and flicking through the pages.

Lyra beamed with pride, like a student presenting her science project to the class. 'I've been doing it for as long as I can remember. I discovered them when I was a child. It was the only place that quietened the voices.' She waved her hands around her head. 'You're all quite noisy.'

'I've heard enough of this. I have more pressing matters to deal with.' Eddington said, clearly troubled by the discussion. He got to his feet and walked towards the door.

'This is serious! I think there's been some kind of weakening of the chronosphere,' Lyra insisted, turning to the Grand Seer for support. 'Like a crack in the mirror. Things are seeping through into the continuum.'

'Maybe that, 'tis a dark and ancient magic for sure,' Kelly agreed.

The professor scoffed. 'There is no evidence of any such thing and there is certainly no sign of a breach.' He turned back towards them. 'We would have detected it in the algorithm!'

And with that he left.

The founder handed the journal back to Lyra. 'You'll have to excuse the professor, Copernicans are not the most open-minded of people. I'm sure he will be instructing his guild to run further tests. In the meantime,' He looked over toward the mirror, 'I think it wise to resist entering the realm until I've had the xenobiologyst's report.'

Lyra looked surprised. 'You're going to send Doctor Shika into the realm?'

The old man nodded. 'I have already sent instructions to prepare for the expedition.'

'I want to go with her!' she demanded. 'I know the paths better than anyone.'

The Grand Seer tilted his head towards the founder and smiled. 'There is none better to be sure.'

The founder considered the idea for a moment, stroking his beard into a point. 'I'll leave that to Kaori. She will be leading the mission. If she agrees then I will not stand in your way.'

Lyra smiled, picked up her journals and placed them back in her satchel.

'She'll say yes, I know it.'

3

PROTECTORATE

Protectorate HQ

Quite possibly the most annoying part of his job, Sabien concluded, was the ridiculous amount of paperwork that needed to be completed after a temporal pursuit.

Protectorate procedure stipulated that every temporal interaction was to be documented and submitted on a separate form, one for every time period.

Since the suspect managed to shift through four separate eras in less than ten minutes, each one of the locations was now effectively a crime scene. They would need to be forensically examined to ensure nothing was left behind or changed in a significant way that would constitute a threat to the future.

The prisoner told the custody sergeant his name was Sebastian Hawthorne, but Sabien knew it was just one of many pseudonyms.

His real name was Silas Wormwood, and he had very good reasons to disavow that particular surname.

The folder sitting on Sabien's desk was impressively thick, one of the largest he'd ever seen. It was a testament to the

Wormwood family's illustrious career on the wrong side of the law.

Taking a sip of his coffee, he opened the file and began by checking the register of open warrants on Silas. There were three outstanding as well as a dozen other crimes that he was wanted for questioning. Everything from dealing in drugs like Hindsight, which gave the user the temporary abilities of a Seer, to dealing in dark relics and knowledge trading.

Taking a sip of his coffee, Sabien settled back in his chair and reacquainted himself with the old case notes.

Silas was the youngest son of a notorious criminal family; there was a long list of Wormwoods on file, each generation worse than the last.

The boy was first apprehended at the age of nine, working for his parents who were gang leaders of a 'Firm' established by his Great-Great-Grandfather over a hundred years before he was born. Between them and the extended collection of siblings, cousins and other dubious progeny, the Wormwoods were responsible for a litany of crimes and organised extortions that the linears would describe as a Mafia.

Apart from Silas, the surviving members were all serving custodial sentences in maximum security prisons – it was inevitable that he would join them eventually.

The boy's fate had been sealed from the day he was conceived.

Sabien was a little surprised to read that, after the arrest of his parents when he was twelve, the Order placed the child under the care of Rufius Westinghouse, a man not widely known for his fostering skills. The old watchman took him under his wing for a while, but as Sabien suspected, his apprenticeship ended badly.

Westinghouse refused to support his application to join the Watch and they parted ways soon after Silas's sixteenth birthday, with Silas joining another watchman by the name of Gideon Ravenscroft. What happened next was a mystery, the records were missing.

'Good catch today, Michael,' said his boss, Chief Inspector Avery, standing in the doorway. 'I'm assuming that you'll want to lead on the questioning?'

'Sure,' replied Sabien, putting down the folder. 'Did you ever have any dealings with the Wormwoods?'

Avery sucked air in through his teeth. 'I was only a constable back then when George Wormwood succeeded his father, still wet behind the ears. He's a nasty piece of work, the spitting image of his old man – the apple didn't fall that far from the tree with that one. And his wife's no better. She was the only daughter of the Flemings, possibly the most detestable bunch of swindlers you could ever meet. Within two years they had become the King and Queen of the Syndicate. Silas didn't stand a chance growing up amongst that rookery of villains. Rumour has it that George got so drunk once, he went back to kill his own grandfather just because someone bet him it would end his existence.'

'I'm guessing he didn't go through with it.'

Avery laughed. 'He did, but it turns out the man wasn't his grandfather after all. Which doesn't surprise me in the slightest.'

'But you caught them?'

The Chief Inspector nodded and turned towards the door. 'With a little help from Westinghouse. Back then he was serving as a Praetorian, protecting the Romanovs. We were too late to save the family, and the Revolution screwed any chance of correcting the timeline. We caught both of them in the Winter Palace, celebrating in the bedchamber of Catherine the Great. They're serving an endless sentence in the bowels of the Château.'

Château D'If was a temporal prison built on an island in the Bay of Marseille. More commonly known as "Château Death", it was the Order's equivalent of Alcatraz. Prisoners who were sent there never returned to the continuum.

'So what happened with Westinghouse?' Sabien asked as they walked down the stairs to the cells. 'Why did he take on the boy?'

The Chief Inspector shrugged. 'I suppose he felt guilty about depriving him of his family. He tried to take Silas under his wing. The kid was a very talented redactor, and a respectable time runner to boot, but the damage had been done. His parents really did a number on him. The records are still sealed of course, but he was basically feral, even the irascible old bastard had to admit defeat.'

Walking down the final flight of steps, the cries of the inmates rose to greet them. Like caged animals they howled and spat curses as they passed. Dirty hands appeared through the bars of the cells holding tin cups and plates, which they clanged together, alerting everyone to their approach.

'Calm down!' shouted the Captain of the Guard, marching towards Sabien and Avery. 'Or there'll be no pudding.'

He was a heavy-set man with one good eye. The other was covered by a patch. This, as every one knew in both the Protectorate and criminal fraternity alike, was Albert Jackson, more commonly known as "One-Eyed Jack".

He wore a long coat with a thick leather belt, on which he kept a wooden truncheon with a brass cudgel.

'Chief,' he greeted Avery, touching his finger to his cap. 'You be here to see Wormwood's boy I'm guessing.'

'I am indeed,' Avery said. 'Lead the way Jack.'

The prisoners fell silent as the guard walked along the stone corridor. Sabien recognised some of them. They were mostly small-time dealers and thieves from the lower ranks, and the most stupid.

The clever ones used them to do their dirty work. These were the expendables, the foot soldiers of the Dark Guild known as the Syndicate.

The cells in the basement of the Protectorate building were constructed from materials with no past, they had been temporally excised of any history.

Detaining a temporal criminal was not a simple task, since the chronology of any normal object could be used to escape. Even One-Eye's clothing had to be kept in a state of flux. In the early days, the Protectorate had used objects from plague ships or leper colonies, undesirable histories that only a fool would choose to take his chances with.

It had taken the work of a brilliant scientist by the name of Alexander Templeton to create a quantum material that was in a permanent nascent state. Coating an object with Temporalite eradicated its history, effectively wiping its memory. It had very little practical use outside of the prison system, but to the Protectorate it was a godsend.

4

XENOS

Xenobiology Lab, Regents Park, London. Present day.

Doctor Shika closed the lid on her laptop and rubbed her temples, trying to soothe the lingering headache behind her eyes.

'More coffee,' she said to herself, going over to the machine.

She had not slept well. Her dreams were plagued by the disturbing memories of her ghast, Ophelia. The harrowing visions of long-dead worlds and the hideous things that dwelled within, lingered in the corners of her mind like cigar smoke after a dinner party.

Ophelia was her symbiote, a non-corporeal entity from the Maelstrom, that bonded with Kaori during a disastrous mission involving a pod of Nethersharks and a defective stun lance. At the time, it saved her life, so a few nightmares were a small price to pay.

She poured herself another cup of black coffee and went back to her desk.

. . .

Opening her laptop once more, the research on the so-called "Shadow Realm" reappeared. It was extremely light on detail compared to the vast libraries of scientific data her department had gathered on the Maelstrom, but that took years to compile and was still nowhere near complete.

The most exhaustive work to date was a small book by a Scriptorian named E.M. Williams. Written over a hundred years ago – it read more like a children's ghost story rather than an empirical study.

Its primary sources appeared to be myths and folklore, oral traditions gathered from hearsay and superstition. Williams's basic hypothesis proposed there were ancient paths running through redundant or forgotten sections of time, dead branches that failed to collapse when the continuum took another route.

After years of extensive research, Williams concluded that the paths were constructed during pre-history by an entity who passed into legend as the "Old King", one the Nordic bards referred to as "The Wanderer", or Odin to give him his proper name. According to her book, the Old King possessed a deep primordial power that had since been lost but whose paths remained, hidden behind mirrors, running parallel to their own.

If it wasn't for her experience with Belsarus, Kaori would have laughed at the thought of it. But in his attempts to travel into the future, the eccentric inventor inadvertently proved there were other dimensions. She had seen one with her own eyes. There was a portal to a mirrorverse twenty floors below her feet, a pocket universe where the universal rules did not apply.

Taking a sip of the coffee, she scrolled through the other documents in the directory until she came to the latest entry:

a report made by Rufius Westinghouse after an attempt to rescue Lyra Cousineau.

Kaori put down her cup and opened the file, which was unsurprisingly short. The watchman was not one for paperwork. In all the years that she had known Westinghouse, she couldn't think of many occasions when the cantankerous old bugger had ever followed procedure. He was too old, too set in his ways, it wasn't in his nature – which was probably why she liked him so much.

Rufius described his venture into the Shadow Realm as: "a dark and ominous place, filled with echoes of forgotten things," and the creatures they encountered as: "fearsome shadow wraiths commanded by an insane overlord."

The other members of his expedition included the Grand Seer, Joshua Jones, and Lyra's husband Benoir. Of them, only Kelly had written a statement, although it was more poetry than actual fact.

In shadows deep, where darkness holds its sway,
A realm unseen by light's unwavering glare,
There lurks a land where nightmares come to play,
And twisted creatures dance in grim despair.

The moon's pale gaze dare not pierce the night,
For fear of stirring horrors from their tomb,
Where spectres roam and haunt the silent sight,
And whispers echo in the spectral gloom.

Beware, ye who would wander in this land,
For madness lurks within its dark embrace,
Where every step may lead to your end,
In shadow's realm, where nightmares hold their chase.

'Doctor Shika?' her assistant interrupted, hovering in the doorway. 'Lyra Cousineau is here. Apparently, she has important information regarding the Shadow Realm?' he added, turning the last part of the sentence into a question.

Kaori hadn't briefed her team on the founder's request as yet, but it was clear that Lyra already knew.

She wants to go, Kaori thought, weighing up the idea. *She does know the realm better than anyone.*

'Let her in.'

Dressed in black combat fatigues, leather boots and carrying a heavy rucksack, Lyra looked as if she had joined a SWAT team.

'Hey,' she said, shrugging the bag from her shoulder and putting it down on a chair. 'I thought you might want to see this.' She pulled out a journal from one of the many pockets of her cargo pants and handed it to Kaori. 'I've tagged the most important pages.'

The doctor was slightly taken aback. This was not the ethereal seer that would muse over the death of a butterfly for weeks. Something had changed, her eyes were hard and filled with a sense of purpose.

'Thanks,' she said, taking the journal.

On the front cover was a hand-drawn illustration; a beautiful ink rendition of a wonderland trapped inside an ornate mirror, like something from Lewis Carroll's "Looking Glass" adventures.

The pages were tagged with tiny coloured post-it notes.

Kaori turned to the first one, which showed a map of various regions with copious amounts of annotations.

'That's Mordor,' Lyra explained, leaning against the desk. 'You probably want to start there, it's where we last saw the Nazgûl.'

'Mordor?'

Lyra laughed. 'Yes, I needed a name for it and that just seemed to fit. The wraiths tend to gather there more than any other region.'

Kaori turned to the next bookmark, the page was covered in sketches of nightmarish creatures. They reminded the xenobiologyst of *Chrysofilia* from the Varnac Nebula, but she held her tongue and held the book up towards Lyra. 'These are the wraiths?'

Lyra nodded. 'Yup. That's how I imagined the Nazgûl would look.'

'How many have you seen?'

She started counting on her fingers, but gave up. 'Could be twenty, or a hundred. It's hard to be sure, the realm has a tendency to hide things when you're actually looking for them. Roads can be especially tricky and never, ever rely on the signposts.'

Kaori was beginning to think it would be wise to take her after all.

'Have you decided who's going with you?' Lyra asked, getting up and going back to her rucksack.

'No, I was just putting a plan together.'

'So, maybe I could come?' she wondered, taking out another book from her bag. 'Because, I do know more about it than pretty much everybody else.'

Kaori tried to think of a good reason to turn her down, but nothing sprang to mind. The founder's directive was pretty clear that she could choose her own team and having a local guide would make things a lot easier.

'Okay, but there will be rules.'

Lyra clapped her hands together like a child and sat down with a new journal. 'I knew you'd say yes,' she said, opening it to a blank page and taking out a pen.

'You're a seer. Of course you knew.'

'Well yes, that's true. Although that won't help us much in the Shadow Realm.' She started writing out a list. 'We're going to need a few things. I've always had to improvise before, but I'm guessing you will be able to get pretty much anything.'

Kaori's brow furrowed as she read the first few items. 'Yeah, pretty much.'

5

SECRETS

Cell 291, Protectorate HQ.

Silas sat in the cell, staring at the wall.

This was not his first prison cell, nor was it likely to be his last. His father used to boast that there wasn't a clink strong enough to hold a Wormwood. Which in the past was true, his old man escaped from all but the last of his prisons – it was one of his many talents. George Wormwood was something of a legend amongst the Syndicate, earning him the nickname of 'Slippery Jack.'

Unfortunately, it was not one of the skills he passed onto his son.

Looking back, Silas knew he didn't have the most normal of childhoods. There was no schooling, no formal education. He learned to read from the stolen manuscripts and rare books they acquired for collectors. Calculus and mathematics were necessary to manage the ledgers and ensure everyone received their fare share of the booty.

It came easily to him. Everyone in his family worked, from the moment they could walk. Silas was the youngest of five children, each one cut from the same cloth as their parents. They were a 'Firm', a criminal enterprise that controlled most of the sixteenth century, and their Empire was expanding.

There was never a dull moment – it was never boring.

Growing up on the wrong side of the Order, Silas realised early on that they were outcasts, doing whatever it took to survive. Loyal only to themselves and the family. His talents as a 'canary' kept them one step ahead of the Protectorate, but it meant they were permanently on the run, never staying in one place or time for too long.

From what he could remember, it had been an amazing adventure. Running 'errands' with his brothers, never knowing that their games were honing their skills, that their parents were training them.

'We all pull together or hang,' was the unspoken family motto. He could still hear his father berating his older brothers when they screwed up. He was a hard man, one who was not afraid to use his fists. Their's was a dog-eat-dog world, one that didn't believe in second chances.

'Don't get caught,' was the closest they came to "good-bye", but eventually they all did. Every member of his family ended up in the Château or dead. Sometimes he wondered if the latter wasn't a better option.

At the age of twelve, they locked up his parents and the Order placed him with Westinghouse, believing that the old watchman would rehabilitate him. Silas tried to be good, to go straight, but it was too late, the old ways were too ingrained.

By sixteen he was out on his own.

There were countless times since then when he had nearly been caught, his sixth sense keeping him one step ahead.

It would take a special kind of Crow, to get one over on him and Inspector Sabien was just that man, a true "Thieftaker".

Silas resigned himself to the fact that it took their best man to catch him.

He smiled to himself, it was all part of his plan.

It would begin with a secret, one that he had been keeping for just such an occasion – his get-out-of-jail-free card.

6

SHADOW REALM

Shadow Realm

Kaori stared into the shimmering surface of the mirror trying to come to terms with the fact that it wasn't reflecting the room in which she was standing.

Taking a deep breath, she closed her eyes, feeling Ophelia stirring beneath her conscious mind.

'It's okay,' she whispered to the ghast, 'go back to sleep.'

The rest of her team were running final checks on their equipment, patiently waiting for their boss to make the first move.

This was one of those singular moments over which she always procrastinated – the decision point, before she committed them to a mission. Putting ten other lives in danger for the sake of research. Usually she would be staring into the dark swirling mass of chaos on the other side of a breach. Standing on the precipice looking into the Maelstrom, wondering if they would make it out alive.

'Okay,' she said to herself, opening her eyes. 'Time to go.'

Lyra was standing beside her, idly twiddling her hair. Kaori got the feeling that she would have stepped through without hesitation if it hadn't been for their safety protocols.

They had sent a probe through twenty minutes earlier, which disappeared without trace. It wasn't unusual, many went into the Maelstrom never to be seen again. Those that returned were usually too damaged to retrieve any useful data from and when they did salvage some images, they generally wished they hadn't.

For some reason, Kaori assumed this would be different. She hoped for at least a few environmental readings before it died, but it wasn't to be. They were going in blind, or at least unprepared for what was to come.

All except Lyra, who was now braiding her hair into pigtails.

'Can we go now?' she asked politely, tilting her head to one side.

Kaori nodded and stepped forward.

It felt as if she had walked through a waterfall of ash.

The air in the world behind the mirror tasted like dust, of desiccated bones and mouldering paper. Like an attic room in an old house closed up for centuries or the tomb of a long-dead pharaoh.

Lyra had assured Kaori that they wouldn't need breathing equipment, but she forgot to mention the smell.

The sky was grey and overcast, and the winds whistled through the crumbling remains of what must have once been a town.

They were standing in an old market square, the surrounding buildings reminding Kaori of the Old Town in Prague. Decrepit half-timbered houses in various states of collapse lined cobbled streets that went off in various directions. The glass in their leaded windows was yellowing and coated with dirt, making it impossible to see inside.

Weak, watery sunlight filtered through a thick layer of cloud, as if permanently frozen in a kind of pre-dawn.

Kaori checked the readings on the monitor strapped to her forearm: the diagnostics were within acceptable tolerances; the air was breathable if a little high in sulphur oxide; there was a bunch of spores floating around that didn't appear to have any lethal pathogens and it was a little on the chilly side.

There were no signs of life, organic or otherwise.

She shivered inadvertently, her ghast stirring. *This is a bad place,* it emoted, not so much in a language, but more of a feeling. *We should leave.*

Lyra took out one of her journals and flicked through the pages until she found a map and handed it to Kaori.

'Welcome to Mordor,' she said, raising her voice over the wind.

Looking at the carefully drawn lines, Kaori could see numerous routes, each redrawn as if Lyra had gone over them countless times. There were hundreds of separate paths, every one with its own set of annotations.

'We need to go this way,' Lyra added, pulling a scarf over her nose and motioning with her right hand. 'It's going to change soon.'

Kaori realised the glyphs in the margins were actually timestamps, ones that Lyra had meticulously captured on many separate occasions.

Pulling her own scarf over her face, she waved to her team and followed Lyra into the town.

7

———

QUESTIONING

Protectorate HQ.

'Silas Wormwood, you are being charged under The Temporal Protection Act of 11,341. Namely, that on the fourth of May 11,519, you did knowingly engage with a primitive culture and attempt to influence their technological development and in doing so change the course of history. How do you plead?'

Chief Inspector Avery looked up from the charge sheet.

Silas simply shrugged. 'Not guilty.'

Sabien was standing behind his boss with his arms folded. 'The Copernicans have retrieved the sword you gave to Moctezuma, your fingerprints are all over it.'

'Doesn't prove anything. I gave it to him as a gift. Cortés would have done the same.'

'What were you doing in Tenochtitlán in the first place?'

Silas leaned back in his chair and folded his arms. 'I was on holiday. I've always wanted to visit the Aztecs.'

Sabien knew his type, he was the epitome of a Time-Breaker. Cocky and self-assured, the kind that were not easily intimidated by authority. Career criminals who saw the Protectorate as an enemy rather than a force for justice.

Breakers knew every loophole in the system; how to move through time without leaving a trace; where to find the rarest artefacts and who to sell them to without provenance. They lived on their wits, and the good ones became very rich.

Sabien knew he was going to need a redactor to get anything like the truth out of this one.

'Are you seriously going to sit there and deny that you stole a crystal skull from Moctezuma's temple?' continued Avery.

Silas smiled and opened his arms wide. 'That was part of the trade for the sword. A fair exchange.'

'So why did you run?'

'I needed the exercise? The banquet he put on for me was quite rich. I'm watching my weight.' He smiled and patted his flat stomach.

'Through three time zones in under ten minutes?'

'It's a new personal best. You know I ran for the Copernicans when I was younger.'

Sabien grunted. 'I've had enough of this bullshit. I'm calling in a redactor.'

Silas's smug expression vanished. Sabien's threat clearly hit home. Protectorate redactors were not the most subtle of mind readers, their techniques were something akin to mental torture. Ex-cons that spoke of it afterwards would pale at the memory.

'Now hold on, gents, let's not get ahead of ourselves. This is a parley is it not? A negotiation.' He held up his hands as if surrendering. 'I have something you may want to know.'

Sabien was half way out of the door.

'Like what? The location of the Syndicate headquarters?'

The prisoner put his hands down on the table. 'First I need to know you'll protect me. I'll be a marked man if I tell you this.'

'That depends on the quality of the information,' said Sabien, closing the door.

Silas's eyes narrowed. 'I'll need some kind of assurance.'

Avery sighed. 'Fine. You have my word that should this information be of use, we'll consider a lighter sentence for your so-called holiday. But I'll still need the name of the man you were working for or at least the whereabouts of the Skull of Doom.'

'Fair enough,' agreed Silas.

'So?'

Silas took a deep breath, and sat back in his chair once more. His eyes flicking between the two of them, waiting for their reaction.

'So, I know how to find Atlantis.'

8

———

WRAITHS

Shadow Realm.

They had been walking along the "Bone Highway" for what seemed like hours. It was hard to tell without a Sun to mark time. Her chronograph stopped working the moment they arrived, it was as if the entire world was on pause.

The gravel crunched morbidly under their boots, each step crushing the tiny skeletons of unrecognisable creatures.

Earlier, when Lyra first led them to the path, the xenobiologysts had stopped to take samples, placing the fragile structures in glass jars. At first, Kaori thought they resembled birds, or tiny mammals, but it was hard to tell exactly, since no two appeared to be from the same genus.

A few members of the team refused to use the road, finding it too gruesome, choosing instead to walk alongside on the grey salt marshes that stretched as far as the eye could see. The marsh was mostly stunted gorse and moss, with waterways winding through it. They smelled stagnant, and the oily pools were a breeding ground for clouds of midges and other biting insects, which swarmed over those that took the side path.

It was a barren, soulless landscape, and Kaori was beginning to understand why Lyra named it Mordor.

'Is it all like this?' she asked, quickening her step to walk beside the seer.

'Oh no. This is by far the worst region,' Lyra replied in her sing-song voice. She took out one of her maps and pointed at various places. 'The valleys of Rivendell are quite beautiful, as are the mountains of Ered Nimrais in Gondor.'

Squinting at the grey horizon, the scientist in her wondered how such a place ever came to exist, what forces would be required to create such a world. *And how was it still here?*

'Does the weather ever change? Are there seasons?'

Lyra shrugged, tilting her head towards the sky. 'It rains sometimes. Black rain, full of ash. I've always imagined that it comes from Mount Doom, but I've never seen a volcano.'

'Does the sun ever set?'

'No, night never comes, I don't think I would like to be here if it did.'

Kaori knew what she meant. It was a depressing, soulless place. As the rest of her team traipsed behind them, she could feel their morale waning.

'We're going to need to stop soon,' she said, looking around for a suitable camp site.

Lyra shook her head and pointed to something in the distance. 'I wouldn't, not yet. Not until we reach the crossing at least.'

The crossing was nothing more than an intersection of old roads. A worm-eaten signpost stood at its centre, listing badly to one side like the mast on a sinking ship. The names of its destinations had been worn away to indecipherable scratches.

Less than twenty yards from the crossing, on an island in

the centre of a small dark lake, stood the remains of a tower. The oily water shimmered in the dull light. Thick stone walls that once had stood defiantly against its enemies were slowly crumbling into a scattered pile of rubble around its base.

One by one, the xeno team tentatively crossed the rotten wooden bridge that spanned the creek.

'We should be safer here,' explained Lyra taking off her backpack and sitting down on a larger piece of rubble.

The others followed suit, clearly happy for a rest. They broke out rations and camping equipment while Doctor Shika and her assistant set up a perimeter of monitoring equipment.

'You won't be needing those,' Lyra said, nodding towards the sensors. 'I'll know when they're coming.'

Kaori smiled. 'I know, but we need the data if we're going to stand any chance of understanding what they are.'

Lyra rolled her eyes. 'Your technology isn't going to help us here. The rules of our universe don't apply.'

Doctor Shika sat down beside her and took out a packet of rice crackers. 'You know I've spent a lot of time in the Maelstrom right?'

Lyra nodded, sipping on a juice box. 'I know. I've read your timeline, and your friend's.'

'You've read Ophelia?' said the doctor, trying not to feel too offended. Seers had a reputation for not respecting people's privacy.

'She's very old.'

'She is,' Kaori agreed. 'I think she's one of the oldest Storm-Kin I've ever met.'

Lyra placed her hand on top of Kaori's. 'She likes you very much, but she knows she's going to have to leave you soon.'

'What?'

Lyra smiled. 'She says you have someone else to protect you now.'

Kaori blushed. 'Ah, yes. Him.'

'Sabien is a good man.'

'He is. Although don't let him hear you say that. His head's big enough as it is.'

Lyra was suddenly distracted, twisting away as if trying to hear something more clearly.

'Are you okay?' asked Kaori.

The seer's eyes rolled back, turning white.

'Lyra?'

'Excuse me, Doctor Shika,' interrupted one of the scientists, his expression a mixture of confusion and fear as he studied his tablet. 'I'm getting some very strange readings.'

Kaori got up and took the device from him. 'Shit,' she exclaimed, looking out across the marshes. 'That doesn't make any sense.'

'Told you,' said Lyra, her eyes returning to normal. 'They're coming.'

She carefully placed her lunch box on a rock and took something else from her rucksack. 'It's going to get dark, really quickly. Have your team pour this in a circle around the island.' She handed Kaori a bag of what appeared to be salt. 'And turn on all of the lamps.'

On the distant horizon storm clouds were gathering. Kaori felt Ophelia stirring, readying herself for trouble. She handed the bag to her assistant. 'Do as she says.'

'But –,' he began to protest.

'Just do it. Then breakout the disruptors.'

Lyra climbed the rubble to get a better view of the oncoming storm. She watched the xenos scrabbling around, frantically unpacking weapons and other strange pieces of technical equipment. The roiling clouds began to take on forms as they approached, as though an army were concealed within in. Silhouettes of dark creatures drifted in and out of sight.

'Five hundred yards,' intoned one of the technicians, his voice struggling to hide the fear.

His colleagues were strapping strange devices to their backs, now looking more like ghostbusters than scientists. They took positions at the edges of the white circle.

9

COGNIZANCE

Protectorate HQ

'Atlantis?' Chief Inspector Avery laughed. 'He's pulling our leg. No one's heard from that station in thousands of years.'

Sabien watched Silas through the one-way glass. The man was pacing around the interview room, reading the various messages scrawled on the walls by its previous occupants.

Atlantis was not the mythical island dreamed up by Plato as an allegory on the hubris of nations, but a scientific research station. No one knew what exactly was being tested, but it suffered a major technical failure and vanished from the timeline, taking the entire team and the island with it.

The Draconians eventually stopped looking for it after years of searching. Although there were still regular reports of sightings, which they diligently investigated with no success.

It was their very own Area 51, the absence of a rational explanation of its disappearance leaving a vacuum for conspiracy and myth to fill. Theories ranged from alien technology, to weather control or advance weapons research.

Attracting the more eccentric collectors, who would pay a small fortune for anything related to the lost mission.

'I think he's bluffing. I still think we should see what the redactors can pull out of him,' Sabien said, turning to face his boss.

Avery folded his arms over his large belly. He was only two years from retirement and was getting more cautious with every case. Sabien could see the cogs turning behind his eyes as he considered the options.

'But Atlantis is a strange choice, don't you think? If you were going to offer something to keep you out of the Château, you wouldn't pick something as wacky as that. Would you? I'd go for the leader of the Syndicate, or at least one of his senior executives.'

Sabien shrugged. 'Who knows what's going on inside his head.'

'Trouble is, if he's taken Cognizance, we won't get anything useful out of him and it'll scramble the mind of anyone who tries.'

Cognizance was a popular narcotic amongst the members of the Syndicate. It enhanced your mental faculties, making you hyper-aware of your surroundings, heightening your senses. It also came with a few useful side effects, giving the user the ability to create a psychic shield, one that could repel any form of mental probing, reflecting the attack back to the redactor a hundredfold.

Avery shook his head. 'No. We've got him on the advanced tech charge. Let's book him and see if a short stay in the Château doesn't loosen his tongue.'

They went back into the interview room.

'What proof can you give us that you know the location of Atlantis Station?'

Silas shrugged. 'Other than showing you. Not much.'

Sabien laughed. 'You think we're going to fall for that one. You'll be on your toes the first chance you get.'

The timebreaker held up his hands, as far as the manacles would allow. 'Guess you'll have to trust me.'

'Or we could send you to the Château and see if a few nights in there wipes that smug grin off your face,' growled Sabien.

10

ARGORYX

Shadow Realm

The island was surrounded by a swirling tornado of phantoms. Ethereal wraiths made of smoke and bone, circled around them, their eyes glowing with a malevolent hunger in the gloom.

Lyra's ring of crystal seemed to be holding them back, but for how long was anybody's guess.

She stood transfixed beside Kaori, watching the xenos' weapons lancing through the spectral monsters with arcing rays of energy. The bright, blue-white beams sliced through their translucent bodies, burning their tattered shrouds but failing to do any lasting damage.

'Baxter, get the argoryx array online!' Kaori barked at one of the team. The man dropped his weapon and opened one of the long black cases. He took out a large silver tube and began to connect it to a series of battery packs.

'Abandon's coming,' Lyra whispered in the doctor's ear. 'We should leave.'

She couldn't explain how she could sense the wanderer approaching, but somehow they were connected. His presence was making her skin itch, goosebumps prickled along her forearms as her blood turned to ice.

A tall, bearded figure appeared through the dark swirling mists, walking across the bridge towards them holding a long staff with a red gemstone embedded in its crown. Kaori thought he looked more like a dark wizard, like Sauron. Blaming Lyra for the Lord of the Rings references, she dismissed the idea and checked the readings on the tablet.

Whatever he was, he wasn't human, the analysis of the gases surrounding him showed exceptionally high levels of carbon dioxide and argon, a toxic atmosphere for most life on earth.

He's not from this world. She thought.

Someone screamed as the wraiths suddenly broke the circle and poured in through the gap.

The shadow creatures descended on the team like a rabid pack of wolves. Black tendrils formed out of their smoking corpses, curling around the bodies of their prey and invading every orifice.

Dropping their weapons, the xenobiologysts fell to their knees, screaming as the dark spirits burrowed inside them.

'WE SHOULD GO NOW!' shouted Lyra, taking out a small mirror and placing it on the floor.

Kaori ignored her, she was too busy trying to help Baxter. Her body was now encased in the heavy shielding of a storm-kin which Lyra assumed must be Ophelia. The armour formed a semi-transparent suit of horned plates that reminded Lyra of one of Benoir's dinosaurs. The wraiths were avoiding her, obviously unwilling to take on the ghast.

The doctor opened the metal cylinder along its long edge, holding the two halves of the tube out before her. 'Now!' she screamed at Baxter, turning her head away as he flicked a switch, a blinding white light flared from inside it.

The wraiths screamed, retreating away from the ribbons of energy unfurling from inside the case. Like slow-moving branches of lightning they spread out towards the spectres.

Abandon bellowed and raised his staff as if to strike.

Before he could deliver the blow, the nearest of the wraiths became entangled in the web of light, which spun itself around the creature like a spider cocooning a fly. The phantom screamed as it was pulled inside the metal casing.

Kaori's ghost seemed to sense the impending strike and hardened as the Old King brought his staff down. His blow glanced off the shell, knocking the cylinder out of her hands and hitting Baxter squarely in the face.

'NOW!' screamed Lyra, grasping the doctor's hand and dragging her towards the mirror.

Kaori resisted, looking back at what remained of her squad as they rose to their feet like marionettes. Their limbs twisted and broken, staring at her with cold, black eyes.

'Wait!' she yelled, breaking free of Lyra and going back for the cylinder.

Standing over Baxter, Abandon raised the staff over his head once more.

The doctor picked up the silver tube, hesitating before turning back to Lyra and taking her hand.

Lyra placed her other hand on the mirror, feeling for the world beyond, she reached into it and pulled them both through.

'We need to go back!' Kaori said, her ghost armour fading. She was still clutching the case, which was covered in Baxter's blood.

'It's too late, they're gone,' said Lyra, studying the surface of the mirror and wondering if the wraiths could follow them. 'Didn't you see their eyes?'

Kaori grimaced, her eyes filling with tears. She looked down at the cylinder. 'What the hell were they?'

'Hell indeed,' agreed the Grand Seer, whose study they were now standing in. 'Spirits, demons, wraiths. All manner of terrors,' he added, taking a black cloth and draping it over the long mirror.

'They took my entire team.'

'And they would have taken you too,' Lyra reminded her, pointing at the metal tube. 'What was so important that you would risk your life?'

Kaori's expression hardened. She checked an LED display on the side of the case.'The only way to learn about them is to capture one. I need to study it.'

'Tis best to weigh the enemy more mighty than he seems,' quoted Kelly.

'There were more than last time,' Lyra said, turning towards the Grand Seer. 'And Abandon was with them.'

'We will need to report this to the founder,' he said, stroking his beard. 'It appears we may need the services of the Department of Psychical Research after all.'

Doctor Shika looked confused. 'Who on earth are they?'

'I found them in 1914,' Lyra explained, 'they're rather unusual. They've been fighting demons for hundreds of years.'

'But they're not of the Order?'

Lyra shook her head. 'No, they're different. They've got their own set of skills.'

'I need to get this back to the lab,' Kaori said, walking towards the door. 'Tell the founder I will have a report for him tomorrow.' There were tears forming in the corners of her eyes once more. 'After I've informed their families of their loss.'

11

CHATEAU D'IF

Château D'If

The night winds swept across the island, whistling through the cracks in the weathered rock and tugging at the cloaks of the guards. Silas shivered as he hobbled between them up the slick, stone staircase that led to the prison.

The walls of the sixteenth century fortress loomed over them. Dark and imposing, they rose into the night sky like a sheer cliff, its temporal shielding shimmering like oil on water over the granite surface.

This was the infamous Château Death. Somewhere behind those battlements his parents were being held in stasis or the "Endless Sentence" as it was more commonly known – held in perpetuity with no prospect of release.

When he was younger, Silas often questioned whether it wouldn't have been better to have executed them. At least then he could have stood at a grave and mourned their passing. There were no visitation rights to this prison, so he was left to wonder what terrible dreams they were having inside their stasis. The rumour amongst the Syndicate was that the prison redactors put you in an endless loop of your worst crime, reliving it through the eyes of your victim. But there was no way to know for sure. Those who entered never left. Which was why they called the entrance the 'door of no return.'

They finally reached the top of the stairs and stopped before an imposing set of iron-studded wooden gates. Twice as tall as a man, they were salt-stained by the ever-present storms that battered the island.

No one had ever escaped from this place, Silas reminded himself. The temporal safeguards surrounding it made it impossible to jump out of, and the isolated location and severe weather made it impossible to survive without a large boat or perhaps a hot air balloon.

Many tried. All had failed. There were stories of inmates who attempted to fly, building gliders and launching themselves from the highest point, only to fall to their deaths. There was even talk of a submarine made from barrels. The ninety-foot waves put paid to that attempt, smashing the vessel against the rocks like a child's toy.

He knew they were likely to be nothing but tales put about by the Protectorate as a warning to his kind. 'Stories to scare the children,' his father used to say. 'Not a cell ever been made to hold Slippery Jack,' he would joke, flexing his massive biceps. And Silas believed him.

At the time his father seemed to be invincible, the rightful King of the Thieves. They were untouchable, the past was theirs for the plundering. It was a golden time in Silas's memory, right up until that day in Russia when they caught them and locked them up. This was one prison Slippery Jack would never manage to break out of.

. . .

The guard hammered his fist on the gate, holding up his lantern to show their faces as the grille was pulled back.

'Watchword?' barked a gruff voice from inside.

'Vigil Temporis,' the guard replied.

The sound of gears grinding into action made Silas's heart beat faster. He took a deep breath, trying not to show his fear. 'Never let them see you're scared,' his father would remind him whenever trouble was brewing. 'Act like you couldn't care if you lived or died. No one wants to fight a man who's got nothing to lose.'

The doors slowly inched apart and the guard took hold of his chains and walked him inside like a dog on a lead.

He'd pictured this moment for nearly ten years.

Walking through the gates, Silas felt the prickling sensation on his neck, a sure sign that they were passing through the temporal shielding.

The courtyard of the Château was circular with stepped rows of cells stacked against the inside of the walls. It reminded Silas of the amphitheatre in Medellín.

'Prisoner four-six-seven,' intoned the guard, handing the chains to the prison warden. 'He's all yours.'

The warden was a thin, wiry man with terrible teeth and eyes that were too close together. He reminded Silas of a rat.

'Four-six-seven. Wormwood. Technology trading with primitive cultures,' the man read from his clipboard. 'That's the full set then.'

He yanked on the chains and started towards the cells. 'We've got your room all nicely prepared. Thought you'd like to be close up with the rest of your family. We like to make special accommodation for our longer term residents.'

The warden chuckled to himself and shook his head. 'We've been wondering how long it would take to get you. There was a book running on it. I'm up to make a pretty penny.'

The prison guards were mostly ex-Protectorate, or, in

some cases, Draconians retired on medical grounds. Whatever this man had once been, he'd clearly seen his share of action. He moved with a stiff, rolling gait, as if one leg were carved from wood, the kind of injury that told stories without a single word.

He stopped at the door and nodded towards the sky. 'Take one last look at the stars boy, you won't be seeing them for a long time.'

12

RETIREMENT

Cap Corse, Corsica. 1616

Rufius sat beneath the shade of a twisted old olive tree, puffing on a long clay pipe and watching the boats sail into the bay. By the look of their colours, they were trading vessels from Livorno filled with wine, cheese and olive oil – as well as the vines he'd ordered a month ago from Tuscany.

This was his favourite time of day. The sun's warmth was slowly fading as it slipped below the horizon, painting the clouds in hues of orange and purple, and casting dramatic shadows over the bay's rugged coastline.

Seagulls called out as they wheeled overhead, circling the weathered Genoese Tower that he made his home on the Northern Peninsula of Corsica. Their cries were a poignant reminder that it was nearly time to start preparing his dinner.

The old watchman put down his pipe and picked up the leather-bound journal. It was something that caught his eye on his last visit to Bastia, a port city less than fifty miles to the south.

His fingers traced the intricate patterns on the hand-tooled calf-skin cover, the texture stirring memories of his first almanac. Rufius smoothed the pages flat, feeling the quality of the sizing and the timeline that flowed beneath it.

He could sense the bookbinder at work. It was imported from Italy because paper was becoming an expensive commodity on Corsica. The influence of the Genoese had increased literacy amongst the Corsican nobility who were becoming avid collectors, amassing grand libraries of classic literature – although most of the peasant folk were still unable to read.

Rufius still found it strange to open a journal to blank pages instead of scrolling lines of temporal calculations and new mission orders. Part of him missed his old almanac, he often wondered what the Copernicans would have done with it – over half of his life was recorded within its pages.

Probably burned it. Too many secrets.

Although it would have been useful to have something to reference while writing his memoirs, because it was proving to be more difficult than he'd anticipated.

When you've lived as long as I have, your memories tend to coalesce, he'd written as the foreword. Above it were several titles crossed out, the current version declared "THE LIFE AND TIMES OF A WATCHMAN," in large capital letters.

Turning to the first chapter, which he called "CHANGELING", he put on his glasses and began to write.

Jorvik 854.

It all began with a sword, a Roman gladius, which I named Gunnlogi.

In my naivety, I thought it to be a magical weapon, one that taught me how to fight. Little did I know I was learning from its history.

I was introduced to the founder after a chance encounter with Dorovir whilst helping my adopted father, Sindri the Smith, sells his goods at market.

In those days, they were not as organised as an Order – we were simply a small group of like-minded individuals trying to make a better world.

I probably wasn't aware of their vision at the time, I was too busy learning how to control my talents. Too fascinated with the past and exploring the worlds that had opened up to me.

Then he noted in the margins:

- Harrison - development of the first tachyon.
- The witch, Maebh - Tuatha
- The formation of the Draconians.

Rufius sighed closing the journal and taking off his glasses. Reflecting on the distant past wasn't an easy task, the details were sketchy at best. His childhood was spent with the family of a blacksmith in the heart of the Danelaw. They treated him more like a servant than a son, but it could have been a lot worse. As Sindri's apprentice he was generally accepted by the village, but he always felt like something of an outsider.

He was less than fourteen-years-old when he first met the founder. Rufius couldn't be exactly sure of his age, since he was never told his actually birth date, instead he adopted the day they found him in the woods – the day after Midsummer, the 22nd June.

There had been so many adventures. His time as a Praetorian meant he had crossed paths with virtually every influential figure in history. He'd lost count of the number of royal heirs and monarchs he had saved from certain death.

The years passed so quickly, more than was evident from the greying of his beard. One of the benefits of temporal dilation was that you tended to live long beyond your natural life span.

But he was beginning to feel his age, as if he was being stretched too thin.

This was only his third month of retirement and things were not quite going as planned. It was nearing the end of August and the vineyard that surrounded the tower was heavily laden with Vermentino grapes. However, the Maître Vigneron who was supposed to organise the harvesting had broken his arm and was laid up for the rest of the summer. If they didn't bring in the crop in the next few weeks it would perish on the vine.

His dream of producing his own wine was not getting off to the best of starts.

Cap Corse was a beautiful remote peninsula in the northern reaches of Corsica. Rufius had chosen 1616 when the Republic of Genoa controlled the island. They built towers like his as a deterrent against the Barbary Pirates whose corsairs frequently raided the villages and ports of the island.

It wasn't that Rufius was particularly searching for trouble, but the odd raid was a welcome change from the otherwise sedate pace of life in the Mediterranean.

He had already earned himself a nickname amongst the locals, 'Capitano,' after seeing off a gang of marauding privateers who were trying to abduct a group of local children. Slave trading was a stock in trade for the pirates. European slaves were taken back to the Barbary States of North Africa and sold into servitude or held for ransom.

Putting the book down, he picked up his pipe, tapped out the embers and refilled it from his pouch. There was hardly any of the *Nicotiana Tabacum* left, the only decent smoke in this era, which meant another trip to Bastia.

Pinto, a Portuguese merchant adventurer, was due in the next week or so and he was bound to have a batch of new pipe weed as well as tales of his travels in South America.

'You really should give that up you know,' said a voice from behind him.

Rufius recognised it immediately as that of the founder.

'It's one of my last pleasures,' he said, getting to his feet.

'Along with the wine.' The founder noted the empty bottle beside his chair.

'Well yes, that goes without saying. It's good to see you old friend.'

There was an awkward silence for a moment, as if the two men had forgotten how to greet each other.

The founder looked out over the bay. 'You've certainly picked a fine spot to hang up your tachyon.'

The watchman relit his pipe and took a long draw on the stem. 'It has a certain something, I have to admit. The locals are mostly friendly. We've a small pirate problem, but nothing I can't handle, and the wine is very quaffable.' He blew out a smoke ring. 'But enough of the small talk. I'm assuming you're not here to discuss the weather?'

Turning back to face Rufius, his old master's expression hardened. 'No, unfortunately not. I wanted to ask you about the Shadow Realm, or more specifically your last sojourn into it.'

Rufius shuddered inwardly. 'Not something I care to repeat any time soon.'

'A few days ago I instructed Doctor Shika to take a xenobiology team to investigate. Kaori was the only survivor, and only then because of Lyra Cousineau.'

Rufius took the pipe out of his mouth and inspected the bowl, tamping it down with his thumb. 'I'm sorry to hear that. It's a terrible place. Feels like you're in purgatory.'

'What did you see when you were in there?'

The old watchman sighed, staring out into the deepening purples of the sunset. 'Something older than time itself. Nothing like the Maelstrom. The world was dead, devoid of life. And the things that pursued us, the "Nazgûl", Lyra called them, they were demons spawned from the very depths of hell – as was the devil that led them. Kelly could only just hold them back long enough for us to escape.'

The founder frowned, in all their time together he couldn't remember seeing his old friend quite so affected. This was a man who'd been lost inside the void of the Maelstrom for years and survived to tell the tale.

'The Grand Seer believes the being you encountered was responsible for the creation of the realm. He calls him the "Old King". I can only assume that he's a remnant from some forgotten branch of time, one that bifurcated from the continuum millions of years ago.'

Rufius grunted. 'Kelly is a madman and a fool, but he did save us all that day. His hocus-pocus actually seemed to affect them. He was rambling on about how it was built on a deep, ancient magic that has been lost over time. I'm not surprised Kaori's technology didn't work, the usual rules don't seem to apply in there.'

'She managed to capture one of them. Doctor Shika believes she may be able to learn something of its origins.'

The watchman's eyes widened. 'Did she now? Well that woman is nothing if not tenacious. If anyone can find a way to defeat them, she will.'

The founder didn't seem convinced. 'Did you know Lyra inadvertently discovered a group known as "The Department of Psychical Research", based in 1914? She believes they have been fighting these so-called demons for some time.'

'Yes, I remember, she mentioned King George's league of extraordinary gentleman.'

'According to her, they've had a great deal of experience in defeating these creatures.'

Rufius's eyes narrowed. 'Ah, now I see, you want me to pay them a visit? Learn how they do it? Have you come to ask me to come out of retirement?'

The founder smiled and patted his friend on the shoulder. 'It needs a subtle approach. Professor Eddington is not convinced there is an issue and the Draconians are too heavy-handed for such a task.'

Rufius scratched his beard and then shook his head. 'Joshua Jones is more than capable of handling this kind of mission. Send him. If he fails, which he won't, I'll consider it, but I'm sure he'll be fine.'

The founder nodded. 'I understand.'

13

JOSH

Rothes Glen House, Banffshire, Scotland. 1892

Josh sat in the kitchen staring at the half-finished glass of wine. He was dog-tired and the dinner wasn't going to cook itself. Caitlin was in the lounge, with their son dozing on her chest. It was Josh's turn to cook, and part of him was secretly wishing they'd picked a century with pizza delivery, the idea of a large pepperoni with garlic crust was rather appealing right now.

He couldn't remember the last time either of them managed an unbroken night's sleep in the last three months. Zack was teething and they were taking it in turns to get up to comfort him. Both he and Caitlin were struggling on very little rest and copious amounts of caffeine, so tempers were beginning to fray.

It wasn't helped by the fact that, since Rufius had officially retired, Josh's workload had increased dramatically. The Copernican dispatchers proposed putting him on 'day' missions so that he wasn't away from his family for so long. Caitlin dismissed this out of hand, pointing out that it was a ridiculous idea – Josh could complete months of missions and still be home for dinner.

Having recently returned to work at the Great Library, she was finding it difficult to adjust. After over a year of maternity leave, the challenge of overseeing the largest collection of books in history was a daunting prospect, made all the more stressful by the chaos she discovered when she got back to her office.

The indexing project, which Caitlin left in the capable hands of her team, had not progressed as well as she'd hoped. Various factions within the library's senior fraternity capitalised on her absence by taking the opportunity to derail the work; hiding entire sections of the catalogue and ruining months of careful planning.

'They're a bunch of children,' she growled at him, when Josh mistakenly asked how it went on her first day. 'And the elder Biblios are the worst,' she added, referring to the venerable curators who all seemed to be over eighty to Josh.

'They've stolen part of the index and are refusing to return it without assurances.'

'Can't you just rebuild it?'

The expression on Caitlin's face made it very clear that was not the right thing to say.

'Do you know how long it took to compile?' she asked through gritted teeth.

Josh shrugged. 'I don't know. A couple of months?'

In retrospect, he could see that he should have gone higher with his estimate, but his sleep-deprived brain wasn't firing on all cylinders. There was shouting, well more like ranting, and door slamming. Everything seemed to be his fault. It took nearly a week before they were back on speaking terms again.

This was when he missed his mother the most. She would have been a perfect grandma, there were enough rooms in this house for her to have a whole wing to herself and a garden that needed a lot of attention.

But she was gone, and Caitlin's parents were planning yet another mission on the *Nautilus*. The most supportive family they had right now were Alixia and Lyra, who came to visit them regularly, and who left an open invitation for them to move back into the Chapter House.

But Caitlin refused – she wanted to prove that she was a capable mother.

'Other people do it. Linears especially. I'm not having someone else raising our son,' she snapped, when Josh suggested getting a nanny.

The founder's summons appeared in his almanac an hour later, right in the middle of dinner. It was terrible timing, it was the first time they had eaten together since Caitlin had gone back to work. They used to have a rule about not having almanacs at the table, but after Rufius retired, Josh was permanently on call.

Zack had finally fallen asleep in a nest of cushions on the hearth rug and the ensuing silence felt like a momentary lull in an air raid.

'He wants to see you?' Caitlin whispered, taking a sip of wine. 'Why?'

Josh pushed his plate away, he'd lost his appetite. 'I don't know. It doesn't actually say.'

Unlike the usual orders from the Copernicans, which were long pages of details and diagrams, the message simply read "A matter of some importance has arisen.".

'I wonder why he contacted you directly? He doesn't usually get involved in mission assignments does he?'

'No,' replied Josh, trying to remember if he'd screwed anything up lately. The note reminded him of the letters his headmaster used to send home to his mother – ones that Josh became very adept at intercepting.

But there was nothing that came to mind, and the last time he saw the founder was at Rufius's leaving ceremony.

'Sim told me that Eddington's locked himself in the map room. They're all working double shifts on something, no one's saying what.' Caitlin yawned and put her fork down, her meal only half-eaten. 'I'm too tired to have any more.'

'I know,' he said quietly, looking over to their sleeping son. 'Maybe we should ask your parents to take him for a few days? We need a break.'

She folded her arms on the table and rested her head upon them. 'Yes. That would be nice. Just so I can get a decent night's sleep.'

'I can't remember what that feels like,' Josh said, getting up from the table and clearing away the plates.

'When do you have to go?'

'Tomorrow morning. Nine am.'

She picked up her almanac and pulled out the fountain pen secreted in the spine. 'I'll message mum. I don't think I could face another stint on my own.'

14

SILAS'S SECRET

Château D'If, Marseille, France.

Silas shambled into the Governor's office in chains.

He looked terrible. His hair was greasy and unwashed, hanging lankly over his face and hiding his eyes. There was a paleness to his skin that spoke of lack of daylight and vitamins. At first, Sabien thought they'd taken away his clothes and given him rags, and then he reminded himself that a few days outside of the temporal prison would equate to months inside its walls.

Temporal dilation was a byproduct of the shielding. The guards were rotated on a weekly basis to ensure they didn't age too quickly, but many retired early after "losing years" inside the Château.

The Inspector stood at the back of the office with his arms crossed while the Prison Governor, Alexandre Dumas, sat behind his desk poring over a report with a thick-lensed magnifying glass.

Dumas was a portly man with huge side whiskers. The gold buttons on his waistcoat were straining against his barrel of a belly, and from the smell of his breath, Sabien guessed the Governor liked a glass of rum or two with his breakfast.

'Number four-six-seven,' Dumas said gruffly, looking up from behind his lens. 'You requested a meeting with your arresting officer.'

Sabien uncrossed his arms and stepped forward. 'Do you have something you want to tell me?'

Silas nodded. Licking his lips and staring at the remnants of the Governor's breakfast. 'I do, but it's been a while since I ate anything that didn't taste like dirt. Do you mind?'

The Governor scoffed, putting down his glass. 'I'd rather feed it to my dogs. You have two minutes. State your business or I'll have you thrown into Endless with your parents.'

Disappointed, Silas cleared his throat and looked at Sabien. 'You asked me if I could give you proof. Well, I can, but there's only one man who'll be able to confirm it.'

'And who would that be?' the Inspector asked, beginning to feel like the man was giving him the runaround.

'Rufius Westinghouse, tell him that I've found the key to the Obsidian Gate.'

15

BRIEFING

**Founder's study. Christ Church College, Oxford.
1668. 9am.**

'Joshua,' the founder said, rising from his chair. 'Thank you for coming.'

'No problem,' Josh replied, looking around the study expecting there to be others. 'What's up?'

The founder shook his head, as if to say 'not here', and walked towards the entrance to his personal library. 'Close the door and come with me.'

Josh did as instructed and followed Lord Dee through the ornately carved arch into the private collection of the rarest books in the continuum.

'I have a rather unusual request,' the founder began, lowering his voice. 'This mission needs to be treated with the utmost sensitivity. In fact it would probably be wise if you didn't discuss this with anyone.'

Josh wondered if that included Caitlin, but decided now was probably not the time to mention it. The old man was being rather furtive, as if about to divulge some terrible secret.

'Okay.'

Lord Dee took a small journal down from the shelf. 'As I'm sure you are well aware, the Shadow Realm has proved to be something of an enigma to the Order. For many years, I believed it to be nothing more than an accumulation of redundant branches, a benign region that posed no threat to us or the continuum.'

Josh grimaced at the mention of the realm. He could still taste the ash in his mouth from his last visit, still see Abandon's glowing eyes and the shadow wraiths surrounding them – it was anything but benign.

'The Grand Seer informs me that your recent expedition was nothing like as uneventful.'

'No,' Josh agreed. 'Not the best.'

'Indeed. This Old King, Abandon, I believe Lyra has named him, is becoming a cause for concern.' The founder opened the book to a page filled with Lyra's illustrations. 'She may have also mentioned to you that during her recent visit to the early twentieth century she happened upon a group known as "The Department of Psychical Research".'

Josh nodded. 'She has.'

Lyra's encounter with King George's monster squad had made for an entertaining after-dinner story. However, Josh was never quite sure how much was actually real when it came to Caitlin's eccentric step-sister.

'Good. Well, it appears we may be in need of their assistance. She believes that they have experience in dealing with Abandon and his demonic horde—'

'Demons?' Josh interrupted, 'are you sure this isn't a job for the Draconians?'

The founder's eyes hardened. 'I sent Kaori Shika and a Xeno team into the realm three days ago. Only the Doctor and Lyra returned.'

'What happened?'

'They were attacked. It appears these "Nazgûl", as Lyra calls them, can take possession of a host body. Kaori managed to capture a specimen, but the others were unaffected by her weapons.'

Josh was beginning to wonder if this wouldn't be more of a job for the Colonel. 'I take it you've been to see Rufius?'

The old man nodded. 'He said you were more than capable of dealing with this.'

'Did he now.'

Josh wondered what exactly the old watchman had said. Inwardly, he was pleased to hear his mentor considered him capable of handling the job, while the rest of him wished he'd agreed to join him – he was beginning to miss the old bugger.

'So what do you want me to do?'

'Visit this Department and learn more about their methods. Preferably without revealing who you really are.'

'Sure,' Josh agreed. It didn't sound like an overly dangerous mission. 'But why all the secrecy?'

The founder sighed. 'Professor Eddington disagrees with my assessment of the threat. I would prefer if, for now at least, we keep this between ourselves.'

16

KAORI

Xenobiology Lab, Regents Park, London. Present day.

'So you nearly died,' said Sabien, staring at the wraith-like creature floating inside the containment chamber. It circled slowly around the glass tube as if stirred by an unseen wind.

'Ophelia protected me,' Kaori replied, tapping on one of the monitoring screens mounted to the side of the chamber. 'As she always does.'

He seemed less than happy with her answer, wrapping his arm around her waist and pulling her towards him. Schrödinger, her sabre-tooth cat, growled at him from the other side of the lab.

'You promised me,' he said, stooping to kiss her, 'there would be no more crazy adventures.'

She kissed him back and then untangled herself from his embrace. 'I don't see you taking it easy. Which battle did you chase that suspect through the other day?'

Sabien shrugged. 'Some Roman thing. I wasn't there long enough to get a good enough look at them, let alone get injured. The suspect was too quick.'

'Or you're getting too slow,' she said, throwing him a mock punch.

He dodged it with ease. 'He was a champion runner when he was younger. Won the Bellador Cup five times in a row. But, seriously, please stop putting yourself in harm's way.'

Kaori laughed. 'It's part of my job. You can't study extratemporal lifeforms from a distance. The only way we're going to be able to defend ourselves against them is if we can study them up close.'

The inspector took a deep breath and let it out slowly. 'I'm not going to change your mind, am I?'

She smiled, stroking the side of his face with her fingers and kissing him once more. 'No, but promise me you'll never give up trying.'

He turned back to the specimen floating inside the chamber. 'So what exactly am I looking at here?'

The wraith was the manifestation of a nightmare. Its body appeared to be made of translucent skeins of flowing smoke. The head was cowled. Beneath it, was what appeared to be an inhuman skull.

Kaori walked around to the other side and tapped on another console.

'It's not like the non-corporeals from the Maelstrom. The physical properties of the Nazgûl are extraordinary to say the least, it's like a projection, it has virtually no physical form.'

Sabien looked confused. 'Nazgûl?'

'It's what Lyra calls them. She's used Tolkien's books as the basis for naming the Shadow Realm. It kind of makes sense, personally I would say it looks more like a dementor – especially when you've seen it with your own eyes.'

'Dementor?'

Kaori sighed. 'You're telling me you've never heard of Harry Potter?'

He shrugged. 'Did he catch one too?'

'Never mind.'

He squinted at the creature. 'And so you're saying it's not really there? How did you catch it?'

'I used an agoryx, it's a semi-sentient organism that produces energy matrices to capture its prey. We use them a lot to collect specimens in the Maelstrom.'

Sabien tilted his head to one side, a look of bewilderment spreading across his face. 'It doesn't look very dangerous. Ugly as sin but not dangerous.'

'This is its dormant state. When they attacked my team they took a very different form.'

She pressed another button and a field generator kicked in with a deep hum. The wraith transformed instantly into a malevolent mutation, reminding Sabien of the demons from his mother's bible. The thing thrashed out at the walls of the chamber with barbed tentacles, its skull growing horns and rows of vicious teeth.

He took a step back. 'Okay, switch it off. Jesus. How the hell do you keep that thing from breaking out?'

Kaori switched the field off and the wraith returned to its dormant state.

'I've modified the stasis fields. I think it's using a form of gravimetric energy, there are certain frequencies that seem to affect it, like detuning a radio.'

'They're using gravity?'

She shook her head. 'It's not that simple, there's something really odd about it. As if it's not complying with the fundamental laws of the universe.'

Sabien shrugged. 'Well, strictly speaking neither do we.'

'You know what I mean.'

He tapped on the glass. 'Well I don't know about you but my gut tells me you should flush this thing out of an airlock.'

Sabien got the distinct impression the wraith was watching Kaori as she walked around the chamber to join him. 'There are more of these in there – potentially hundreds.

If they find a way to break through into the continuum we're in real danger. I've seen what they can do.'

There were tears in her eyes as she wrapped her arms around his neck. 'They took my team Michael. We didn't stand a chance.'

He kissed her neck. 'It's okay. You'll find a way. You always do.'

17

GOODBYE

Rothes Glen House, Banffshire, Scotland. 1892

Caitlin's parents were only too happy to take their grandson for a few days. They were testing a new engine on the *Nautilus* and were planning to go to the Permian to collect samples for Alixia.

'I was thinking I might go with them,' Caitlin said, packing a selection of Zack's toys into a bag.

'I thought you wanted a break,' Josh replied, trying to convince his son to eat his breakfast. This was his second attempt, the first having been splattered over the kitchen floor.

' I know, but Mum's happier with a socket set than a nappy, and dad has a habit of dropping things.' She appeared from the study carrying a large rucksack stuffed with books. 'Anyway, I could do with an adventure, feels like I've been stuck in one time for too long.'

He could tell from the look on her face that she'd already made her mind up.

Caitlin put the rucksack down. 'What did the Founder say?'

Josh knew better than to lie. She had an uncanny knack for knowing when he wasn't giving her all the facts. 'He wants me to go and check out a group called the "Department of Psychical Research".'

Caitlin frowned. 'The guys that Lyra met? The ones that pulled her out of Loch Ness?'

'Yes. He wants me to learn more about them.'

'Doesn't sound like an emergency. What about your other work?'

He paused, his tired brain unable to think of a suitable excuse. 'It's a bit delicate. I think it's got something to do with whatever Eddington is working on, the founder told me not to mention it to anyone.'

She folded her arms over her chest. 'Including me?'

Josh gave up trying to persuade Zack to eat any more and turned towards her.

'He didn't say that exactly.'

Caitlin removed Zack's bib and wiped his face in one fluid motion. 'Is Lyra going?'

'Not as far as I know. Just me.'

She lifted their son out of his high chair and balanced him on her hip. Her eyes narrowing. 'Feels like there's something you're not telling me Joshua Jones.'

He looked at her sheepishly. 'There may be demons.'

'Djinn?'

'No, something else. When we were trying to find Lyra in the Shadow Realm, we bumped into some pretty nasty things. She called them "Nazgûl".'

'Like the Black riders from Tolkien? Ring Wraiths?'

Josh shrugged. 'I don't know. I haven't read it.'

Caitlin raised her eyebrows. 'Then I suggest you do, or at least find out more about them. They're not something you want to mess with, unless you happen to possess the one ring to rule them all.'

She bent down to kiss him. 'Or go and see Lyra.'

Josh found the young seer swimming with a pod of unusual-looking dolphins in the flooded caverns under the Chapter House.

While she dried her hair with a towel, Lyra told him about the various members of the department, about Lieutenant Murray, Davey and Cobham, the meeting she had with King George V and his Secretary of State.

'Davey is sweet – even when he turns into a wolf. Murray is always grumpy. He's a vampire who lost the love of his life to a stryzga. The King needs to stop smoking and lose a bit of weight, but he's very polite. I've never really spoken to Cobham, not unless you count the time he was possessed by Abandon. He's got metal legs.'

'And they fight demons?'

She nodded. 'Yes, they're very organised. They have a war room deep in the vaults of the Tower. Edward Grey runs the whole thing, he's the Secretary of State, or something. There are bases all over the world. I was sent to one in Shanghai. Well I stowed away on one of their airships, but you know what I mean.'

Josh began to understand why the founder wanted to keep this mission a secret from Eddington. The professor was not a great one for fairy tales or flights of fancy, especially when he couldn't predict the outcome.

'Do they know where these demons are coming from?'

Lyra shook her head. 'No, but once I saw Abandon, I knew it must be from the Shadow Realm. I told the Grand Seer, and he spoke to the founder. They sent a Xenobiology team in with me, but it didn't end well.'

Her eyes filled with tears. 'Kaori lost a lot of her friends.'

Josh assumed the limitations on knowing about his mission didn't apply to Lyra and told her about how the founder was sending him to the DPR to learn about their tactics.

Lyra suggested the best option would be for him to introduce himself as her friend. 'Anything else would take too much explaining. They're a suspicious bunch, they take their secrecy very seriously.'

She continued. 'When I first met the King, he thought I was a clairvoyant, a medium like Lieutenant Murray's beloved Georgiana. I thought it was easier to stick with that. He even asked me to join his department, which I politely refused, but His Majesty said I would always be welcome.'

'I'm not a seer Lyra, I don't think I could play a convincing psychic.'

She pursed her lips as she considered the options, then smiled. 'No, maybe not, but I think I know who you could pretend to be.' She took hold of his hand. 'Come with me.'

18

SABIEN

Protectorate Archives.

Inspector Sabien slid the safety grille aside and stepped out of the elevator. The clattering of the metal shutters woke the archivist who was sleeping with his head on the counter.

The man was clearly surprised to have a visitor. Sabien assumed that he didn't get many from the way he was dressed. The regulation uniform for an administrative officer was a single-breasted tunic with a high collar and silver buttons, much like the uniform of the Victorian Metropolitan Police. The archivist, whose name tag declared him to be "Arthur Watkins", was wearing a maroon cardigan and a pair of fingerless gloves.

'One moment,' Watkins muttered under his breath as his hands fumbled around on the counter looking for his spectacles.

'There we are,' he said, putting them on. 'Now, how can I be of assistance?'

Sabien handed over a large file. 'Is this everything we have on the Wormwoods?'

'Ah, yes,' The man said, weighing the heavy report with

both hands. 'Wormwoods, this would be the most recent cases.' He squinted at the label on the cover, reading off the codes as he typed them into an antiquated keyboard and pulled a lever.

A bell sounded somewhere and a small ticket appeared from a slot with a clunk.

'There are five other volumes on that particular family,' the archivist said, handing Sabien the punched card. 'This will take you to them directly.'

The inspector took off his glove and held the card, allowing his fingers to read the timeline of the indentations. They showed him exactly where the other reports were stored in the vast archive. It was an efficient indexing system, one that the Scriptorians had tried and failed to emulate.

But these weren't the case files he was looking for.

'Do you have anything on Silas? The youngest son, after the arrest of his parents?' He flipped open the report and tapped on the note appended to the last page.

Watkins whistled between his teeth. 'The juvenile seal, that makes things a little trickier.'

'Trickier how?'

The archivist leaned on the counter and beckoned Sabien to come closer. 'Just in case they might be listening,' he whispered. 'I'm not strictly supposed to allow it, but there is a way.'

Sabien was beginning to think the man had spent too long on his own down here.

'Okay,' he replied. 'So what does it involve?'

Watkins nodded and took out a wad of pink forms from a draw under the counter. 'You'll have to fill these out in triplicate, and get them signed by your superior.'

'Or?'

The man's eye narrowed slightly, a sign that Sabien's instincts were correct, there was always another way to skin the proverbial cat.

'Or, you could make a small donation to the Archivist's Benevolent Fund,' he pushed a battered old tin towards the inspector. "For those who served silently", was scrawled under the letters "ABF".

Sabien was sure the acronym was more likely 'Arthur's Beer Fund', but didn't have the patience to go through the standard procedure. Watkins looked close to retirement age. He'd obviously failed to progress along the usual career paths within the Protectorate, meaning he must have screwed up so badly that curating the archives was the only option left to him.

He took some change from his pocket and deposited it into the tin.

'Much appreciated,' said Watkins, swiping the tin away and under the counter before Sabien could change his mind.

The archivist went back to his card machine and began punching in a new set of numbers.

There was no ding when the next card appeared, which was a different colour.

'Here,' he said, offering Sabien the ticket. 'It'll self-destruct in two minutes so I suggest you be on your way.'

The card took him to a random part of the archives. Sabien found himself standing on an iron gantry beside a tower of metal cages that stretched up into a distant ceiling. He inserted the card into the small slot on an intricate locking mechanism. There were a series of clicks and whirrs before the door rose up like a portcullis.

The shelves were stacked with cardboard boxes, each labelled with a series of letters and numbers that he guessed were part of the indexing system.

Checking the ticket, he found the corresponding box and took it down from the shelf. It was remarkably light, and when he took off the lid he could see why. There was only one slim file inside, a manila envelope with the words "S. Worm-wood. #182938/JV – Not for distribution," stamped on the front.

Sabien took out the file and placed the box back on the shelf.

Pulling up a case of books, he sat down and opened the envelope.

19

TOWER OF LONDON

Department of Psychical Research, Tower of London. 20th August, 1914

The London of 1914 was a far cry from the city Josh had known. This one seemed to be caught between two centuries – the old and new. Its roads were lined with a chaotic mix of horse-drawn carriages and early motor cars. A tram advertising Bryant & May matches weaved between them, its upper deck filled with men in brown suits and women wearing large hats.

There was a heavy scent of coal smoke in the air, reminding Josh this was still the age of steam. The buildings around him were stained with soot, it seemed to settle on everything.

The street was a bustling hive of activity. Food stalls lined the pavements, each one painted with gaudy signs declaring *"Piping-Hot Pea Soup, Hot Eels and Pickled Whelks for sixpence"*. Shopkeepers in long white aprons stood outside their stores with trays of samples competing for trade with the hawkers who called out as they pushed their handcarts.

• • •

At the corner of Tooley Street, Josh passed an old man selling newspapers. The headline read "GERMAN FORCES OCCUPY BRUSSELS."

He bought a copy and tucked it under his arm. Pulling the brim of his bowler hat down a little lower, he looked just like any other business man on his way to the office.

It was difficult to imagine that at this point in history, no one had experienced a World War. The British Government declared war against the German Empire sixteen days ago, sending its Expeditionary Force to France three days later.

No one knew the horrors that were to come; the Battle of Tannenberg wouldn't start for another few days, but would result in the annihilation of the Russian second army. Hundreds of thousands would die in less than five days.

This was the calm before the storm.

Walking across Tower Bridge, Josh stopped for a moment to take in the view.

There were no high rise offices dominating the skyline in this time. Through the smog he spotted the gilded urn on the top of the Monument and beyond that, the dome of St Paul's.

There was something more sophisticated about this version of London. It was understated, more elegant somehow without the glass and steel monoliths rising above it. Although some of the buildings on the South Bank look as if they were about to collapse.

Below him, the River Thames was choked with barges and boats filled with coal and cargo. The smell rising off the water was terrible. All manner of rubbish was being churned up in their wake, it was like an open sewer.

He turned back towards the Tower.

It was still a formidable sight. A storybook castle in the heart of the City, the kind he used to draw in his diary on those long nights when his mother was sick.

Josh had never actually visited the Tower of London, even though he'd lived within a few miles of the capital for most of his life.

He knew very little about it. The notes in his almanac told him it was built by William the Conqueror in 1070, and used more as a prison rather than a defensive stronghold, dominating the city as a symbol of Royal power for centuries until it became a tourist attraction.

His mother could never afford to send him on school trips to places like this. It was a shame because it would have made history classes a lot more interesting.

Instead, his lessons consisted of an endless list of boring dates and events, learning about dead politicians whose achievements had no real bearing on what was going on in Josh's life. Neither Gladstone nor Disraeli were going to repeal any acts that would save his mum, or get him out of trouble.

Josh wondered what his teacher, Miss Fieldhouse, would say if she could see him now. He could still hear her lilting Welsh accent trying to inspire them on those tedious afternoons spent staring out of the classroom window while she waxed lyrical on the Poor Laws of 1834.

If he'd known then that one day he would be able to travel back into the past, he probably would have paid more attention, but hindsight is a wonderful thing.

Navigating through the course of history was like following a map, but surviving for any length of time in the past required local knowledge and insight. Rufius's first training mission taught him a hard but valuable lesson – blending in is key.

The French Revolution was not a healthy place for a South London car thief who couldn't speak the language.

. . .

As he passed through the West Gate of the Tower, Josh made a mental note to bring Zack to see places like this when he was older. He knew Caitlin would laugh at the idea of walking around the exhibits like a linear, but he wanted to make sure his son experienced something like a normal life, the kind Josh always dreamed of, and have all the things that he never could.

He tried to look inconspicuous, mingling with the other visitors as they filed past the stoney-faced yeoman.

Once beyond the portcullis, he followed Lyra's instructions, making his way to the inner ward and through a series of narrow passageways until he came to a small studded oak door in the side of one of the towers.

'Open up!' he said, rapping his knuckles on the door.

'Who goes there?' came the gruff response.

'A King's man.'

'And which King would that be?'

'Richard, Cœur de Lion,' replied Josh, praying that they hadn't changed the password.

He was relieved to hear the grating of long iron bolts being drawn back behind the door.

Behind it stood a man dressed like a Norman knight, his helmet appearing to have a large magnifying lens welded into the face plate. *This must be Mortimer*, Josh thought, remembering Lyra's warning that he was a seer of sorts, a reader of minds.

Josh took off his hat and stepped into the elevator.

'Where to?' asked Mortimer.

'Basilisk Vault,' replied Josh, standing to one side to let the man close the shutters.

'Basilisk,' repeated the guard, his cyclopean eye staring at Josh as he pulled the lever.

There were a few moments of uncomfortable silence as

they descended rapidly through hundreds of levels. Josh could feel the man's mind probing his, they were childish fumblings compared to the mastery of the Grand Seer.

Slowly, Josh released the intuited memories of the author, Herbert George Wells, exposing enough of the man's past to be convincing. It was a diversionary tactic that Lyra knew would be too tempting for the old doorman, who was an avid reader of Wells's work.

'You don't look much like a writer.' Mortimer observed, 'and you look a lot younger than I imagined.'

Josh was wearing a tweed three-piece suit, his tachyon hanging on a gold chain from the waistcoat. He thought he looked every part an Edwardian author, or at least from the photographs of Herbert at the time. Although Josh drew the line at growing a moustache.

'Have you read any of my work?'

Mortimer seemed to relax a little, taking off his helmet and producing a book from inside his tabard. 'It's my favourite,' he said, handing it to Josh. 'Would you sign it?'

Josh took the book and examined the cloth cover. 'The Time Machine,' was emblazoned across the front in brown lettering with an Egyptian Sphinx sitting above the words: 'H.G. Wells.'

'Sorry, I don't have a pen,' Josh said, feeling the timeline unwind at his touch. It was a first edition, published by Heinemann in 1895.

'Please, use mine,' said Mortimer, his face flushed and rather sweaty. Josh was still getting used to the man having two eyes when he handed him a fountain pen. 'Can you make it to Morty? That's what my friends call me.'

Josh wasn't sure the man actually had any real friends, but did as he was asked. Accessing Herbert's signature was not too difficult, it was part of the package of memories that Josh had absorbed a few hours earlier.

H.G. Wells was an honorary member of the Order, having

been proposed by several Grandmasters including Eddington, Derado and the founder himself. The writer was given
privileged access to the Antiquarian archives and taken on
more than one trip back into the past.

When he died, he left his mind to the guild. Lyra took Josh
to him before he left for 1914.

Handing the book back to Mortimer, Josh tried not to
think how much it would be worth if it ever got sold at
Christies.

The elevator came to a stop and the seer put his helmet
back on and shoved the book inside his clothes.

'Thank you sir,' he said, bowing slightly as he pulled back
the grille.

'You're welcome,' Josh replied, still a little taken aback.
'Take it easy.'

'I will try.'

20

CME

Greenwich Observatory. Present Day.

Sim hated being so close to the Frontier. The temporal uncertainties in the present made every hair on the back of his neck stand up, not to mention the electromagnetic interference from all of their technology.

But someone from his department had to check the Standard Random Coefficient and it was his turn.

As one of the least desirable tasks amongst the Copernican actuaries, SRC duty was allocated by means of a lottery. It should have been a rota, but Eddington thought it would be a little more interesting to leave the selection to chance – it was the closest the Stochastic Professor of Probability ever came to playing a joke.

And Sim's number had come up, again, for the third time this year. Considering the number of candidates, he was beginning to wonder if the lottery was truly randomised after all.

· · ·

The task wasn't too onerous. The observatory at Greenwich was equipped with everything he could possibly need. All that was required were a few hours of his time while he took readings at regular intervals from a seventeenth-century Bernoulli Distributor installed by the Astronomer Royal in Flamsteed House.

In the present day, the house, and more importantly, its Octagon Room, was a museum displaying exhibits of the original devices used by John Flamsteed to draw his map of the heavens for Charles II. To a Copernican, the collection was a treasure trove of important scientific discoveries. Each artefact carried its own unique history, chronologies that Sim struggled to resist investigating while he waited the tedious twenty-minute interval between readings.

The SR coefficient was an important factor in their probability calculations. 'Without evaluating the level of random, there is no way to compensate for the unlikely,' Professor Eddington would quote on a regular basis. It was his mantra, a prayer to the gods of chance.

No two periods in time carried the same SRC, but the one closest to the Frontier was by far the most significant. As all Copernican actuaries knew only too well, it was the final reading before the future became the present.

He checked his tachyon, it would be at least another four hours before he would have collected enough data for the test and his stomach was beginning to rumble. The café in the Royal Maritime museum at the bottom of the hill was only ten minutes away. If he timed it correctly, he could be there and back between one reading.

Closing his almanac, Sim tucked it inside his robe and made his way to the exit.

The café was about to close when Sim arrived and the choice of sandwiches was extremely limited. Choosing the least stale looking option, he took his place in line behind a group of students trying not to stare at their outlandish clothes.

Unfortunately, he was wearing his travelling robes, which made him look more like an extra from a Harry Potter film than a member of the public. In hindsight it probably would have been wiser to change into something more contemporary, but denim made him itch – as did most of the modern fabrics.

'Hey Malfoy,' said one of the students, who sounded like an American and was wearing a NASA t-shirt. 'Show us your wand.'

Sim smiled. This wasn't the first time he'd heard that, part of him would like nothing better than to show them what he was truly capable of.

What would Josh do? He wondered. His friend was the only person Sim knew that had spent most of his life in this unpredictable era.

'Good one,' he replied, waving his finger in the air. 'Expelliarmus.'

They all laughed, which Sim assumed was a good thing.

The old woman behind the counter swore under her breath. She was obviously having issues with the till, complaining about the 'bloody card machine not working' and asking 'if anyone could pay in cash?'.

Having had the foresight to bring the appropriate currency for the era, Sim walked to the front of the queue while the students complained about the lack of "contactless" and waved their mobile phones at the assistant.

Leaving the café feeling rather pleased with himself, Sim noticed everyone was staring at their screens. They all wore the same bewildered expression, like a child who'd accidentally broken their favourite toy. Some were shaking them or holding them up in the air as if trying to get a better signal.

By the time he climbed back up the hill to the observatory,

it was clear that there was something wrong with the telecommunications network.

There was also something very odd about Standard Random.

Sitting down to eat his sandwich, he took a second and then a third reading to be sure that the Bernoulli wasn't just playing up. They were all wildly different compared to the ones he logged that morning.

Standard Random was indeed being very random.

One of the staff from the Royal Observatory burst into the building just as Sim was making a note of the fourth reading and beginning to wonder what on earth was going on.

The man was in his forties, with a mop of dark hair and a slightly manic expression. Around his neck hung a lanyard with his observatory ID, stating his name as 'Prof. Brian Cox.'

'Have you got a signal?' the man asked, waving his phone in front of Sim's face. There was a very clear 'NO SERVICE' notification at the top of the screen.

'No, sorry,' Sim replied. 'I don't have a phone.'

For a moment, the astronomer seemed lost for words, looking at Sim as if he'd said something unthinkable, then blinked and carried on. 'Listen, I've been monitoring solar activity. I think there might have been a CME.'

Sim had no idea what the man was saying. 'What's a CME?'

Professor Cox gave him another look of bewilderment, and Sim wondered if he was about to ask who he was and what he was doing here, but he shook off the concern and turned back towards the door. 'Come with me, I need your help.'

· · ·

They walked quickly around to the observatory, its domed roof was already opened to the sky.

'I've been studying the sun,' the astronomer explained, taking a large bunch of keys out of his pocket. 'I've never seen anything like it.'

Once inside the building, they climbed a spiral staircase until they reached a door that led out onto the roof.

'Where are we going?' asked Sim, following the man carefully around a narrow ledge to the entrance of the dome.

'The Great Equatorial Telescope,' the man replied as if Sim had just asked the most ridiculous question he'd ever heard.

The interior of the dome was filled with a metal scaffold supporting a large copper telescope.

'Everything electronic is fried,' Brian said, pointing towards the blank digital displays. 'I've been recording the solar activity over the last few weeks. It's been showing an unusual level of magnetic reconnection and filament eruption. The latest plasma release was off the scale, causing a massive coronal mass ejection. If my calculations are correct, it will create one of the most intense geomagnetic storms the Earth has ever experienced.' He threw his phone down and took off his jacket. 'I should have seen this coming.'

Rolling up his sleeves, the astronomer grasped the wooden handle of an iron crank and started to wind. Slowly, the entire dome began to move.

'Would you mind giving me a hand?'

Sim took over while the astronomer went to check the positioning on the finderscope.

'Okay, stop there,' he said, holding up one hand.

He positioned a mirror under the eyepiece.

'You can't look directly at the sun, it would blind you,' he explained, adjusting the glass so that it projected the image onto the inside of the dome.

Sim stared up in amazement at the solar surface. Loops of

pure energy were issuing from the edges of the star, massive bursts of plasma exploding out towards the earth.

'What causes it?'

Professor Cox shrugged. 'Areas of highly concentrated magnetic flux in the photosphere. Usually they dissipate without erupting. But this one was massive, larger than the Carrington Event I suspect.'

Sim was only half-listening, mesmerised by the ever-changing patterns. 'Sorry, Carrington Event?'

'In September 1859, two British astronomers, Carrington and Hodgson, recorded a similar level of activity. The magnetic storm was so strong that the induced current set fire to telegraph stations all over the world. Back then, they were fortunate to be not so reliant on semi-conductors.' The man looked out of the dome aperture as the sound of a low flying plane passed overhead. 'The power grids are down and so is the GPS. It must have knocked out the satellites. Let's hope they have a contingency plan for this.'

Sim realised he needed to report this. Whilst the professor was busy studying the solar activity, he took out his almanac – only to find the usually animated pages were filled with static text.

His last readings on the SRC were still waiting to be acknowledged. Nervously, he opened his tachyon. The dials were frozen. Just as with the Linear's phones, there was no connection to the temporal network.

An icy knot was forming in his stomach as Sim went over to the large telescope and ran his fingers over its metal surface. He failed to sense its history. Somehow the Sun's magnetic interference was preventing him from reading its chronology.

'You okay?' the astronomer asked, watching Sim with a curious expression.

'I need to get back,' Sim replied, realising he might have

been acting a little oddly to a Linear. 'Professor Eddington will want to hear about this.'

The man scoffed. 'Not, Arthur Eddington? Surely he's been dead for eighty years?'

Sim ignored him and pressed the homing button on his tachyon.

21

BASILISK VAULT

Basilisk Vault, Tower of London. 22nd August 1914.

The Basilisk Vault wasn't quite what Josh expected, looking more like a private library than a museum of monsters.

Walking along the shelves, Josh studied the spines, stroking the old leather bindings with his fingers and sensing their histories. These were some of the rarest first editions and original manuscripts in existence: Lord Byron's memoirs, lost works by John Milton, and the expedition diaries of Captain Robert F. Scott. Hundreds of missing books that Caitlin would give her eye teeth to add to her collection.

'And who do we have here?' came a deep voice from the shadows, followed by a puff of cigarette smoke.

'Herbert Wells, your Majesty,' Josh said, bowing low.

King George V stepped out from behind one of the stacks, holding a book in one hand and a cigarette in the other. Dressed in a houndstooth three-piece suit, his hair was slicked back, with a full moustache and beard peppered with grey.

'Wells? The name rings a bell – no relation to the author I suppose?'

'One and the same, sire,' Josh replied, allowing the natural cadence of Herbert's speech patterns to take over from his own.

The King smiled and offered his hand. 'I am a great admirer of your work Master Wells. If only there was such a thing as a Time Machine. One wonders what mistakes could have been avoided eh?'

'Indeed,' Josh replied, shaking it firmly. 'It is only when Time is nearly over that one realises how absurd it is to take Time for granted,' he quoted from the novel.

The King nodded in agreement, patting him on the shoulder. 'Wise beyond your years. Now tell me what the devil are you doing in my vault?'

'I'm a friend of Lyra.'

George's thick eyebrows raised at the mention of her name. 'Madame Cousineau? Well now, yes, talented medium. Saved one of my boys. How the devil is she?'

'She's well, sire. She mentioned your department when we were discussing the subject of my next book over dinner.'

He took a long drag on his cigarette. 'Did she now? A book you say?'

'Obviously I would obscure the source. She explained that your organisation has been a closely guarded secret for generations, but I think it has a certain mystery to it, one that would enthrall my readers.' Wells's words flowed through him easily now, the intuit had embedded more strongly than he'd imagined.

'Very wise. I have to admit, there is a certain appeal to the idea of having our work memorialised by such an accomplished author. Even if most would think it nothing more than a flight of fantasy.'

'I was hoping to meet the members of your extraordinary

group. Learn more about them first hand, perhaps even join them on a mission?'

The King's eyes narrowed. 'This is not something for the faint hearted, Mr Wells. Our work deals with the darkest forces, borne from the depths of hell itself.'

Josh nodded solemnly. 'Lyra has explained. I am prepared.'

'Well then,' George said, slapping Josh on the back. 'Let me introduce you to my men.'

War room, Tower of London. 22nd August 1914.

The Secretary of State reminded Josh of a bird of prey. Edward Grey was the epitome of a Government official; dressed in a long frock coat and pinstripe trousers, his silver hair swept back and oiled in place, hawk-like eyes watching everything with a cold, calculating stare.

Grey was talking to three unusual-looking men, who bore a striking resemblance to Lyra's description of her rescuers: Murray, Davey and Cobham. They appeared to be discussing the deployment of forces on a map of Great Britain carved into a long mahogany table – none of them seemed to be able to agree on the right strategy.

Lyra mentioned the war room, describing its pneumatic messaging system and situational maps of the world decorating the walls, but she hadn't done it justice.

It was a hive of activity. A constant stream of messages were being processed by a team of uniformed auxiliaries moving small magnetic symbols across the various charts.

Josh estimated there were at least a hundred sites marked on the four walls.

King George seemed in no particular hurry to interrupt their discussion, lighting another cigarette and chatting casually to one of the auxiliaries.

'My apologies, your majesty,' said Grey, finally coming

over to join them. 'We've had an incident at Bosworth Field. There's been a sighting of a Tudor army.'

'The ghosts of the War of the Roses?' exclaimed the King. 'Haven't we got enough to contend with the blasted Bosch traipsing all over Belgium?'

Grey bowed his head slightly. 'Yes, your majesty. Indeed we do. Unfortunately the demonic horde seem to be capitalising on the conflict.'

'Bloody poor show.'

'So, who do we have here?' Grey asked, as Lieutenant Murray and Davey came over to join them.

The King blew out his cheeks and cleared his throat. 'This is a friend of Lyra Cousineau's, an author no less, you may have heard of him. Herbert, or rather, better known as H.G. Wells.'

The Secretary of State's lips stretched into a thin smile, reminding Josh of a cobra about to strike. 'Indeed I have,' he held out a hand. 'A pleasure to meet you. I am a great admirer of your books.'

Unsure of what to say, Josh simply shook the man's hand firmly.

'He wants to chronicle our work, use it in his next book,' George added proudly. 'Can't think of a better man for the job.'

Grey nodded, but behind him Josh could see that Murray wasn't convinced. The Lieutenant's eyes darkened as he examined Josh. When Lyra first mentioned that he was a vampire, no one took her seriously, but being in close proximity to him, Josh was beginning to believe it. His skin was paler than paper with dark purple veins threaded beneath. When he spoke, Josh thought he caught a glimpse of fangs.

'I thought we were supposed to be a secret organisation,' Murray protested. 'We don't know anything about him. How do we know he won't put us all in danger?'

'He's H.G. Wells, one of the finest writers of the age,' insisted the King. 'Have you not read War of the Worlds?'

The vampire sneered. 'My life is strange enough, I've no need for fiction.'

'Any friend of Lyra's is a friend of mine,' added Davey, winking at Josh.

'We don't have the luxury of choosing our battles,' Grey reminded them, 'nor our comrades. The King has agreed to let him observe our work – we shall show him every courtesy.'

Lyra warned Josh that Murray would be the must difficult member of the team to convince.

'Tell him you studied the arcane, while researching the Island of Doctor Moreau. That you have an in-depth knowledge of the occult.'

Josh took a deep breath and let the memories of Wells take over.

'Lyra informs me you're battling a demonic horde. I've had some experience with such creatures whilst working on one of my earlier novels. I was actually present at a seance with Sir Oliver Lodge and Conan Doyle when the demon Astaroth took possession of the medium. I read the St Michael Prayer while the other gentleman performed an exorcism.'

Grey seemed impressed, but the vampire's mood showed no sign of improving. 'We'll need more than fancy words to defeat the spawn of Hell. As Madame Cousineau knows only too well.'

One of the auxiliaries approached the Secretary of State and passed him a note, which he read and then wrote a hasty reply before returning it to her.

'Gentlemen, enough of this. I just learned that the British Expeditionary Forces are massively outnumbered and taking heavy casualties from the German First Army. They're retreating towards a town called Mons in Belgium. There are reports that fallen soldiers are taking up arms once more. The dead are rising. Lieutenant, I have ordered that an airship be prepared, you depart in the next hour.'

22

NASA

Gravity Recovery and Climate Experiment. NASA, JPL, California. Present day.

David Fellowes took off his glasses and rubbed his tired eyes. It was four o'clock in the morning and he should have left hours ago, but there was no point, the data displayed on his screen would have kept him from sleeping anyway.

Joining the Gravity Recovery and Climate Experiment (GRACE) as a research assistant back in 2018, David was part of the follow-on team from the original mission which was created in 2002. They were studying the Earth's gravitational forces and how they affect the movement of the oceans.

The data came from two satellites orbiting the Earth which measured the variations in its gravity from the constant redistribution of water across the planet.

The latest readings were overlayed on a topographical map of the globe like a heat-map, showing the ocean bottom pressures in various shades of red and blue, indicating increasing or decreasing anomalies.

Something was very wrong with the picture.

David had verified the data three times, comparing it with

the scans from the previous weeks. There was nothing wrong with the telemetry, everything checked out.

The distribution of the seas was changing rapidly, the kind of activity recorded during the earthquake off Japan in 2011 – except there were no reports of any quakes from the USGS early warning system.

Although the solar activity might be a factor, he thought to himself, taking a sip of cold coffee and wishing he hadn't.

His department received an email about the coronal mass ejection from NOAA, the National Oceanic and Atmospheric Administration, in case it may be a threat to their satellites, but all of their equipment was safely shielded. They were NASA, every risk had been identified and mitigated against.

David turned back to the email he'd been drafting to his counterpart in the German Research Centre for Geosciences, who were co-funding the GRACE follow-on experiment. A copy of the latest scan was sitting above the half-finished report. He was struggling to find terms that didn't sound like something from a biblical apocalypse, but nothing else seemed anywhere near appropriate.

Rereading the text, he sighed, deleted the paragraph and typed a simple question.

'Is this the end of the world?'

23

SABIEN

Protectorate HQ. 1890

The first few pages of the juvenile report read like something from a Dickens novel. It was a social worker's nightmare. The boy's childhood was a litany of petty crimes, escalating as he got older. It was clear that his parents treated their children as nothing more than slaves, to them they were just another member of the gang, who were ruled over with a strong hand or a belt.

Silas, being the youngest, was mostly cared for by his older sister Meg, until she died of tuberculosis when she was fifteen.

There was hardly any mention of the other siblings, their profiles were probably in the doorstop of a separate file on the Wormwood "Firm". Sabien had arrested a few of them, but never the parents, they were too clever. George and Lillian were always ready to let one of their kids take the blame. The elder brothers, Walter and Finneas, were notorious tomb robbers, both died whilst attempting to steal the body of Attila the Hun.

Studying the dates on the charge sheet, Sabien could see

the frequency of arrests reducing over time. As he got older, Silas clearly got better at avoiding capture.

One thing that stood out in all of the notes was that he never spoke. Not even when they took him away from his parents at the Winter Palace.

The interrogators who interviewed him about the Romanovs noted his lack of cooperation, and looking back through the old cases, it was clear that Silas had been taught not to speak to them.

It was always the way with criminal families like the Wormwoods, indoctrinated from an early age to distrust any form of authority. "Keep your mouth shut" could have been their family motto.

'So what changed?' Sabien asked himself, turning to the section on his time with Westinghouse.

The years he spent under the watchman's mentorship could not have been more different. There were copies of his school reports for the four years he attended the academy. Silas took to it like a duck to water, gaining high marks in all the required subjects, and excelling in athletics. His house master wrote: "It is clear the boy has come from a troubled background, but his keen intellect and obvious talent have overcome many of the shortcomings that would have held others back."

Rufius seemed to have put him on the straight and narrow, there was no criminal activity or at least none that was reported. He seemed to have found an outlet in his time-running, winning the Bellador cup for the next four years in a row.

On his sixteenth birthday, for reasons unknown, Westinghouse refused to sponsor Silas's application to join the Watch. Their relationship ended that day, and they went their separate ways.

· · ·

The next entry was two years later, entitled:

ASSASSINATION OF JFK.

The report referenced three other case files, which Sabien could see by the codes were highly restricted, eyes-only documents. The synopsis in Silas's notes stated that Rufius was part of the Praetorian guard assigned to protect President Kennedy. Silas and Ravenscroft were one of the other teams assigned to the mission, along with three others. Their task was nothing more than sentry duty, keeping watch on the outer perimeter of Dealey Plaza in November 1963.

Silas failed to spot Lee Harvey Oswald entering the Texas School Book Depository, claiming at the time that he was dealing with an issue involving a pro-Castro demonstration.

The investigation into the incident concluded that Silas was not directly responsible for the crime. Although, there were rumours that it was actually a Syndicate hitman by the name of L'Oscurità, who was responsible for the shooting, and that Oswald was indeed nothing more than a 'Patsy'.

Westinghouse on the other hand, never forgave his former protégé.

For Silas to ask for an audience with his mentor was a very strange request indeed.

Sabien closed the file, he needed to talk to the old man.

24

MONS

Mons, Belgium. 23rd August 1914.

Josh stood at the edge of the battlefield looking out over the massacre.

The sun was setting behind the Nimy Bridge, its weak rays tainting the evening mist with a sickly yellow hue. Hundreds of soldiers lay dead across the cratered field, their broken bodies half-submerged in the cloying mud.

Lieutenant Murray had given them a situation briefing on the flight, which he begrudgingly allowed Josh to join. In the cramped cargo hold of the airship, Murray told about the British Expeditionary Force.

Comprising over ninety thousand men divided into two corps, they were some of the best trained and most experienced of the European armies of 1914. Their training focused on rapid-fire marksmanship meaning that the average soldier was able to hit a target fifteen times a minute, at a range of three hundred yards with his Lee–Enfield bolt-action rifle.

These men were the best the British Army could muster, and they were in trouble – something was preventing their enemies from staying dead.

. . .

It was clear from the carnage surrounding them that the
Royal Fusiliers had dealt a terrible blow to the German
advance, but the overwhelming size of General Von Quast's
forces were too much to hold back – the British Forces were in
retreat.

Josh resisted the urge to take out his almanac and ask Sim
what happened next. It was unusual to be experiencing
history in real time, without the benefit of the Copernican
actuarial department or the backup of the Dreadnoughts.

The founder's instructions were clear: don't reveal who
you are, learn how Murray's team dealt with the threat, and
don't change the outcome of WWI.

The stench of the bodies was beginning to turn his stomach. Everything about this place reeked of death. Time
seemed to be standing still, as if it were holding its breath,
waiting for something to happen.

Lieutenant Murray and his team were picking their way
carefully amongst the corpses searching for any sign of activity. They carried strange devices that reminded Josh of something his grandad would use for testing batteries.

He wasn't sure what exactly they were looking for, but he
made a mental note to steal one of the machines the first
chance he got.

Murray marched over to him, his boots and trousers
stained with the grey mud.

'Have you seen enough?' he asked. 'You seem a little off
colour.'

The vampire's eyes were dark, and his teeth longer than
usual, protruding out over his bottom lip. Josh wondered if
being this close to so much blood was too much of a tempta-
tion for him.

'Does this bother you?' Josh asked. 'You seem a little pale too.'

Murray leaned in closer, his lip curling to expose his fangs. 'Would you like me to show you what I'm capable of?'

Josh shook his head. 'No. I've read Mr Stoker's work.'

'Hey Mr Wells,' interrupted Davey, who was still in human form. 'Can I show you something?'

The tension broken, the Lieutenant returned to his search.

Josh followed Davey until they reached one particular body.

'Do you see the mark?' The big man said, kneeling down beside the corpse.

Josh knelt down beside him and studied the grey skin of the man's face and neck. On one side a dark stain had appeared, like a bruise in the shape of a ring with a cross through the centre.

'I've seen it on other bodies, before they turn,' Davey continued, 'we call it the black mark. I thought you might know what it means, being a man of letters an all.'

Looking closely, the skin appeared to be burned, as if the soldier had been branded. It wasn't a symbol Josh recognised, but it was an opportunity to ingratiate himself with Murray. The only way to find out was to go into the victim's past.

'Give me a moment,' he said, placing his hand on the man's chest. 'To pray for his soul.'

'Sure.' Davey stepped away, putting his hands in his pockets and bowing his head.

Reaving was something Caitlin warned Josh about so many times. Accessing the chronology of the recently deceased was a dangerous undertaking, one that could lead to places with no way back.

Closing his eyes, he slowed his breathing and searched the corpse for any sign of a timeline.

There was nothing.

A yawning void engulfed him. A nothingness that went

beyond anything he had ever experienced in the Maelstrom. There was a total absence of being, as if all the ties to this world had been cut loose and the man's life had simply drifted way.

He moved his hand over the mark, and felt a chill run down his spine – as if someone just walked over his grave. It triggered a vision of a vast tomb. An ancient, alien place, whose cold granite walls were carved with similar strange glyphs. There was a deep, sonorous sound, like a thousand voices chanting as one in a language he couldn't understand. And beneath it, somewhere buried below the stone, a malevolence stirred in the darkness, another mind sensing his presence.

It lasted less than a second and was gone, but it left Josh with a sense of foreboding. He knew that something evil dwelt there, and that he was destined to meet it.

'Rest in peace,' Josh whispered, taking his hand away. The mark was already fading from the man's skin.

Davey wiped his eyes with the sleeve of his coat. 'That was good of you. No one usually bothers. My Papa used to say there was no point – we're all doomed to hell.'

Josh got to his feet and brushed the dirt from his trousers. Looking around at the field of bodies. 'I'm not sure about hell, but it's something close.'

Davey tilted his head like a dog catching the scent. He glanced over towards Lieutenant Murray and then back to Josh. 'Something's coming. You should probably go back to the ship.'

His body began to transform. The jacket split along the seams as bulging muscles covered in coarse fur burst through. Davey's jaw deformed, long fangs tearing through the skin as his face cracked and twisted unnaturally until it formed into the snout of a wolf.

'Prepare yourselves,' Murray shouted to his men, pulling out a long silver sabre.

In the fading light of dusk, Josh caught the faintest movement as the dead began to stir. His heart beat faster as he watched the ruined corpses slowly rising to their feet.

Davey bounded off into the mists, tearing into the men with tooth and claw.

The vampire turned to smoke and disappeared. Cobham and the rest of the squad were planting unusual looking objects at strategic points across the ground. At first, Josh thought they were mines, but as the team came closer, he saw they were canopic jars, the kind that Egyptians used to store the organs of their dead during mummification.

'Demon traps,' said Cobham, handing him a case of them. 'They're drawn to essence. Plant them five feet apart in a circle around you. It will give you some element of protection.'

Josh took the first and stowed it in his bag, then placed the others around him. By the time he positioned them all, the battalion of the undead were only a few yards away.

He took a deep breath and braced himself – zombies were his worst nightmare, it was the way they moved – awkwardly as if controlled by unseen strings.

Murray coalesced out of smoke beside Josh. 'There's too many,' he said, levelling his sabre at the oncoming horde. 'We need to get back to the ship.'

The first of the undead approached the outer edges of the circle. Its dark eyes focused on Josh, lurching towards him, one hand clawing at the air between them.

When it reached the site of the first half-buried jar it paused and the slack-jawed head twisted at an odd angle to stare down at the ground.

As if the invisible puppet master cut through its strings,

the body collapsed to the ground in a heap. Tendrils of dark smoke wound out from its mouth, eyes and nose, as the demon's spirit curled into a spiral and poured into the jar.

Four more fell quickly behind it.

Davey carved his way through the wall of shambling men behind them, leaping over the heads of the last to land next to Josh. He was a magnificent beast, standing over nine feet tall, his muzzle and claws stained dark red. Without a word the werewolf picked him up and carried him away towards the airship.

The airship ascended swiftly from the ground, offering them a birds-eye view of the scale of the outbreak. There were literally hundreds of reanimated corpses stumbling across the battlefield towards the bridge. Beyond it they could see the British Forces encampment, where the men didn't stand a chance.

'What were they?' asked Josh, trying to maintain the pretence of being an author and taking out his almanac to make notes.

Murray ignored his question, studying the ground with a pair of binoculars. 'We need to take out the bridge.'

'I'll go,' said Cobham, shouldering a bag of what Josh assumed were explosives.

'You've got less than ten minutes,' estimated Murray.

Cobham nodded and walked off the observation deck, the servos in his metal legs whirring and clicking as he went.

Josh noticed the pitch of the turbines change and the airship turned slowly towards the river.

'We don't know,' said Davey, answering Josh's question. He had returned to his human form, but there were still rapidly healing scars on his hands and face. 'They're not like the others.'

Josh pretended to make notes with his pencil. 'How did you know they were coming?'

Davey grimaced. 'There's a smell, like rotten eggs.'

'Like sulphur?'

The big man shrugged. 'Don't know what that is, but it stinks.'

Cobham dropped down from the airship on a rope, his legs allowing him to cover the distance to the bridge in a few bounds, far faster than any human dead or alive.

They watched him place the dynamite at the end nearest the advancing German dead, rolling out a long fuse wire as he crossed the span to set a second bomb on the British side.

'Two minutes,' declared Murray.

The undead were nearing the river, the bridge narrowing their formation, forcing them into a column.

'He's not going to make it,' said one of the squad.

'Quiet!' barked the vampire.

In the twilight of dusk, they saw the line of orange light streak across the bridge, signalling that Cobham had lit the fuse. Josh realised he'd purposely waited until the undead were crossing to create the most damage.

Seconds later the entire structure erupted in a ball of fire, blasting parts of bodies and timber in all directions, illuminating the night's sky.

Those who avoided the blast marched on regardless, as if driven by some unseen drum, falling into the fast flowing river and were washed away.

Josh realised he'd been holding his breath and let it out.

'Any sign of Cobham?' asked Murray, scanning the ground with his field glasses.

Whilst everyone was distracted in the frantic search for their colleague, Josh decided it was a good time to leave and took out his tachyon.

25

———

ONE OF EVERYTHING

Central Repository of Misplaced Artefacts, Baker Street, London. 1863

To Sim's amazement, he found himself in a long, dark corridor lined with shelves of umbrellas, Gladstone bags and the strangest collection of hats.

There was quite a distinctive smell, which reminded him of the cloakroom at the Chapter House; the musty aroma of many damp, well-travelled coats.

Time travel was based on a set of fundamental rules and Sim was beginning to wonder if he may have broken the most basic of them. He certainly wasn't where he intended to be – this was not Copernicus Hall.

Realising he was still holding his tachyon, he consulted the concentric dials of the brass chronometer. They were locked in a singularly unusual configuration – all their temporal markers were set to zero. As far as he could recall, this was impossible, unless it was broken, which never happened. Tachyons didn't fail, they were manufactured to the highest Antiquarian standards, it was simply unthinkable.

The only exception involved Grandmaster Konstantine

hardwiring the Mark VI with remote detonators, but he was under the influence of an Aeon at the time, so that hardly counted.

The tachyon was by far the most reliable piece of temporal equipment the Order had ever produced and they certainly didn't take you to random locations.

Sim tapped the metal casing with his finger, and then shook it vigorously next to his ear to see if something had come loose. Pressing the homing button multiple times seemed to have no effect – the thing was totally dead.

'Are ye lost?' asked a Scottish woman from somewhere beyond a large rack of overcoats.

'Hello?' replied Sim, parting the coats to find a wall of precariously stacked suitcases. 'Who's there?'

The head of an older lady with frizzy grey hair appeared from between two battered steamer trunks plastered with labels from exotic locations.

'When huv ye come fae?' she asked, stepping out into the passage.

The woman was less than five feet tall, wearing a leather waistcoat, white blouse and a patchwork skirt. She crossed her arms and studied him from behind a pair of half-moon spectacles like a disappointed headmistress.

Sim wasn't quite sure how to respond. 'Erm. The present? When are we exactly?'

The woman shrugged. 'Depends on yer calendar. Ah'm guessin' fae yer dress that ye'll be usin' Holocene, so 11.863.'

'It's not a dress.' Sim replied.

She tutted, turning on her heel and walking away. 'Copernicans, always so damn literal. Come wi' me.'

Sim hesitated, looking around for any sign of an exit.

'The chances o' findin' yer way oot o' here on yer ain is less than nine tae one,' her voice echoed down the passage as she turned a corner and disappeared out of sight.

Sim didn't like the sound of those odds and hastily followed the sound of her footsteps.

They spent the next thirty minutes navigating the labyrinth that was the "Department of Misplaced Artefacts", as the woman, who eventually introduced herself as Evelyn Montgomery, liked to call it. Which certainly explained the eclectic collection of random objects lining the shelves. It surpassed any Antiquarian storehouse that Sim had ever visited. There were rusting pieces of old steam engines, iron keys, undergarments, hats and the strangest assortment of false teeth, eyes and coins jammed into specimen jars.

As far as Sim could see there was a total absence of an organisational system to the placement of things – stuff was just piled on top of each other in a massive disorganised jumble.

Eventually they arrived at what he assumed was the central office.

Josh was loitering at the front desk looking despondently at his tachyon.

'Sim!' he said, his face lighting up. 'What the hell are you doing here?'

Sim was pleased to see his old friend too. There was an awkward moment when he thought Josh might actually try and hug him, but it passed quickly and he settled for a handshake. 'Trying to get home,' Sim replied.

'Me too.' Josh leaned in and whispered. 'Any idea when we are?'

'No. Trapped in some crazy old lady's Cabinet of Curiosities by the look of the place.'

Evelyn had disappeared behind the beautifully carved oak counter. There were sounds of drawers being opened and closed. 'Ah can hear ye, ye know. Ah might be auld, but Ah'm no' deef.'

'When were you?' Sim asked Josh, lowering his voice.

'1914. They sent me to investigate a zombie uprising in World War One,' Josh replied, leaning against the polished counter top.

'Dae ye mind?' said Evelyn, standing up behind the desk and wiping down the surface with a cloth. 'This is an antique.'

'Who are you?' asked Josh, 'and what is this place?'

Evelyn placed yet another pair of glasses on the end of her nose. 'Gentlemen, ye have the honour of finding yersels in the Central Repository o' Lost or Misplaced Artefacts.'

'And how exactly did we get here?'

The old woman laughed. 'Sorry, forgive me, but ah never get tired o' hearin' that question. Obviously, yer tachyons malfunctioned. There's a failsafe built intae the device that dumps ye here if it cannae safely locate the endpoint. It's no' somethin' that many ken exists, mainly because they are so damn reliable, but Rufius insisted..'

'Rufius?' Josh exclaimed.

'Westinghouse. Aye, the watchman, dae ye ken him?'

'Yes,' they both responded in unison.

Her eyes glazed over a little. 'Ah huvnae seen that auld codger in a hunner years. Noo, those were bonnie times, nae mistakin.'

Sim and Josh exchanged a knowing look, both wondering if they'd discovered one of Rufius's old flames.

A large Maine Coon cat appeared beside Evelyn, breaking her out of her reverie. 'Galahad! Far hiv ye been, loon?' she said, running her hand lovingly over its back.

'So why did they fail?' asked Sim, taking out his tachyon once more. The clockface was still frozen.

'Happened to me too,' said Josh, producing his Mark VII. 'No idea why.'

Sim held his next to Josh's to compare, both dials were

stuck in exactly the same configuration. 'Maybe there's something wrong with the new models.'

Evelyn grunted, putting the cat back down on the floor. 'I think I've got a few Mark II's in here somewhere, if yer interested?' She waved her hand at the wall of small wooden drawers that stood behind her. 'They were always ma favourite.'

'If it's not too much trouble,' replied Sim politely.

'No trouble, dearie.' The old woman wandered off, talking to her cat who was following behind.

'It's not just that,' said Josh when she was out of earshot. 'The timelines are all out of whack too. I thought it might be something to do with the event I was dealing with.'

'The zombie army? Was it a breach?'

Josh shook his head. 'No, not exactly. More like a kind of mass possession. There was no sign of an aperture and the creatures weren't like anything from the Maelstrom. I tried to trace one of their timelines, but just got the faintest image of a tomb, that was it.'

Sim's brow creased. He took out his almanac from an inside pocket and turned to a page with a long list of numbers. 'I was at the Frontier taking readings on the Standard Random Coefficient. There was some unusual solar activity, the astronomer at Greenwich Observatory called it a Coronal Mass Ejection. All the electronic devices were affected, mobile phones, computers, satellites – basically anything with a semi-conductor. I assumed that it was also interfering with my ability to travel. My almanac is offline too, the last set of readings didn't send.'

Josh took out his own journal. The pages were filled with static text like a normal book. 'What does that mean?'

Sim closed his journal and shrugged. 'Something's interfering with the sympathetic link. I'd say there was an eighty-four per cent probability that it's related to the CME.'

• • •

Evelyn returned carrying a tray of old tachyons, most of which looked like they'd been through a war. Scratched and dented, some had parts of their casing hanging off.

'They're no in the best of shape, you ken, but you're welcome to try them oot.'

Sim picked one up and studied it. 'Same issue,' he said, holding it up to Josh.

They examined all of them. Each one had stopped at exactly the same time.

'So it's not just us,' concluded Sim. 'Something's very wrong with the continuum.'

'We need to get back,' Josh agreed, conscious of the fact that Caitlin and Zack were with her parents right now and wondering if the *Nautilus* could get affected too.

Sim sighed looking around at the piles of random junk. 'Indeed we do. I'm just not quite sure how.'

Evelyn tutted and crossed her arms. 'Jist typical o' the Oblivion Order, aye lookin' at the glass half empty. There are other ways tae travel, ye know.'

Josh glanced at Sim, who raised his eyebrows and shrugged. 'And how would you do that exactly?'

Evelyn placed the first pair of spectacles on top of her head and grinned. 'Wheesht! Using the hive network, o' course. Follow me.'

'What is this place?' Josh wondered aloud as they followed her along a corridor lined with door keys on tiny hooks.

'I told ye, it's a repository,' said Evelyn proudly. 'The largest single collection o' lost, misplaced an' disowned artefacts in history.'

Josh thought it looked more like an enormous junk shop, but decided to keep that to himself.

'So you're an Antiquarian?' asked Sim, running his fingers

along a shelf of dusty antique Viking helmets. There was no sign of a timeline.

'I was once,' she began, turning a corner into a passage full of sarcophagi. 'But this is aw tegither independent o' the Order. My da started it before I was born. He was something of a free thinker and no' a big fan o' the rules an' regulations imposed by the Protectorate.'

'How much stuff have you actually collected?' Josh asked, passing the entrance to a warehouse-like hangar. It was filled with old furniture and what appeared to be an old double-decker bus stuffed with gaily-coloured velvet cushions.

'We used tae joke that we ha' one of everything,' she replied. 'Naw, I think we pretty much dae.'

Sim spotted another cat prowling between the stacks.

'Is it just you and the cats?'

Evelyn nodded. 'Keeps the rodents under control. Although ah'm no' sure if ah've created a cat population problem instead. Ah cannae keep track o' them aw these days.'

'How long have you been here?'

She scratched her head. 'Weel, that's a tricky question. Ah wis twenty-four when ah left the Order tae come an' work wi' ma da. He died ten years later. Ah stopped countin' efter that.' Evelyn shrugged. 'Does nae matter, time's a storm in which we're all lost.'

They came to a circular metal door. It looked like the kind of thing that you would find on a submarine only much larger.

'Ma da wis never yin tae trust the Order's technology. He believed we should be free tae wander the timelines without everyone knowin' our business. He built his own secret routes intae the past, called the Hive. It's a non-hierarchical network based on nodes that connect moments together like cells in a honeycomb. Da wis something of a genius, although when ma died he found it hard tae cope. Without her, the indexing of things became a wee bit unmanageable, and he became obsessed wi' finding a better system, but never managed it. Hence the chaos we find ourselves in.'

She pressed her ear against the metal door and rapped her knuckles on it. There was a hollow echo from inside, like dropping a stone into an empty water tank.

'Hmm.'

'Can this Hive network get us back to the Copernicus Hall?' asked Sim. 'Or the House of the Hundred?'

'Certainly can.' Evelyn groaned, straining to turn the large wheel in the centre of the door. 'Those and aboot nine hundred or so destinations. Da wis quite a nautonnier in his time. He connected most of the significant events in the last two thousand years, although others have rather abused it since.'

Looks a lot like an airlock, thought Josh, beginning to wonder what was on the other side.

As she pulled the door open, there was a slight hiss, followed by a prickling sensation that reminded him of the first time he'd touched the medal in the Colonel's house.

Inside was a small room, the walls were covered in an old fashioned switchboard, plugs and wires hung from wooden panels that covered every inch. It smelled like the old valve radios that his grandad use to collect in his shed.

A telephone began to ring, setting off a series of other bells along the corridor outside.

'Excuse me for a moment,' Evelyn said, putting a headset over her wild hair and plugging it into the switchboard.

'Baker Street one-eight-six-three, how can I help you?' she spoke in a polite RP English accent into a small microphone. '1742, yes of course, one moment.' She plugged in another cable and walked along the board until she found the relevant socket and plugged it in. '1742, routing you now.'

She closed the call and took off the headset.

Sim studied the boards in amazement. Every socket had a small brass plaque with the year etched into it.

'Your father created this?'

Evelyn nodded, her face beaming with pride. 'Afore he lost Mama and his most o' his marbles. 'Twas his passion. A completely redundant network undetectable by the snooping Copernicans. Nae offence.'

Sim smiled. 'None taken. It's amazing. How does it work?'

'And who's using it?' added Josh.

Her expression changed. 'Unfortunately, ma da took the secret o' its connectivity tae his grave. Ah think it's something tae dae wi' quantum entanglement, but dinnae quote me on that. Da told me once that the nodal nature o' the network meant it would never break doon, it's self-correcting. As for who's usin' it, the whole point is that it's anonymised. We get the calls, we route them, we dinnae ask questions.'

'But how come no one knows about this?' asked Sim.

'No one within the Order at least,' Josh corrected him.

Evelyn winked at Josh and rubbed her hands together. 'Ah think we're gonnae get along famously. Noo, when exactly did ye want tae get tae?

'England, 11-668,' replied Sim.

'We dinnae need tae use Holocene coding for this, dear. It only goes as far back as the first millennium. 1668 it is.' She plugged in the end of a long wire and pointed towards two kiosks at the other end of the room. 'Jist pick up the receiver, and ye'll find the rest looks after itself.'

The telephone reminded Josh of something from an old gangster movie. The receiver was made from Bakelite, a twisted cord hung down from a wooden box with a brass mouthpiece and a dial. There was a symbol of a bee etched into the centre.

Josh picked it up and placed it next to his ear. There was a sound, like distant music or voices, he couldn't quite make it out. 'Hello,' he whispered into the microphone.

A moment later he was standing inside a store cupboard beside Sim.

26

WRAITH

Founder's study. Christ Church College, Oxford. 1668.

The thick glass lens rested on a brass stand in the middle of the table. It reminded Josh of the screen from one of the early television sets people bought to watch the Queen's coronation in 1953.

He was waiting with the founder and the Draconian Grandmaster, Derado, for a call from the Head of the Xenobiology Department, Doctor Shika

A bell pinged and a pale green video image flickered onto the lens. A breakthrough in temporal communications that the Antiquarian engineers were calling "Chronovision". The picture was from the present, streaming directly from Kaori's laboratory.

'Good morning gentleman. As we suspected, the wraith does not belong to any known genus or species we've encountered,' she began, pointing at the entity floating in the chamber behind her.

Her voice was slightly out of sync with her lips, but it was still incredible to think it was being transmitted from three hundred and fifty years in the future.

The founder nodded, casually stroking his beard into a point. 'So, not of the Maelstrom?'

'No.' She tapped a sequence of keys on her console and the picture was replaced by a series of chemical formulas scrolling over the lens surface.

'Not of this or any other world,' Kaori's voice continued. 'It's essentially a gaseous entity. Its form can change on demand, the molecular structure solidifying when required. I've never seen anything like this in the chaos realm.'

Grandmaster Derado squinted as he leaned in closer. 'And you say there are more of these?'

'Hundreds more,' the Japanese doctor replied, the picture returning to her camera feed. 'They took out a squad of my best men in under three minutes. Nothing we threw at them made any difference, none of our weapons had any effect. Only the argoryx, which uses an energy matrix to capture its prey.'

'And the man that led them?' continued the Draconian Grandmaster.

'Certainly looked human,' Kaori replied. 'But my readings told another story. He was exhibiting supernatural abilities, and was exerting some kind of influence over them. He also had a staff.'

Derado scoffed. 'A staff?'

'I know this is going to sound a little crazy, but he looked like a wizard, with a red gemstone in the crown. I didn't really get time to check it out, since he was trying to beat me with it.'

'And they took possession of your entire company?'

Kaori nodded, blinking back tears. 'They did. Every one of them. They didn't stand a chance.'

'I watched an entire battalion of dead men get back to their feet,' said Josh, coming to stand beside the founder.

'When was this?' she asked, a look of confusion replacing the grief.

'1914.'

The founder cleared his throat. 'Ah yes, sorry Doctor Shika, I should have mentioned that I sent Joshua to investigate an unusual event at the beginning of the First World War. Lyra discovered a group operating under the auspices of King George V, they call themselves "The Department of Psychical Research". They were formed to fight these creatures. He has only just returned.'

Josh grimaced at the thought of what he witnessed. 'I didn't see Abandon, only the zombies. The DPR were using jars, like Egyptian funeral ones, they called them "Demon Traps". I managed to keep hold of one, it has something that draws the spirits out of the host body.'

He placed the jar on the table in front of the lens, assuming that was where the camera would be, although there was nothing obvious.

'Don't open it,' advised Grandmaster Derado.

'I'll need to examine it,' added Kaori. 'Can you have it shipped to the lab?'

'Of course. We'll ask the Antiquarians to store it in the appropriate vault,' said the founder, picking up the jar and examining it. 'Not Egyptian though. I would hazard that this is more likely of Mesopotamian origin.'

Josh hadn't realised until now how easy it was to send artefacts into the future. It was a simple case of putting them somewhere safe and waiting. They would be instantly available to Kaori's team.

'It must be using some kind of attractor, like flies to rotting meat. Did they have any other weapons?' asked Doctor Shika.

'There was a device, some kind of scanner, it looked like my grandad's old voltmeter. And there was a mark on the bodies.' He drew the symbol on a piece of paper and held it up to the lens. 'Burned into their skin like they'd been branded. I tried to weave with one of them and it took me to a tomb, somewhere alien, not like anything I've ever seen.'

'You performed a reaving on a possessed body?' exclaimed Derado, crossing himself and muttering something under his breath. Josh had never taken him for a religious man until that moment.

'Have you been feeling okay? No headaches or loss of consciousness?' asked Kaori.

Josh shrugged. 'No, I feel fine.'

'And these men, did they manage to suppress the uprising?' asked the founder.

'No, we were completely overrun. We only just made it back to their airship.'

Kaori still looked concerned. 'I think you should see Doctor Crooke. Get him to take a blood sample to be sure you didn't pick up anything else like typhus or influenza.'

'I think we need to call a meeting of the High Council,' suggested Derado.

'I agree,' said the founder. 'Thank you, Doctor Shika, please keep me updated on any progress you make on the jar. Joshua walk with me.'

The image faded away to a small dot on the lens and disappeared.

Josh followed the old man out into the corridor.

'Have you managed to reach the *Nautilus*?' Lord Dee asked as they climbed the stairs.

Josh shook his head. 'They're not responding. They were on a mission to collect samples from the Cisuralian for Alixia. Caitlin and Zack have gone with them.'

The founder sighed, taking out his almanac, the pages were filled with hundreds of new messages. 'No, I've received similar reports. It appears temporal travel is being disrupted. Professor Eddington is proposing we implement an immediate lockdown, no unnecessary journeys until we can identify the problem.'

Josh wondered whether he should mention the Hive network, but something stopped him. If it were discovered, there was a good chance Evelyn would shut it down. It was the only stable way to travel, and he needed it if he was going to find Caitlin.

27

THE NAUTILUS

Maelstrom.

Caitlin had just finished feeding Zack when the *Nautilus* suddenly dropped out of warp, although it made no odds to her son, who was now fast asleep in the makeshift cot.

The ship's turbines were making a strange noise, like the cyclical whine of a jet engine throttling down. She tried not to worry, but Caitlin could tell from the look on her mother's face that something was wrong. There was a certain way her brow furrowed as she checked the gauges and dials on the control panels, biting her bottom lip in the same way that Caitlin did.

Without a word, her mother unbuckled herself from the pilot seat and climbed down the ladder into the engine room.

'Where are we?' Caitlin asked her father who was poring over the navigation console. He scratched his head and shrugged like someone who hadn't the faintest idea. Which was mildly annoying considering he was supposed to be the best navigator in the guild.

'I think we're in the Maelstrom. There's no sign of linear time.'

'The Maelstrom?' Caitlin exclaimed, going to the observation window. 'I thought we were supposed to be in the Permian?' she continued, lowering her voice as Zack stirred.

'We were, up until a minute ago,' her father agreed, checking the screen once more. 'The nav is showing us as less than five thousand years from our destination.' He thumped the side of the console with his fist. The display flickered and went out.

'That's not good,' he muttered to himself.

A moment later, her mother's head popped up through the hatch. The ends of her hair appeared to be singed.

'We've lost power,' she said, reaching out for a toolbox that sat nearby. 'We've basically dropped out of the continuum. Her induction loops have failed, I can't see why. There's nothing obvious.'

Dragging the box towards her, she began sorting through the various tools, dropping the ones she didn't need onto the deck with a clank.

'Shhh!?' Caitlin snapped, going over to check on her sleeping son. 'So we're stuck here?'

Juliana seemed to finally find the thing she was looking for. 'For the moment yes, but I know this ship like the back of my hand. I'll find the problem don't you worry.'

Caitlin took a deep breath and sat back down on the leather sofa. 'I'm trying not to.'

Her mother climbed out of the hatch and put down the wrench. 'Thomas, put the kettle on will you. I think we could all do with a strong cup of tea.'

Her father nodded and went off to the galley.

'I know you're worried,' continued her mother, coming to sit down beside her. 'But your father and I have spent most of our lives out here. We know how to survive. If something is broken, this is the perfect place to find a replacement. It's the best junkyard you could ask for.'

Caitlin shrugged, fighting back the tears. 'I know, it's just

Zack, I don't want him to spend too long out here. Lyra says he's already able to sense the timelines around him. Who knows what he'll pick up in this place.'

Her mother nodded. 'The shielding on the *Nautilus* should keep him safe. I built her to withstand the worst that the Maelstrom could throw at us.'

Her father returned with a tray laden with biscuits and a large pot of tea. A cup of Earl Grey and four chocolate bourbons were exactly what was needed to boost morale.

'How are you coping with work?' her mother asked, pouring another round of tea into china cups she'd clearly stolen from the USS Enterprise.

It was an obvious diversionary tactic, but Caitlin welcomed the chance to talk about something more normal.

'God! They're a bloody nightmare. No one can agree on anything. The Taxonomists are actually holding the Darwin collection hostage until we agree to hold talks about their revisions of the Life Sciences section.'

'Scriptorians can be very territorial. Your grandfather was always complaining about the in-fighting, he used to make a joke about how many indexers it would take to change a lightbulb.'

Caitlin smiled, she'd heard variations of this one before. 'How many?'

'It doesn't matter, by the time they finished arguing about whether it belongs under home appliance or lighting – the sun would have risen. It wasn't very funny, but then most Scriptorian jokes aren't.'

'Did you ever wonder whether you chose the wrong guild?' Caitlin asked, picking up another chocolate biscuit and dunking it in her tea.

Her mother sighed and put her arm around her daughter. 'We all do at some point. Your father switched, and there have been times when I wondered if I wouldn't have been more suited to the Antiquarians. I even went to one of their New Year's Eve parties, they're not exactly the most gregarious of groups, but they do have the best fireworks.'

A tremor rocked the ship, as if the hull of the ship were grating along the side of a large rock. Zack woke with a start, and immediately started crying. Caitlin picked him up and cradled him.

'What the hell was that?' Her father said, coming out of the galley.

Her mother was already at the observation window.

'Something's out there, probably attracted to the shielding. It's never good to idle too long in one place.' She picked up the wrench and made her way to the hatch. 'I need to get those engines back online.'

28

OBISIDIAN GATE

Cap Corse, Corsica. 1616

Sabien had crossed paths with Rufius Westinghouse on several occasions, none of which had ended particularly well. They were like oil and water, the old watchman making his disapproval of the Protectorate very clear.

Regardless of his personal animosity towards them, Westinghouse was still regarded as something of a legend amongst the members of the Order.

Having been one of the founder members, he had earned his place on the High Council. However he never took it, preferring to remain a lowly man of the watch than wear the chains of a Grandmaster.

Within the Protectorate, he was considered a maverick. There were many of Sabien's fellow officers who would like to have seen him put away for his unconventional approach to managing the timelines.

But he got results.

.   .   .

'What the hell are you doing here?' The old man's voice boomed across the vineyard as the inspector made his way up the hill towards his tower.

The inspector decided it was wiser to approach from a distance, and on foot, rather than appear on his doorstep. The watchman was notoriously quick-tempered and quite deadly with a wide array of weapons – a combination that could be potentially lethal when surprised.

'I have a question to ask you,' Sabien shouted, raising his empty hands into the air in surrender. He knew there was a very good chance the old man was aiming a musket at him at this very moment.

'I'm retired,' came the response, his voice nearer than before, but still Sabien couldn't locate the source. 'Not that you lot seem to be taking it seriously.'

'I know, but this is a special request. One that only you would know the answer too.'

The watchman stepped out from behind a row of vines. Holding a flintlock pistol in one hand and a sword in the other.

'My eyes aren't as good as they were,' he explained, tucking the pistol into his belt. 'Put your hands down you fool. I'm not about to shoot one of the Protectorate's finest.'

Sabien relaxed and lowered his hands.

Rufius sheathed his sword. 'We've been having some trouble with Barbary pirates around these parts lately. You have to be on your guard,' he said, nodding towards the tower. 'Come on. I've got a feeling I'm going to need a drink.'

'It won't take long.'

'Indulge me. Seems to be my week for visitors.'

The interior of the tower was crammed full of packing boxes and steamer trunks. Books were stacked randomly in corners and old brass artefacts hung from the low beams.

'You'll have to excuse the mess. The Antiquarians insisted I take everything out of storage and this place hasn't quite got enough capacity. Methuselah is coming over later to add another couple of rooms.'

Rufius picked up a cardboard box from an old chair and placed it precariously on top of another pile. He dusted off a bulbous old bottle and pulled the cork out with his teeth.

'This is Rumbullion, the locals call it "Kill-Devil". I had a case of it brought back from the West Indies. 1650 was a particularly good year,' he began, pouring two large glasses and handing one to Sabien. 'So what is this burning question that you're wanting to ask?'

'We arrested a suspect last week. He was trading knowledge back to the Aztecs. It was a routine arrest, or at least I thought it was until he started talking about Atlantis.' He took a long, slow sip of the brandy.

Rufius chuckled and sat down in the chair. 'Atlantis? Don't tell me, he knows where the key to the Obsidian Gate is.'

Sabien looked surprised. 'Yes.'

'This suspect of yours wouldn't happen to go by the name of Silas Wormwood by any chance?'

The inspector nodded.

'Hah! Did he give you a run for your money?'

'Four epochs in under ten minutes.'

Rufius smiled. 'He's slowing down. When I knew him he could do seven easily in that time.'

'And the key?'

The watchman took a slug of rum and poured himself another. 'It was something of a running joke, pardon the pun. The boy was under my charge for a while, after his parents were put away. I used to use Atlantis as one of his training missions.'

Sabien looked confused. 'It went missing thousands of years ago. No one has been able to find it.'

'Twelve thousand, if you believe Plato. Which we both know was nothing more than a story, but Silas didn't. The point of the exercise was to explore how far he would go before giving up the search.'

'And the key?'

'Hah, I have it here somewhere.' Rufius stood up, went over to a large chest of drawers and began routing through it. 'I told him that there were four gates into Atlantis. Each with their own key. All he had to do was follow the chronology of the Obsidian key and it would take it there. An island of untold wealth and riches. The boy's eyes nearly popped out of his head. Here we are.'

Rufius held up a long metal key with an ornate fob. 'The Obsidian Key.'

He handed it to Sabien.

The inspector took off one of his gloves and felt the cold iron. His face a mask of concentration.

'Do you see the trick?'

'It's a displacement key,' the inspector said, handing it back.

Westinghouse grinned. 'Not just any displacement key. A master. One with more timelines than a Stryzga after the Battle of the Somme.'

'And one of them leads to Atlantis?'

Rufius sucked air in through his teeth. 'Well, that's the rub. I might have made that part up.'

'So, there's nothing to support his claim.'

The watchman held up a finger. 'Now, I didn't say that. The man who sold me the key swore on his grandmother's life that he bought it from a sailor who worked on one of Templeton's supply ships.'

'Templeton?'

'The Director of the Chronomatic Research Institute, he was stationed on the island. Before it disappeared.'

'So it could lead us to Atlantis?'

Rufius scratched his beard. 'In theory, yes, but highly unlikely. It would require another vestige, something to isolate the relevant strand of time. But it's a moot point, nothing remains that could be used to trace it. Templeton managed to blow himself and his team out of existence. No one has ever made it back from Atlas Station.'

29

INFINITY ENGINE

Copernican HQ, 1688.

Professor Eddington was surrounded by a dense lattice of swirling timelines. The holographic model of the last twelve thousand years twisted around him like the filaments of a thousand lightbulbs. His face was a mask of intense concentration, but it was clear to Sim that his master was struggling to control it.

The professor's hands wove through the layers of the temporal model with the precision and poise of an orchestral conductor, fighting to maintain its complex formulaic structure.

Observing in silence around the perimeter were the members of the High Council: Grandmasters of the Guilds and their senior advisors.

'Increase entropic reversion and reduce the causality index by two points,' Eddington instructed his team of actuaries through gritted teeth.

Sim's hands instinctively moved to a set of brass levers and carefully adjusted each one, watching the needles slowly creep across the dials.

With subtle gestures, the professor focused on a particular series of dates and read them out in turn. 'American Independence 11.776 – good, Gutenberg Press 11.440 – as it should be, Battle of Hastings 11.068. Damnation!'

The tension in the room was palpable. Sim could feel the sweat beading on his forehead. None of them had ever seen their master work so hard to control the Infinity Engine, but the temporal model was losing cohesion.

'There's nothing more I can do,' he admitted, holding up his hands in defeat. The glowing lines faded away until they found themselves standing in the dark.

'It appears Master De Freis's hypothesis is correct. Something is disrupting the chronodynamics of the continuum.' Eddington dabbed at his brow with a handkerchief as the lights were switched on.

Deep in thought, the founder walked into the centre of the room. 'These are dark days indeed,' he began in a low, sombre voice, 'never in our history has the continuum faced such a threat. Our members must be protected at all costs. Have they all been located? Are they safe?'

Eddington looked like a broken man. 'We have lost contact with them, my lord. Their almanacs and tachyons are no longer temporally synchronised. We are effectively blind.'

There was a collective intake of breath from the rest of the room, all of the grandmasters looked deeply concerned. The Copernican Guild prided itself on always being able to advise the Council on the best course of action, their statistical analyses were the basis of every decision that was taken – they never failed.

'Do you at least have some idea what might have caused it?' asked Derado. The Draconian Grandmaster was dressed in full battle armour, as if he'd just returned from a mission.

The professor took a deep breath, pausing to gather his thoughts before answering. 'Without any data, it would only be a hypothetical answer. A strong gravitational field, like that of a black hole, perhaps – one that could distort the fabric of space-time. It would certainly have to be a massive object. Simeon's report of the solar activity at the Frontier may be a sign, but I cannot say with any certainty.'

Lord Dee turned to the members of the council. 'Grand-masters, I suggest we suspend all missions and begin plans to retrieve your members immediately. Compile a list of last known locations. Every one needs to be found and returned safely. Derado, assess the threat-level. Those stranded in the most dangerous eras will need to be prioritised. Has anyone managed to contact the *Nautilus*, do we know where she is at this moment?'

There was a moment of silence and many blank expressions.

'I've still not managed to reach them,' said Josh, stepping forward.

'Do you think their engines could be affected?' the founder asked, turning towards Eddington once more.

'I cannot say my Lord. Statistically it is very likely.'

30

LYRA

Xenobiology

Lyra studied the wraith with the fascination of a small child visiting the zoo for the first time.

The creature coiled endlessly inside the glass chamber like a swarm of ghostly eels. A formation it assumed the moment Lyra entered the laboratory.

Watching her over the top of her laptop screen, Kaori realised she hadn't really thanked the seer for pulling her out of the Shadow Realm, although she still wasn't quite clear how she did it.

'Do you know what it is yet?' asked Lyra, her wide eyes transfixed by the turmoil.

'I've narrowed it down to one of three things,' replied the doctor, getting to her feet and walking over to join her.

'It has a similar energy profile to *Draconaris Subix*, but doesn't exhibit the same atomic signature. The mass spectrometer puts it squarely in the non-corporeal realm and yet we can clearly see it with the naked eye – and for some reason it's emitting the same form of beta waves as a *Taxian Kalasaur*.'

Lyra shook her head. 'No, not a Kalasaur, I can feel it.'

Kaori tilted her head slightly. 'You can sense it?'

The seer frowned and placed her hand on the glass. 'As if it's singing a very sad song. There are no real words, just a series of emotions, like a whale calling out to her lost calf.'

Doctor Shika tapped a series of keys on one of the consoles, and a waveform appeared on the screen. She studied the oscillating lines for a moment and then keyed in another sequence of commands.

'What is it?' asked Lyra.

'Well, this is a Theta wave,' she pointed at the first of the lines. 'It's four to seven hertz. And that's the Beta wave running at thirteen to thirty.'

'They're brain waves.'

Kaori's eyes widened as she realised. 'Why didn't I think of that? Yes, this is the kind of activity you see in a human brain when it is dreaming.'

Lyra smiled and took her hand away from the glass. 'Dreaming, yes, that's what it feels like.'

The doctor stared back up at the creature. 'So part of this was once human?'

'Once. Yes, but now it's something else.'

31

PARABOLIC CHAMBER

Chapter House. 1668

'What if they're trapped in the Maelstrom?' asked Josh, pushing his food around the plate with his fork like a petulant child. The boar was up to Methuselah's usual standards, spit-roasted over an open fire, but he wasn't really hungry. It was difficult to focus on anything other than finding Caitlin and Zack.

'I'm sure they're safe wherever they are,' Alixia tried to reassure him. 'The *Nautilus* is one of the finest vessels I've ever travelled in, and she's with her parents, who are very accomplished Nautonniers.'

It was true, the *Nautilus* was one of a kind. The High Council considered commissioning a fleet of them, but the Antiquarians were having trouble replicating her design – even with Juliana's help. Their engineers were beginning to believe they would have to be constructed inside the Maelstrom, which brought its own complications.

'I know, I keep telling myself that, but it's not working,' Josh replied.

'And the *Nautilus* has gravimetric compensators,' added

Sim, who knew everything there was to know about the time ship. 'They should be able to reduce the effect of the temporal fluctuations.'

It sounded convincing, although Josh really had no idea what Sim was talking about; his mind was elsewhere. All he could focus on was that his family were in danger and there was no way to help them.

'What am I suppose to do? I can't just sit around here hoping they're going to turn up.'

Alixia clapped her hands together and the entire dinner table fell silent.

'Josh is right, we shouldn't sit here wringing our hands like old fishwives. Many of our people are stranded, we should be preparing to take them in as soon as the founder has found a way to rescue them. Phileas, Lyra, I want you to help your father prepare the secondary wings, he's going to need to attach at least a thousand more rooms. As for the rest of you, we're going to need to stock up on medical supplies and food. Sim and Josh, come with me.'

No one questioned Alixia when she used that particular tone of voice, it had an underlying threat that spoke to the inner child in all of them. As one, the guests rose to their feet and filed out of the door.

'Where are we going mum?' asked Sim.

'To your father's parabolic chamber, if nothing else Josh should be able to communicate with Caitlin.'

The parabolic chamber was a small, circular room with a domed roof. The cylindrical walls were covered in mirrors configured to create an infinite number of reflections of any subject that stood at its centre. It was Methuselah's personal project, a lensing device that could locate anyone who had intersected with your timeline. A form of temporal telescope – one that could also be used as a communications array.

Josh took a deep breath and stepped inside the chamber.

'I'd keep your eyes closed until you're in the middle,' Sim advised from the doorway. 'Helps me to cope with the vertigo. Keeps me from wanting to throw up quite so quickly.'

Josh took his advice, putting his hands out to steady himself.

'Okay, you're there,' whispered Sim, closing the door. 'Now focus on a memory of Caitlin or Zack, the chamber will do the rest. Good luck.'

Opening his eyes, Josh was greeted with a thousand reflections of himself. The wave of vertigo was intense, like standing on the ledge of a very tall building and trying not to stare at the drop. The lensing effect wasn't helping, it created myriad versions of reality, each one showing a slightly different variant of what he was about to do next.

Taking another long breath, he tried to recall the first time they met in the library. There were so many other versions of that day, but the very first was still there, tucked away in a corner of his mind. Josh could see her beautiful smile as she came over to help him, the way her hair fell over her face when she was looking through the book on Stauffenberg and the bright sound of her laugh.

Suddenly, the chamber darkened, the mirror images around him changing until Josh was standing in the void of the Maelstrom. A vast empty space surrounded him, it was absolute and, for a second, he lost his train of thought.

'Where are you?' he whispered, searching the darkness for any sign of life. As his eyes slowly adjusted, he glimpsed gossamer-like threads of time drifting past him, eddies of temporal energy cast adrift into the nothingness like cobwebs on the wind.

It felt like a hundred lifetimes since his last visit to the Maelstrom, but the memories of his battle against the Djinn were still as vivid. Somewhere in this chaotic realm were the remains of Dalton and the Nihil. Josh wondered if anything truly died in the non-linear realm.

The lensing image shifted inside the chamber. Following his thoughts it took him towards a dark ruined planet surrounded by an asteroid field. As he flew between the vast chunks of black rock, Josh knew this was all that remained of the Nihil home world.

Quickly realising his mistake, Josh re-focused his attention on Caitlin and Zack, clearing his mind of any other thoughts but them.

In the blink of an eye, he was standing on the bridge of the *Nautilus*. Caitlin and her mother were busy at the controls, while her father held the baby.

'Josh?' exclaimed Caitlin, looking a little confused. 'Is that you?'

'You can see me?' he asked, his voice echoing around the chamber.

She walked towards him holding out her hand, titling her head as if trying to get a better view. 'Kind of, you're like a ghost.'

Josh smiled. She looked as if she needed a hug. He reached out to touch her face, but felt nothing. 'I'm using Methuselah's parabolic chamber. It's kind of weird. Are you okay?'

Caitlin's lip trembled, the way it usually did before she was about to cry. 'No, something's wrong with the engines. We're trapped here.'

Her mother interrupted. 'It's the gravimetric drive. The compensator has burned out. No idea why, but I need you to send in another one, there's a spare in the hangar.'

'Okay,' Josh replied. 'Is Zack all right?' Looking past them towards the bundle in his grandfather's arms, thinking about the last time he'd held his son.

The image twisted for a moment and refocused on a

different scene. Some hours had passed by, they were now in the galley, feeding his son.

'Sorry, I lost my train of thought for a second.'

'It's been nearly six hours,' Caitlin snapped, the fire returning to her eyes. 'Try and stay focused and listen carefully. Mum says you need to bring a new compensator and a fifteen-gauge torque spanner. We've got limited power and something big keeps testing the ship's defences. Your best bet is to get the Draconians to open a breach near the Mordant Quadrant. We should be able to pick you up in there.'

The picture dropped out once more and he was back in the void. There was no time to explain that the Order was in lockdown, that all missions should be postponed. He would have to find an unofficial way into the Maelstrom.

And he knew just the man for the job.

'What did she say?' Sim asked as they made their way down the stairs.

'They're stuck in the Maelstrom, their engines are fried, and they need spares: a gravimetric compensator and a torque spanner. Can you pick them up?'

Sim looked confused. 'Of course, but how are you going to get into the Maelstrom?'

'I know someone.'

'Bentley?' Sim said, remembering the red-headed artificer who'd once saved his family. 'I should have guessed.'

When they reached the ground floor, Arcadin was sitting in a chair placed against the front door. The blind doorman got to his feet and bowed. 'Master Jones and Master De Freis, I'm afraid I have been instructed to bar the door, no one is to leave.'

'We understand,' said Sim, motioning Josh to go into the changing rooms. 'How are you keeping? I hear that father has been working on a new doorbell?'

While Sim kept him talking, Josh crept into the cloakroom and found his locker. Quickly changing into his travel robes, he took the photograph of Caitlin and Zack from the inside of the door and slipped it into his almanac.

Half way along the row of cabinets was a wooden panel with a Bee carved into it. He pressed the symbol and the hatch popped open, inside was an old Bakelite phone.

'Baker Street 1863, how can I help you?' came the voice of Evelyn through the receiver.

'Ascension Island, 1927,' said Josh.

'Putting you through.'

32

BENTLEY

Draconian Headquarters, Ascension Island. 1927.

Bentley was nearly unrecognisable. His physique had changed considerably since Josh last saw him, fighting the Djinn during the Fire of London. His red hair was cropped short and the chubby, awkward body that Darkling used to make fun of, was now taught and muscular beneath his Draconian uniform.

He held himself with a self-assured confidence, like a soldier.

'Hi Josh,' he said with his usual smile, extending a hand. 'How are you?'

'Bentley, you're looking good,' Josh replied, shaking it firmly. 'You're an officer now?' he added, noticing the pips on his friend's collar.

'Field Artificer, First Class,' Bentley said with pride, his cheeks reddening. 'That's what they give you for saving the continuum apparently.'

'And a few medals besides,' Josh added, pointing at the coloured bars on his tunic.

Bentley shrugged. 'I was just doing my duty.'

Josh looked around the atrium. A Master Sergeant was organising his squad, barking orders as they formed themselves into a line. 'Yeah, on that note. I could use your help. Is there somewhere we could talk?'

'Sure.'

Thankfully, Bentley's quarters were on one of the lower levels of the lighthouse. There were no lifts in the Draconian headquarters and there seemed to be a policy of taking the stairs at a run.

As expected, his room was filled with half-finished inventions.

'Do you still have a breacher?' Josh asked, picking up something that looked remarkably like a pineapple made from copper wire.

'Yes. Two actually,' said Bentley, hastily tidying away a pile of washing into a cupboard. 'I've managed to miniaturise the main components, soon it'll nearly fit in your pocket. Why, do you need one?'

Josh sat down on the bed and told him about the events of 1914, how the dead rose from the battlefield and his problems with getting back home. Bentley sat on his bed, listening intently without interrupting.

'They're probably using some kind of quantum redundancy, each node able to act as a router,' he explained, when Josh mentioned the Hive Network, his technical brain intrigued by the science behind it. 'Self-correcting. Brilliant.'

'Whatever is causing it, the *Nautilus's* engines have been affected, Caitlin and Zack are on board. They're trapped in the Maelstrom.'

A klaxon sounded somewhere below them and Bentley got to his feet, his body tensing. 'The whole garrison's been put on high alert. No one's told us why, but the Dreadnoughts are being prepped for immediate action.'

'There's something wrong with the timelines. People are stranded all over the past. They need the *Nautilus* to rescue them.'

'Why not use the Hive Network?'

'That could get complicated. The woman who runs it isn't a fan of the Order and I'm not sure it even goes back far enough. Look, I need to get into the Maelstrom. Caitlin says the ship is being attacked, she needs those parts.'

Bentley nodded, his jaw clenched as if preparing for battle. 'Of course, let's go.'

Sim was waiting in the Nautilus's hangar when Josh and Bentley appeared from a storage room.

'Well that was unusual,' said Bentley, looking back towards the storage cupboard, the symbol of a bee still faintly glowing on the door.

'Yes, it takes a bit of getting used to,' agreed Sim. 'I had to make three separate calls to get here. Do you have a breacher?'

Josh nodded at the large leather satchel the young artificer was carrying. 'Apparently it's pocket-sized.'

'Well, nearly,' said Bentley, taking off the bag. 'Where do you want to open it?'

'I think Hangar Bay Two is closed for maintenance, we shouldn't be disturbed in there.' Sim was carrying a heavy-looking bag of his own.

'Did you find the spares?'

Sim nodded. 'Yes and a few other provisions, just in case it takes longer than expected to pick you up.'

Josh took the bag from Sim and gave him a hug. 'Thanks mate, you think of everything.'

Sim seemed a little taken aback by the outward show of affection. 'It's my job, remember, Copernicans are hard-wired to think of every eventuality.'

. . .

Hangar Bay Two smelled of oil and burned metal. It reminded Josh of his grandad's garage. The man was an engineer with a love of all things mechanical, and tinkering under the bonnet of his old Jaguar XJ6 was one of his favourite distractions. 'Keeps him out of trouble,' his grandma used to say.

Josh couldn't remember his grandfather ever driving it, but he always wondered if he took after the old man with his love of cars.

Sim was right, the hangar was unoccupied. The half-finished tail section of another *Nautilus* hung suspended inside a huge scaffold at the far end of the bay, while the parts of one of its plasma cannons were lined up along a workbench.

Bentley's face lit up like a kid in a toy shop. His interest was immediately drawn towards the array of lethal components. 'Is that a pulse modulator?' he asked, picking up one of the more intricate pieces. 'Looks like they're using the new Heinlein power converter.'

'Bentley, I need that breach now!' Josh insisted, pulling him away.

Reluctantly, Bentley put the modulator down and looked around. 'That should do,' he said, pointing at a blank wall.

Taking the breacher out of his satchel, he placed it carefully on the floor and attached a battery pack. He fiddled with something on the side until it made a series of whining clicks and began to vibrate. To Josh it looked like nothing more than a series of flashlights bound together by a copper coil.

'Um, I wouldn't stand so close. It can be a little temperamental,' Bentley warned, taking a few steps back.

Sim and Josh glanced at each other and followed his advice.

The device grudgingly flickered into life. Like a lightbulb on its last legs, it made a weak attempt to project an image onto the wall and then expired with a "Phut" and a puff of blue smoke.

'Bollocks,' muttered Bentley, kneeling down beside it. 'It does that sometimes.'

After a few minutes of more fiddling with screwdrivers and a great deal more swearing, a faint beam projected out of the device and onto the wall.

'Okay, give it a second to warm up,' said Bentley, getting to his feet and brushing the dirt off his trousers.

As the beam grew brighter, the circular spot on the wall expanded. The intensity increased, the surface of the concrete began to vibrate and distort, bubbling up like old paint under a heat gun.

'I've found a way to consolidate the disruption fields using photons,' explained Bentley proudly. 'It can also work the other way, closing off a breach in seconds.'

Sim stared in wide-eyed amazement as the seemingly solid wall dissolved away, leaving a perfect circular window into a dark void beyond.

'This is incredible,' he gushed. 'Do you know what this could mean for our frontline defences?'

Bentley nodded. 'I'm planning to build it into a suit, or maybe a helmet.'

'Sorry to break up the moment, but I have to go,' interrupted Josh, stepping towards the black hole. 'Do I just walk through?'

The artificer shrugged. 'I guess so.'

'What do you mean you guess?' said Josh, the pitch of his voice raising slightly. 'Haven't you been through yourself?'

Bentley shook his head. 'No, not as such. I've sent a few objects in there, and they seemed to be okay.'

'What kind of objects?' asked Sim.

It was clear that he didn't really want to answer the question, his eyes dropped to the floor. 'Well, a couple of books and a coffee cup.'

'So nothing living?'

'And a plant.'

Josh tried to control his anger. 'You're telling me that the only actual test was on a geranium?'

Bentley scowled, folding his arms across his chest. 'Orchid actually.'

Sim shook his head. 'This is crazy Josh. You can't go through there, you've no idea if you'll survive.'

'Caitlin and Zack are dead if I don't,' Josh replied, hoisting the heavy bag onto his shoulder and moving closer to the aperture.

'Wait!' said Sim, taking out a full-face diver's mask from his pack. 'Wear this.'

Josh looked confused. 'I'm not going underwater.'

'No, but the air pocket you'll take in with you won't last for ever. It's got a built-in rebreather, should be good for three or four hours at least.'

Josh put it over his head and Sim checked the straps, tapping him on the shoulder when he was done.

He could feel the warmth of the room being sucked into the hole. It was cold, the kind of creeping chill that leeched into the bone. Before him, there was nothing but an inky blackness and no sign of the *Nautilus*.

Whispering a silent prayer to whichever gods might be listening, he stepped into the void.

33

MAELSTROM

***Nautilus*. Maelstrom.**

'Can you see him?' asked Caitlin, hovering behind her mother, who was bent over a reclaimed P-scope from one of the WW2 battleships. They both watched the radar for any sign of contact as the luminous green line arced around the screen.

'Not yet,' her mother replied through clenched teeth. 'It would be a little easier if you gave me some space.'

'Sorry.' Caitlin stepped back. 'It's just I thought he'd be here by now.'

They were running on auxiliary power and the batteries were getting low. After three long days cruising through the Mordant Realms, there was still no sign of Josh.

'Try to remember it's all relative, honey. A day in here could be less than a minute in the continuum. We've no way of knowing how long it will take him to get the parts and convince the founder to let him try and find us.'

'Or if they'll let him come in at all,' said her father.

'Thanks for the positivity Thomas,' growled her mother.

'Would you mind keeping watch out of the oculus in case I miss something? And check on Zack while you're there.'

'Sure.'

Once her father was out of earshot, her mother continued. 'So, let's assume Josh is resourceful enough to find a way into this chaos. His presence should attract the attention of the storm-kin. With any luck we'll be able to detect a change in the underlying chaos patterns before they get to him.'

Caitlin shivered inwardly at the thought of Josh drifting alone in the dark surrounded by a swarm of nightmares. 'Could you try to be a bit more reassuring? You're starting to sound like Dad.'

Her mother put her arm around her daughter and pulled her in for a hug.

'When you've survived in here as long as we have, you learn that there's no point in trying to predict what's going to happen. Living in a permanent chaotic state takes some getting used to and keeping your sense of humour definitely helps.'

'I don't know how you do it,' Caitlin whispered into her hair.

'I think I see him!' shouted her father, pointing at something through the window. 'Fifteen degrees off the starboard bow. There's a cluster of storm-kin activity.'

Her mother kissed her cheek and went back to the scope. 'Yes, I can see it. Caitlin, take over here while I get the ship into position.'

The lack of stimulus was playing tricks with Josh's mind.

Staring into a total void, an abyss, would eventually drive the sanest man to madness and Josh's imagination was already conjuring up the worst kinds of nightmares.

Shapes formed out of the darkness, creating monsters that circled around him like sharks stalking the prey.

'They're not real,' he whispered to himself. 'It's all in your head.'

Closing his eyes, he focused on his breathing. Sim was right about the mask, the pocket of air that surrounded him was shrinking and there was no sign of a suitable place to land as yet.

It was impossible to tell how much time had passed since he entered the void. In reality he knew it was not passing at all. The Maelstrom was timeless, a hard concept to come to terms with when you were drifting through it. There were no stars to determine which way was up – it was totally disorientating.

Every so often a bubble of time would float by like a pocket of lost moments sealed inside a snow globe. They were always too far away to reach or looked too unstable to even attempt to enter.

He was beginning to wonder if Caitlin would ever find him.

We'll find you. Her words echoed in his mind.

'We're closing in on his position,' noted her mother. 'Thomas go topside and get the boat hook ready. Caitlin, hold her steady while I shut down the engines.'

'I can handle a boat hook,' insisted Caitlin, who was already half way up the ladder into the conning tower.

'Fair enough,' muttered her mother. 'Thomas, come and take over. The left rudder is sticking so keep an eye on it.'

Caitlin stepped out of the hatch and grabbed the handrail, attaching her safety line to it.

The view from the conning tower always took her breath away. The silence of the inky blackness was deafening and the darkness was absolute, so much so that it was hard not to imagine you'd gone blind. The lack of stars or planetary objects made it impossible for the brain to orientate itself, or gauge distances.

In this case it made it easier to spot Josh. Caitlin could see a nebula of luminous shapes moving off the starboard bow. Their semi-transparent skin was similar to that of a jellyfish, trailing long, vicious tentacles as they floated around him.

'Hurry up,' she barked into the speaking tube. 'He's being surrounded by Medusozoa.'

She lifted the boat hook from its holder. It was over six feet long with a nasty looking barb at the end.

Josh could see luminous creatures approaching. It wouldn't be long before he'd have to deal with them, but he was ready. He was the Paradox after all, his existence was anathema to them, his timeline was toxic to the Djinn.

There was something quite hypnotic about the way they moved, like bloated, bioluminescent man-o-wars, their long manes trailing behind them. No one would have called them beautiful, especially as they came closer and he could see the contents of their many stomachs.

The corpses were in various states of decay, reminding him of the army of undead on the battlefields of Mons.

He had a slight phobia about zombies.

When he was younger, they could never watch a zombie movie. The thought of rotting carcasses crawling towards you was the true stuff of nightmares. His mother spent hours trying to calm him down after the first episode of the Walking Dead. Not that Josh should have been watching it at such an early age, but she was always so tired, leaving him in charge of the remote control while she snoozed in her chair.

Now he'd actually witnessed the dead rising, something

that the DPR were having to deal with on a daily basis, and whatever was possessing them had come from the tomb.

There was something about that place that made his skin crawl, a malevolence that lingered like a wound that wouldn't heal.

But that would have to wait, first he would have to deal with the giant jellyfish.

The *Nautilus* carved a path through the swarm of semi-transparent Medusozoa, its hull shielding taking a battering as their tentacles scraped along the armour plating. Caitlin ducked as a curtain of vicious looking barbs swept over the conning tower.

'Josh!' she screamed into the void, but it was useless, the sound died the moment it left her lips.

The ship broke through the mass and entered a clearing, Josh's body floated in the centre, surrounded by blackened, crystalline bodies. The tentacles shattered like glass as she swung the boot hook out to catch him.

On her third try she hooked his coat and pulled him in.

He looked dead, pale and lifeless.

'Josh?' she whispered, pulling off his mask and kissing his face, cradling his head in her lap.

Slowly, his eyelids flickered open and he began to shiver. 'Hey,' he groaned, a smile lighting up his face. 'You took your time.'

'Well,' she replied, tears rolling down her face, 'you know what it's like, took a wrong turn at Tycho Station.'

They laughed and she pulled him close, feeling the chill on his skin fading away.

34

LYRA

Xenobiology laboratory. Present Day.

'Are you sure you really want to do this?' asked Doctor Shika, placing a mesh of electrodes onto Lyra's head and attaching the cables.

The seer adjusted the wire netting, pressing the copper contacts down on her temples. 'It's just like any other mind, the intuit will let me speak to it.'

Kaori didn't look convinced. 'You've seen what these creatures are capable of.'

Lyra nodded. 'I have, when they're under Abandon's control, but this is different.' She took out one of her notebooks from her satchel and opened it on a blank page. 'Don't forget I've met their master and sent him packing.'

Pulling a fountain pen from the spine, she wrote 'The Wraith,' in a beautiful copperplate at the top of the page.

'I like to make notes,' Lyra explained. 'Don't worry if it looks like a load of gobbledegook, it's my own form of automatic writing. I'll understand what it means.'

The doctor shrugged, and turned back to the console.

'Okay, I'm going to initiate the connection in three, two, one...'

Lyra took a deep breath and closed her eyes.

There was always some form of sensory overload when she made contact with another sentient being. It was something all seers learned to cope with. Often it felt like a tsunami of intense emotions, usually anger or grief, but other times it could be more subtle like a summer breeze or the caress of an absent lover.

The wraith was hollow and cold, like a night wind in the middle of winter. An icy wave washed through her mind and she shivered.

'You okay?' asked Kaori, checking the monitor. 'Your body temperature just dropped two degrees.'

Lyra nodded. 'No more talking.'

The song she heard before rose from the darkness. It was a haunting melody, filled with dissonant chords that resonated mournfully around in her head. There was a pattern within it that sounded familiar, reminding Lyra of a tune she once heard Uncle Georges play at the Cirque d'Histoire.

Clair de lune? She wondered, letting the thought escape into the void. She began to hum the opening bars.

DEBUSSY? an alien thought emoted into her mind, it was vaguely human, taking her a few seconds to deconstruct. Unlike speech, an intuit was mostly a combination of symbols and emotions.

YES. Lyra replied.

WHO ARE YOU?

She couldn't quite locate the source of the question, there was no structure to the wraith's thoughts, just a fleeting glimpse of something vaguely tangible.

I AM LYRA.

HAVE WE MET BEFORE? came the response, there was a hint of a threat buried beneath it.

WHO ARE YOU? she replied, ignoring its question.

There was a long pause. Lyra could sense something behind the veil, as if there was a discussion going on in another room that she couldn't quite hear.

I AM/WAS DEVLIN.

Lyra scribbled the name down on her note pad.

HELLO DEVLIN. CAN YOU TELL ME WHAT HAPPENED TO YOU?

Again another long pause. In the darkness Lyra saw shapes begin to coalesce, small glowing lights like fireflies flickered in and out of existence as if something were being rekindled inside the creature's mind.

I WAS TAKEN.

TAKEN? BY WHOM?

SEE.

A memory suddenly burst through the oily fog and enveloped her mind.

Devlin was standing inside an ancient temple, the dark walls adorned with alien hieroglyphs and astronomical maps. Lyra couldn't sense his body, but she could see through his eyes. It was a strange feeling, as if his consciousness was disconnected from the physical plane. It was the same sensation that she'd experienced when using Abandon's gift.

Something stirred in the darkness, and Lyra realised there were others standing beside him. She could sense Devlin's fear, the man was part of a team who'd been sent into this alien mausoleum with no idea of what they would find.

Instinctively, Lyra knew they were no longer on Earth. It didn't quite feel as though they had left the continuum, but there was an unusual texture to this world. It was hard to quantify, something about this environment was different, she realised it smelled like the Shadow Realm – of dust and ash.

Dressed in heavy battle armour, the other members of his squad set off. Moving mechanically through the labyrinth, their faces glowed like Halloween masks inside their glass helmets.

Devlin was no soldier, he was a linguist, his head filled with questions. He tried to decipher the glyphs on the walls. Thousands of pictograms ran through his mind as they descended deeper into the tomb-like structure.

Somewhere ahead there was a small explosion, and he took cover as dust and rubble rained down on them.

She could feel him fighting the urge to turn back, to run, it took every ounce of his courage to get back to his feet and move on.

After a few minutes, Devlin reached a blasted door, one that led into a lower chamber. The advanced team had obviously used shape charges to breach the three-foot-thick slab of granite door that now lay in broken chunks around the hole.

Inside was a tomb with a sarcophagus of what Lyra assumed was a king or a priest. The effigy carved into the lid bore little resemblance to a human, its head was almond shaped with three eyes, the body must have been at least twelve feet long.

The rest of the team were already working on opening the sepulchre while Devlin focused on trying to decipher the inscription on the sides.

HERE LIES MAL-SHAJAN THE MARTYR, THE WARRIOR KING OF THE Q'THARIAN, WHO VALIANTLY GAVE HIS LIFE TO DEFEAT THE DEFILERS OF DRAAXON

The memory suddenly faded.

SEE?

WHERE WERE YOU?

BARAD-DUR.

A final symbol flashed in her mind, a circle with a cross through its centre.

The connection between them became unstable, as if something else was attempting to take control of the conversation, trying to stop Devlin from sharing his memories.

Lyra opened her eyes and looked down at her notes which were a mass of hastily scribbled sets of pictograms in the same style as those on the walls.

'What did you see?' asked Kaori.

'I'm not sure,' replied Lyra, taking off the net of electrodes. 'He said he was in Barad-dûr.'

The Japanese doctor frowned. 'Barad-dûr? The Dark Tower in Lord of the Rings? Sauron's stronghold on the plateau of Gorgoroth in Mordor.' Kaori knew her Lord of the Rings lore better than most. Barad-dûr was Sauron's central stronghold in Mordor. She had played more than one D&D campaign around that terrible fortress.

'The Dark Tower,' whispered Lyra, flicking through her almanac until she found a map of Mordor. Holding it up to the wraith, she tapped on the illustration of a black tower. 'Barad-Dûr?'

The writhing creature froze momentarily, as if studying her notes.

'I think we can take that as a yes,' noted Kaori.

35

NAUTILUS

Nautilus. **Maelstrom.**

Josh sat on the old leather sofa cradling his son in his arms and recounting the events of the last couple of days.

Caitlin's mother was busy replacing the compensator and her father was preparing a stew in the galley. The smell reminded his stomach that it had been a while since he'd eaten anything substantial.

'So you can't weave at all?' Caitlin asked, when he finished.

Josh shook his head. 'Not accurately. The tachyons are offline and timelines are out of whack. They're trying to work out how to bring everyone back safely. That's why they need the *Nautilus.*'

'And what about this Hive Network?'

'I don't think it goes deep enough into the past. And, well the woman who runs it is a little eccentric to say the least.'

Caitlin frowned. 'Eccentric how?'

'She's got a lot of cats.'

'Doesn't mean she won't help us.'

'Her father wasn't a fan of the Order, especially the Protectorate, he built the network as a way to travel anonymously.'

She scowled. 'This is an emergency.'

'I'm not sure she cares. Although maybe if Rufius were to ask her—'

'She knows Rufius?'

Josh smiled. 'Yeah, there was a definite twinkle in her eye when she mentioned him.'

He missed the old man, the last four years was like one long, wild adventure and having the Colonel by his side had always made everything okay. It was strange not having him around. Rufius was like a permanent fixture, a piece of the furniture and life hadn't been the same since he retired.

Zack squirmed and began to grumble.

'I think he's hungry,' Josh said, handing him back to Caitlin.

She held up her hand. 'Oh no, this one's all yours, there's a bottle on the stove. Welcome back honey.' She kissed him and walked towards the galley.

Caitlin's mother appeared from the engine room.

'Ten minutes and we'll be good to go.'

36

STAR CHAMBER

Star Chamber.

The auditorium of the Star Chamber was dark and empty, signifying this was to be a closed session. Guards were posted at the doors to ensure the High Council were not to be disturbed.

Josh, Caitlin and the Makepieces watched from the witness box while the Grandmasters of each guild sat solemnly on a raised crescent-shaped bench listening to Professor Eddington speak. Pacing across the chequered floor, he wore his formal Copernican robes, so dark a shade of blue as to be almost black, which only added to the sombre nature of the meeting.

'My investigation into the volatility of the continuum has identified a series of critical junctures that are rapidly diverging from predicted norms. These include events in the early twenty-first, the sixth and the eleventh centuries. Our calculations predict that these deviations will begin to proliferate throughout the surrounding eras.'

'And are you any closer to knowing what is causing this

disruption?' asked the founder, his deep voice resonating throughout the empty chamber.

The professor bowed his head. 'I cannot give you a definitive answer my Lord. I have ordered the difference engines to be thoroughly overhauled and am in the process of recalibrating the Seldon compensators.'

'I think I might be able to shed some light on that,' said Caitlin's mother, getting to her feet and striding onto the floor. 'The *Nautilus's* engines draw their power from the gravitational field. It relies on a consistent level of energy, much like an aeroplane wing uses the lift from the air currents that pass across it.' She held up one hand to demonstrate the flow. 'Something is affecting those fields, and by association the temporal vortices of the continuum.'

For once, the professor seemed relieved at the interruption, listening intently to her explanation. 'Yes, that would correlate with my findings.'

'My compensator burned out trying to deal with the fluctuations. It was like being in a force nine gale in the middle of the Atlantic without a rudder. The waves were gigantic.'

'And what could cause such a storm?'

Neither Eddington or Caitlin's mother had an answer.

The founder ran his hand over his beard, combing it into a point. 'And how goes the recall?'

Eddington cleared his throat. 'We are currently limited to slide rule calculations, plotting the last known locations of the members by hand. It is a rather laborious process.'

'Exactly how many are stranded?'

Eddington stiffened, folding his hands behind his back. Something Sim only saw him do when he was in deep contemplation or delivering bad news.

'Four hundred and five have safely returned using unconventional means, but seven hundred and twenty are still in the field. Sixty per cent are Draconian, twenty-two are Antiquarian, the rest are Scriptorians.'

The founder turned towards Juliana. 'And the *Nautilus*? Is she fit to fly?'

She shook her head. 'No, my Lord, the engines are shot. They need to be rebuilt.'

'How long—'

They were interrupted by a commotion at the entrance to the chamber.

'What is it?' snapped the founder, clearly annoyed at the disturbance. One of the clerks walked over and handed him a note.

'Inspector Sabien would like to address the Council on a matter of great urgency,' the old man read aloud.

'What does the crow want?' growled Grandmaster Derado.

Chief Inquisitor Mallaron looked uncomfortable, obviously unaware of his officer's intentions. 'I've no idea.'

The founder waved his hand. 'Let us hear what he has to say. Admit him!'

Inspector Sabien strode confidently into the chamber, looking every inch the officer in his Protectorate uniform.

'Inspector Sabien, what could be so urgent that you interrupt a Security meeting of the High Council?' snapped Mallaron.

'My apologies Chief Inquisitor. I believe I have information that may be relevant to the current situation we are facing.'

Before Mallaron could respond, the founder stepped in. 'Pray continue Inspector.'

Sabien bowed his head slightly. 'Thank you, my Lord.'

He turned to address the Council. 'Grandmasters, I recently apprehended a suspect trading future technology with the Aztecs. During his interrogation he intimated that he was willing to trade information regarding the whereabouts of Atlantis in return for favourable terms.'

'Atlantis?' exclaimed Derado, raising his hands and shaking his head.

'My thoughts exactly,' agreed the inspector. 'This is not the first time that a suspect has tried to reduce their sentence with spurious tales of the lost island. But in this case there were extenuating circumstances.'

'Such as?' asked Professor Eddington.

'Sorry, but how is this relevant to our current crisis?' interrupted Derado once more.

'Let the man finish,' ordered the founder.

Sabien waited for the chamber to settle and then continued. 'The suspect in question is Silas Wormwood. The son of a notorious band of outlaws, who were all imprisoned during the Romanov crisis. Silas was taken into the care of Rufius Westinghouse and trained as his apprentice for four years.'

Josh sat up a little straighter at the mention of his old mentor, who obviously had a soft spot for small time criminals it seemed.

'I visited Westinghouse, who verified the information that Wormwood gave me.'

'He's telling the truth? He actually knows the location of Atlantis?' the founder asked.

'It appears so my lord.'

'And this is relevant how?' Derado repeated, anger flushing his cheeks. 'Atlantis has been missing for nine thousand years. We gave up looking for it centuries ago.'

The founder got to his feet and walked into the centre of the chamber. 'Because, my learned friends. The island was once home to a research station, one that its Scientific Director, Alexander Templeton, spent many years constructing.'

'Templeton? The crackpot that killed three of his team trying to put them on the moon?' said Derado.

'One and the same. Alexander was a genius. Let us not

forget that his work on quantum tunnelling has proven invaluable to the Order,' added the founder.

'What exactly was he doing on this research station?' asked Derado.

Sabien held up a report. 'Officially it was a deep time observatory, but I can find no detailed records of the project.'

The Draconian Grandmaster sneered. 'Whatever it was, it blew the island out of existence.'

'He triggered the Carrington Event,' said Eddington suddenly looking remarkably animated. 'His attempt to reach the moon caused a Coronal Mass Ejection, in 1859. There were reports it caused fires at telegraph stations due to the levels of electromagnetic activity.'

'Similar, perhaps, to the interference witnessed by Master De Freis at the Frontier?' mused the founder. 'It appears we may have found the source of our anomaly.' He turned to the inspector. 'Has Wormwood shared the actual location?'

Sabien shook his head. 'No my lord, he refuses to tell me. He's demanding to speak to Westinghouse directly.'

'Why don't you just redact him?' insisted the Inspector Mallaron.

'We believe he may have ingested a drug commonly known as Cognizant. Any attempt to read his mind would be dangerous, potentially fatal.'

There was a moment of silence while everyone processed the information. Eddington looked deep in thought as he paced around the floor of the chamber.

'Professor, what would you suggest?' asked the founder.

The Copernican appeared not to hear him, his lips moving silently as he considered the options.

'Professor Eddington?' repeated Lord Dee.

The professor held up his hand, raising his index finger.

'Firstly, if indeed the island has returned, we will need to confirm its position. I will deploy temporal monitoring buoys at strategic points in the continuum, there is an eighty-seven per cent probability that we should be able to triangulate the readings and find the source. Once we have a fix, the Antiquarians will need to send a technical team to investigate.'

'And Wormwood?'

The professor grimaced, shaking his head. 'Do with him as you will. I think it's highly likely that he's playing us for fools. I would not countenance the word of a common criminal.'

37

RUFIUS

Cap Corse, Corsica. 1616

'Does anyone actually know what the meaning of retirement is?' Rufius bellowed down from the top of the hill as Josh and Sabien climbed the rocky path towards his tower.

The inspector raised his hands in mock surrender and stopped at the bottom of the stairs. Josh quickened his pace, taking the steps two at a time until he reached the top.

The colonel was standing in the middle of a vegetable garden. He looked well, his skin bronzed by the sun, but there was more grey in his beard than Josh remembered.

He gave the old man a hug.

'Enough of that,' said the watchman, patting Josh on the back. 'It's good to see you too boy, but what brings you here with him?' He nodded at the inspector who had taken shelter from the midday sun in the shade of an olive tree.

'We need you,' replied Josh.

Rufius scowled. 'It's that serious?'

Josh nodded. 'The continuum is unraveling. Eddington believes there's some kind of anomaly disrupting the timeline. It's affecting our ability to weave. Hundreds of members are trapped in the past. No one can travel through the sixth and there are parts of the eleventh that are unreachable too.'

'So, how the hell did you get here then?' Rufius asked, picking up the tools he'd been using.

While he cleaned the mud from them, Josh explained about the Hive Network.

'Evelyn Montgomery!' Rufius sighed, putting down the trowel. 'Well I haven't heard that mad old bat's name in fifty years. I knew her father, craziest fruitcake in the Order.'

Clearly the colonel wasn't as keen on Evelyn as she was on him, thought Josh.

'We really need your help,' he continued, 'The founder thinks that Silas may be our only hope of finding what is causing it.'

'Yes, Sabien's already been to see me about this. I'm afraid you may be betting on the wrong horse with Master Wormwood.'

'Is he that bad? He can't be any worse than me can he?'

Rufius chuckled, stroking his beard. 'True enough. When I first met him, I thought he was salvageable. That all of those years in the company of ne'er-do-wells could be repaired. At the beginning it seemed to be working. He's very talented, reminds me a lot of you, but the Wormwoods buried their evil deep into the marrow of his bones and eventually his true nature rose to the surface.'

Josh couldn't imagine what it would take to lose the old man's respect and friendship. 'What did he do?'

The watchman sighed and looked out to sea. 'He let a good man die.'

It was clear that Rufius didn't want to discuss it further. He took the tools to a small wooden shed hunched in the shadow of the tower.

Josh followed him. 'Will you help us? At least hear what he has to say?'

'Do I have any choice? Will you leave me in peace if I don't?'

38

FISH OR FOUL?

Xenobiology laboratory. Present Day.

The Grand Seer was unusually still and quiet.

Lyra was beginning to wonder if he had entered into a trance. There was no way to tell from where she was standing.

The wraith swam around the glass cylinder like an enormous black eel, its body folding in on itself in some infinite loop.

Doctor Shika sat at a control desk, waiting patiently for Kelly to say something. She wasn't convinced they shouldn't have gone directly to the founder, but Lyra insisted. The man was the most powerful seer in the Order, but his esoteric ways were anathema to her scientific conditioning.

'Do you hear it?' Lyra asked him, in a hushed voice.

'Indeed I do,' whispered Kelly. 'A mournful lament and no mistaking.'

'Was it human?'

He tilted his head to one side and closed one eye. 'Once, but no more. His body rests somewhere beyond my reach. Full fathom five thy father lies,' Kelly quoted under his breath. Reaching up with one hand and placed it upon the glass. 'What art thou now?'

'Something we've never encountered before,' answered Kaori. 'A xenoform with the ability to change its physical shape at will. The creature is a psychic manifestation of pure energy. It doesn't match anything we have in the database.'

'Neither fish nor foul,' pondered Kelly. 'And yet it roams in the Shadow Realm?'

'Abandon seems to be able to control them,' Lyra agreed.

'The Old King, with silvered crown and eyes that hold the weight of eons, commands the twilight realm where fairies dance in moonlit glades and creatures of the dark whisper ancient secrets. His dominion stretches beyond the mortal veil, where night-born beings heed his silent call and shadows bow in reverence to his timeless reign,' Kelly recited the opening chapter of E.M Williams's book.

'I think we need to go back,' said Kaori.

'Back into the Shadow Realm?'

The doctor nodded. 'This time we'll be prepared. We can defend ourselves.' She picked up a small device. 'This should keep them at bay, like a kind of force field.'

Kelly took his hand from the glass and turned towards her. 'You'll need my help, I will prepare a few things of my own.'

'I'm coming too,' said Lyra.

39

SILAS

Chateau D'If

The granite walls of the prison cell were covered in thousands of tiny scrawled messages. Scratched into the grey rock with broken fingernails, they were the only remaining record of its previous occupants. By the stench of the place, they had still been alive when it was last cleaned.

Rufius had smelled worse.

Watching through the bars as Silas slept on his straw-lined cot, Rufius realised it was nearly ten years since they parted ways – that meeting did not end particularly well.

Rufius still had the scar to prove it.

The boy he once knew was gone, and yet he couldn't shake the feeling that he let him down somehow.

The prisoner's hair was matted and tangled, his clothes in tatters.

'How long has he been in there?' Rufius asked the guard.

The man coughed, his breath stank worse than the cell. 'Elapsed time? Over a year. Real time, he was nicked last week.'

This was the maximum security prison for the most

dangerous men and women in history. The Château was a truly terrible, but necessary, deterrent. The old watchman witnessed first hand the damage that a rogue agent could do to the timeline. There were inmates confined within these walls that intentionally caused the death of thousands of innocent linears, some by their own hand and others by their actions. The Endless Sentence was the closest thing the Order had to capital punishment.

Doing time in the Château meant losing a considerable part of your life and he knew that most inmates never left. Imprisoned within a stasis chamber, they would age at a standard rate, living out a normal lifespan like any normal human. The Protectorate had considered accelerating the rate of aging, thus reducing the time required to hold them and releasing them back into society as octogenarians, but it proved unreliable.

In the cell across from Silas were the frozen bodies of his parents. The Governor had decided to give their son a harsh reminder of what the Protectorate were capable of.

Rufius was part of the team that uncovered the plot to overthrow the Romanovs. The Wormwoods were senior members of the dark guild, known as the Syndicate, and with their leader, Rasputin, they had conspired to bring down the Russian monarchy and trigger the rise of the Soviet Union.

'Wake up!' the guard shouted at the prisoner, rattling his baton along the bars. 'You 'ave a visitor.'

Silas groaned and turned over.

The sound woke the other prisoners, triggering a cacophony of cries and complaints. Hands sprouted through the cell bars like flowers, each holding tiny slivers of mirror to get a better view of what was going on.

'Silas,' added Rufius, 'I believe you have something important to tell me.'

The man stirred at the sound of his old mentor's voice.

'Is that really you?' he whispered, rising from the bed and shuffling over to the bars. 'It is,' he added squinting at the light from the guard's lantern. 'I was beginning to think you wouldn't come. Do you have anything to drink?' He licked dry, papery lips.

Rufius took out his hip flask and handed it to him, trying to ignore the state of the man's fingers.

'Well I did. So, now, would you mind telling me what all this business with Atlantis is about? Have you lost your mind?'

Silas swept the greasy hair away from his face, and drank deeply from the flask, savouring every drop as the colour slowly returned to his grey cheeks.

He handed it back with a nod of gratitude. 'Thank you.' Then turning towards the jailer. 'Do you think we could have a little privacy?'

The guard remained still, his jaw clenched, his beady eyes trying to burn a hole in Silas's skull.

'If you wouldn't mind?' added Rufius.

The man grunted and reluctantly moved off, shouting at the other inmates to keep quiet as he walked down the corridor.

Silas waited until he was out of earshot before continuing. 'So, they actually sent you. I wasn't sure. You know, after the last time. Well, good. Anyway, I've found it, old man. Or at least a way to get to it.'

'With the Obsidian key, yes I've heard the tale.'

Silas smirked. 'No, I just needed to get your attention and Sabien was my best chance. What I've got to offer has far more provenance than those wild goose chases you used to send me on.'

'It's been missing for over nine millenia. What exactly is it you think you've found?'

Silas wagged his finger. 'Ah, now, let's not get ahead of

ourselves. First things first, you have to get me out of this godforsaken place.'

Rufius scoffed, folding his arms over his chest. 'That wasn't part of the deal.'

'You owe me,' Silas growled, baring his yellowing teeth like a caged animal.

'I owe you nothing!' the watchman exclaimed. 'I gave you a chance to be something better, far better than they ever gave you.' He gestured towards the stasis chambers of Silas's parents.

'You took away the only people who cared about me. Tried to make me into something I wasn't. No one asked you to. And when I didn't measure up to your expectations you threw me away like a rotten apple.'

Rufius lowered his voice, conscious of how quiet the other inmates had become. 'You let JFK die. How was I supposed to react? You're lucky I didn't hand you over to the Protectorate myself. I gave you enough chances and you threw them back in my face.'

'It was a mistake. I was a kid. You could have gone back and changed it!' Silas hissed through gritted teeth. 'Isn't that the point of being a watchman?'

'Have you learned nothing of our ways? I wasn't allowed. The Copernicans are still trying to unravel the consequences of that day.'

Silas laughed. 'The Copernicans and their stupid rules. Haven't you ever wondered what it would be like not to have to answer to anybody else? To be free of all this,' he waved his hand around in the air. 'Order?'

'I've heard enough. Guard!' Rufius started to walk towards the exit.

'Where are you going?' Silas called after him, 'don't you want to know where Atlantis is?'

Rufius stopped and turned around. 'What exactly is it that

you think you've found? Because the Obsidian Key is still sitting in a drawer in my study.'

'What I've *heard*, is that there's a piece of equipment coming up for sale, and I know the man who's selling it. He owes me too.'

Rufius scoffed, rapping on the door. 'Hah! Is that it? The thieves market sells more of Christ's sacred toes than there are lepers to take them from.'

Outside in the courtyard, Josh and Sabien were waiting.

'Well?' asked the inspector.

Rufius shook his head. 'If he knows, he's not telling us anything until we release him. Personally, I think he's bluffing, it's all part of some game he's playing.'

'I can have him released into my custody,' said Sabien.

The Watchman laughed. 'Hah! And he'll slip away the first chance he gets.'

The inspector held up a pair of unusual handcuffs. 'Not with these he won't.' He handed them to the Watchman.

Rufius examined them closely. 'Chronologically bound to your timeline?'

The officer nodded. 'If he moves more than fifteen minutes away from me, he's pulled back into my present location.'

The watchman scratched his beard. 'I still wouldn't trust him. If nothing else he's the fastest timerunner I've ever met.'

'Do we have a choice?' Josh said. 'If he knows where Atlantis is.'

Rufius sighed. 'I don't suppose we do, but mark my words, he's up to something. The Wormwoods never did anything that doesn't benefit them.'

40

DECISIONS

Founder's study.

Rufius paced around the room like a caged bear. It was less than three months since he had retired and Josh could tell the old man was not entirely comfortable being back amongst the Order.

He never thought the old man would spend his last days pottering around in a vineyard. Josh always assumed he would go down in a blaze of glory.

There was still a fire in his eyes, and his beard and hair were neatly trimmed, which was something Rufius always did before starting a mission – it was a kind of ritual.

'So, he is refusing to tell you?' repeated the founder.

Rufius shook his head. 'Not until he's released. Inspector Sabien here thinks he can keep him on a tight leash, but I know him better than any of you. The man is a consummate escape artist, amongst many other things. He'll be on his toes before you notice he's missing.'

The founder sat behind his desk, one hand stroking his beard as he considered the situation. 'Professor Eddington is convinced that triangulation is the most pragmatic approach, and I have no doubt he will succeed, but I see no reason why we shouldn't follow a two-pronged strategy.'

'Wormwood told him there's an artefact coming up for sale on the dark market. You know what that means,' said Sabien.

The founder nodded. 'The Syndicate.'

Rufius scoffed. 'If the object actually exists and it's in their hands, we'll have little choice but to negotiate and their price will be a high one.'

'We don't negotiate with the Dark Guild,' added Sabien. 'It's against everything we stand for.'

'Even if it meant saving the continuum?' replied the founder. 'Surely our prime objective outweighs any other consideration.'

'If,' Rufius began, 'If we take Silas at his word, and this artefact is not just another ruse. What on earth are we going to do with it? Does Eddington have any idea how to stop whatever is causing this?'

The founder shook his head. 'Not as yet. Nor a way to travel safely through time, other than using the *Nautilus* which he has commandeered for the deployment of the triangulation buoys.'

'There is another way,' Josh suggested. 'It might get us close enough.'

The room fell silent as the others turned towards him, their eyes filled with a mix of curiosity and expectation.

'It's not an extensive system,' Josh explained. 'And it's anonymous, used by those who would rather not be tracked, and the woman that runs it may not want to help the Order.'

'Criminals,' muttered Sabien.

'It's called the Hive. I don't know quite how it works, but it seems to be hardwired to different points in the last thousand years. Like a phone network.'

'Why have we never heard of this?' asked the founder, turning to Sabien, who simply shrugged.

'Because they didn't want you to,' Josh replied.

'I knew her father, Tobias Montgomery,' added Rufius. 'The man was something of a paranoid genius.'

The founder looked troubled, as though he didn't recognise the name. 'And they travel without artefacts? Without weaving? Who is using it?'

'The Syndicate,' declared Sabien. 'It would explain a great deal of the problems we've had in tracing them.'

'Who are the Syndicate?' asked Josh.

Rufius glanced at the inspector. 'Do you want to take this one?'

Sabien nodded. 'They're are an organised crime cartel, a secret guild of assassins, thieves and black marketeers. The Protectorate have never been able to infiltrate them, they're protected by dark seers and redactors who can detect our presence. They also use drugs to enhance their abilities. They trade in illegal artefacts, dark relics, memories and knowledge. We believe their headquarters are located somewhere in the nineteenth century, but none of our attempts to find them have been successful.'

'They are also responsible for some of the worst disruptions in history,' added Rufius. 'Never mention their name in front of Eddington. He goes a particular shade of purple.'

The founder rose to his feet. 'I believe we will have to make some concessions if we are to save the continuum. We will have to put aside our differences and parley with them.'

Sabien and Rufius both folded their arms.

'I vote we leave him in the Château for another couple of weeks. He'll tell us what we need to know eventually,' said the inspector.

'For once we agree on something,' the old Watchman said.

The founder shook his head. 'Ironically, we may not have the luxury of time, from what I've read in Eddington's latest reports the disruption is worsening.'

41

CHAPTER HOUSE

Chapter House

'It seems this may be our last meal together for some time,' said Methuselah, getting unsteadily to his feet and clapping his hands to get their attention.

Alixia raised one of her eyebrows, her husband was clearly drunk.

'He's going to regret this,' whispered Caitlin, watching him pick up his glass. 'There'll be words.'

Rufius was holding Zack, trying to convince him to eat something that Josh assumed was a carrot. The old man was making goofy faces, sticking his teeth out like a rabbit and make their son giggle.

'I've got another assignment,' Josh said, trying not to make it sound too important.

She turned towards him. 'I guessed as much,' nodding at the old watchman. 'It must be bad if you've dragged him out of retirement. Can you tell me what it is this time?'

Josh sighed. 'That wasn't by choice. Anyway, we're going in search of Atlantis.'

Caitlin coughed, nearly spitting out the wine she was drinking.

'Atlantis?'

'It didn't sound so crazy in my head, but yes, the founder thinks it's connected to the problems with the timeline. Something to do with a crazy scientist called Templeton.'

She turned towards him, her eyes widening. 'Alexander Templeton? The one who put a team on the moon?'

Josh nodded. 'Yes. Anyway, he was working on some top secret project on Atlantis and apparently they've found an artefact that could help us get there.'

'The island that's been missing for thousands of years? What kind of artefact?'

'No idea,' he said with a shrug.

She frowned. 'And where is it?'

'Apparently the Syndicate have it.'

Caitlin swore under her breath. 'You're going to meet with the Dark Guild. Are you mad?'

'It can't be that bad. I grew up on the wrong side of the tracks remember.'

She took his hand. 'I know you did, but these aren't like the street gangs of South London. These are the scumbags of history, they're bottom-feeders, there isn't anything they won't do.'

'I can handle it. And I've got the Colonel to watch my back.'

Her lips tightened into a line. 'I'm coming with you.'

'You can't. It's already been decided.' He nodded towards his son. 'Anyway, someone needs to look after Zack.'

Her cheeks flushed, and she gritted her teeth. 'Who decided? Why don't you stay at home and look after him. I'll go off and save the world!'

Josh could see there were tears forming in the corner of her eyes. She was right, of course, she could easily take his place. There had been many times when her ingenuity had saved his life, but that was before the baby. Something changed in him after Zack, he couldn't explain it – he felt the need to protect them both.

'I'm sorry, I wish we could do it together, but I don't know what else to say.'

She shook her head. 'You didn't even consider it. That's the problem.'

42

LILLY PATEL

Antiquarian HQ. British Museum.

'My name is Elizabeth Patel, but you can call me Lilly,' the curator introduced herself. She was a tall Indian woman with long black hair and dark eyes. She wore the standard brown robes of an Antiquarian with a motif of an astrolabe stitched into the breast of her waistcoat in gold thread.

They were gathered in the middle of a science museum, surrounded by exhibits of what appeared to be brass spacecraft.

'I am the Keeper of the Astronomical Archives. I'm also the resident historian on the works of Alexander Templeton and his Department of Chronometric Research.'

Inspector Sabien stood guard beside his prisoner, who Josh thought bore a remarkable resemblance to an actor whose name he couldn't recall. Since being released from the Château, Silas had been given a clean set of travelling robes, a shave and a hair cut. He was manacled to Sabien with a pair of temporal handcuffs, but even still, his eyes were bright, constantly moving as if ready to run at the first sign of trouble.

Rufius was on the opposite side of the group, trying as hard as he could to stand still, but failing miserably.

'The founder has asked me to brief you on Templeton's research,' she continued, taking a helmet out of the Colonel's hands and putting it back in position on the stand.

'I've prepared a short presentation.'

Lilly was in her thirties, with a strong accent, which Josh would have placed around Birmingham, although he'd never actually ventured north of Watford. She spoke with the same demonstrative tone as a school teacher, one who wouldn't take any nonsense.

The lights dimmed and an image projected on to a screen on one of the walls. It showed an old sepia-toned photograph of a group of scientists. The man in the centre stood proudly holding a model of a space capsule, his hair wild and unkempt, reminding Josh of Doc Brown from Back to the Future.

Like a mad professor.

'Alexander Templeton was a genius. His pioneering work in quantum tunnelling led to many innovations that we take for granted today. From stasis fields used in healing chambers to the ability to travel into the deep past, further than any vestige could take us.'

'And prisons,' added Silas.

Lilly seemed a little surprised at the interruption, but carried on nonetheless. 'Yes. His technologies have also been used in containment facilities, but much more besides.'

She pressed a button on the side of the magic lantern and the image changed to a photograph of three astronauts standing on the moon. Their spacesuits were nothing like those developed by NASA in the 1960s, but heavily modified deep-sea diving suits with brass helmets.

'His most significant achievement was in 1859 when Alexander put three members of his research team on the surface of the moon. Something that was not achieved in linear time for another hundred and ten years.'

'How did he do that?' asked Josh, failing to hide the disbelief in his voice.

The Antiquarian took a deep breath. 'The short answer is that we don't know. The mission was deemed a failure after the entire team was lost. Templeton destroyed the equipment in a fit of rage and the department was disbanded shortly after.'

'He was manipulating gravimetric fields,' said the founder, stepping out of the shadows. 'Professor Eddington has strong evidence that his generators affected the sun's photosphere, causing a coronal mass ejection.'

Lilly bit her lip, her face flushing with anger. 'There was never any proof,' she protested.

'No, but some would say that his next experiment was proof enough. My apologies Lilly, please continue with your presentation.'

She nodded and changed the slide once more.

The image was a blueprint plan of an island laboratory, showing an extensive complex on many levels.

'His final project was originally designated as a "temporal observatory," a celestial array to study the deep past of the solar system, built on a remote island in the Atlantic. It was known as Atlas Station.'

'Atlantis,' said Rufius. 'Call it by its real name.'

Lilly ignored the interruption.

'The station was run by a team of over a hundred specialists, all experts in their field, they studied the chronologies of our universe and the planets within it.'

'From what I remember, he was obsessed with space,' added Rufius, walking over to the map. 'Their are rumours that he was attempting to reach Mars when he went missing.'

'We have no idea what the reasons were for the disappearance,' corrected Lilly.

The watchman scoffed. 'He made an entire island vanish. That generally doesn't happen while you're simply "observing" something.'

Lilly switched off the projector. 'Why exactly are you here? No one has taken any interest in his work for years.'

They looked at each other and then at the founder.

The founder cleared his throat. 'There is a very high probability that the current issues with the continuum are connected to Templeton's research. Silas here believes that an artefact has come up for sale on the Dark Market that will help us find Atlas Station.'

'The Thieves Market?' asked Lilly, her eyes widening. 'I thought that was forbidden.'

Silas laughed. 'For the likes of the Order, it is, but I have certain associates, one of whom tells me they have located a probe from Atlas Station.'

Her eyes widened further still. 'A DC6? Do you know what that means?'

'Indeed I do,' Silas said, a smug grin on his face. 'This may be the first contact we have had with Templeton's station in thousands of years.'

There were tears in Lilly's eyes. 'I have to see it.'

'It's too dangerous,' said Rufius, shaking his head. 'Especially with the challenges surrounding travelling at the moment.'

'I don't care,' replied Lilly, her jaw clenching. 'I have spent my entire career studying the man's work, you're not denying me the chance to find him.'

Rufius shrugged. 'Don't say I didn't warn you.'

The founder smiled benevolently. 'Lilly, this isn't a usual mission. There is a great deal of uncertainty, we will likely be collaborating with the Dark Guild.'

She folder her arms. 'It doesn't matter. If there's the slightest chance of meeting Alexander I'm going.'

'As you wish.'

'So, now that's settled where do we begin?' Rufius asked, staring at Silas. 'Where will we find this so-called associate of yours?'

'Lisbon, 1760,' replied Silas.

'We will split into two groups,' Sabien began. 'I will accompany Silas to the meeting. Jones and Westinghouse will wait outside and ensure we're not disturbed.'

'I'll join the meeting,' insisted Lilly. 'To verify the probe,' she added as Sabien began to protest. 'You have no idea what it looks like.'

'I doubt you'll get to see it,' Silas said, stepping forward and forcing Sabien to move with him. 'No one is stupid enough to keep something so valuable so close to the market.'

'Have they set a price?'

Silas shook his head. 'Usually something this valuable would go to auction. Sealed bids. But, this particular dealer has no qualms with a trade, if the right artefact was offered.'

43

THE NAUTILUS

Nautilus repair workshop

Her mother was lying under the starboard engine when Caitlin walked into the engineering bay. The *Nautilus* floated a few feet off the ground, its sleek, brass hull half-hidden under scaffolding.

An army of Antiquarian artificers were working on various parts of the ship. The blue-white flare of arc-welding torches lit up the hangar as they rushed to repair the damage, filling the air with the smell of solder and scorched metal.

'How's it going?' she asked, handing Zack to his grandfather.

'Your mum's been working all night,' he replied, his own eyes ringed with dark shadows. 'She's mainly surviving on tea and chocolate bourbons.'

'I can hear you, you know,' her mother said, sliding out from under the engine on a wheeled sled. 'Professor Eddington needs us to deploy the triangulation buoys and the engines need a complete overhaul before we take her out again.'

Caitlin glanced at the timeship's deeply-scored hull. A

cold shiver ran down her spine as she remembered the sound of the storm-kin scraping their spiny tentacles along it.

'You seriously think she'll survive another geo-magnetic storm?'

Her mother wiped her grease-stained hands on an oily cloth before kissing her grandson and handing him one of her screwdrivers to play with.

She placed her palm lovingly on the side of the ship. 'The old girl's survived ten years in the Maelstrom. I've over-hauled the gravimetric compensators and upgraded the dampening fields on both turbines, so she should be fine. Anyway, we're going to stay out of the continuum for most of the journey. The effects of the gravitational instabilities don't apply to the chaos realm.'

Caitlin scoffed. 'No, just the Djinn to deal with in there.'

Juliana nodded towards the bow of the ship where the engineers were lowering the plasma cannons into place on giant winches. 'Your father's having the guns mounted, just in case.'

Caitlin wasn't convinced. 'The moment you breach into linear time you could be facing a tsunami.'

'I'm fully aware of the dangers,' her mother replied, taking a large spanner from her toolbox, 'but what choice do we have? If we don't find the cause of this and shut it down, things are only going to get worse. Eddington says that NASA detected a change in the gravity field that's affecting the moon.'

'What?'

Her father was extracting the screwdriver handle from Zack's mouth. 'I heard that there have been reports of freak tidal waves in 1990.'

'The moon? I don't understand, how can it affect the moon?'

'Gravity darling,' her mother explained, tightening one of the bolts on the turbine housing. 'Whatever's disrupting these engines is also affecting the fields surrounding the earth. The same fields that hold the moon in Earth's orbit.'

Caitlin folded her arms. 'I'm coming with you.'

Her mother shook her head. 'You're safer here.'

'None of us are safe if we don't fix this. Zack can stay with Alixia, you need all the help you can get.'

Her father handed his grandson over. 'You know there's no point arguing with her, honey. She's as stubborn as her mother.'

'Fine,' Juliana said, 'I'll take that as a compliment.'

44

THIEVES MARKET

Thieves Market, Lisbon, Portugal. 1760

They followed Silas through the maze of narrow alleys and passageways of Lisbon's Alfama district. The route was so complex Josh was convinced the man was doing it intentionally so that none of them would be able to find their way back.

'Where exactly are we going?' he asked as they walked out into a bustling market square.

'The dealer we're going to meet isn't under the Syndicate's protection, so he tends to move about,' Silas said, looking around as if trying to get his bearings.

'Balthazar,' growled Sabien. 'You're taking us to Balthazar Al-Mansoori?'

Silas grinned, walking into the crowd. 'I didn't realise he was so well known.'

'The infamous Marchand de L'ombres?' Rufius asked. 'The Shadow Merchant?'

'One and the same,' replied Sabien, trailing after Silas.

. . .

Night was falling and the moonless sky was deepening into rich shades of violet and purple. With the setting of the sun the bazaar came to life. Under the glow of a thousand lanterns the illuminated stalls seemed to transform, everyday goods replaced by the most unusual array of artefacts.

There were booksellers offering pages from rare manuscripts and alchemists touting essences of old memories, shabbily-dressed merchants selling clothes and mementos that looked as though they were stolen from a grave.

The place smelled of spice and exotic foods, and Josh felt his stomach groaning at the delicious aromas, reminding him how long it had been since his last meal.

'So this is the Thieves Market?' asked Lilly, looking around in wonder.

'Indeed it is,' said Rufius, waving away an over-zealous trader. 'Keep one hand on your tachyon, it's also a training ground for pickpockets.'

Silas led the group through the market, weaving through the crowds of unsavoury characters, who eyed their group suspiciously as they passed by. These were "the great unwashed", as Rufius would call them, those who lived outside of the Order, ones who made their living on the fringes.

By the look of them it wasn't an easy life, Josh thought, trying not to stare. He could relate to that, he spent most of his teenage years doing whatever it took to survive.

Eventually they reached a white church-like building decorated with blue tiles.

'He's in there,' said Silas, pulling Sabien to one side. 'But you're going to need to release me. I can't look like your prisoner when we go inside.'

Sabien shrugged, taking a key out of his pocket and twisting it in the central lock that connected the two bracelets.

'It works just the same,' he said as the manacle chain separated leaving one circlet on each of their wrists. 'They're entangled. I can still find you.'

'Understood,' Silas said, pulling his sleeve down over the metal ring. He turned to the others. 'Wait here.'

'Not a chance,' said Rufius. 'We're all going in.'

Silas's brow furrowed, his eyes narrowing with a hint of resentment. Josh could see there was still tension between him and his old mentor. 'There will be a Sensor on the door. You'll need to be prepared.' He held out his hand. 'I'm going to need some money.'

The watchman grumbled as he dug some gold coins out of his purse. 'You know I'm retired, this is coming out of my pension.'

Silas ignored him and walked over to an apothecary stall. He carefully selected a handful of jars, then haggled over the price for what seemed like an eternity. The ill-tempered trader was less than happy with the outcome, shouting insults at Silas as he returned to the group.

'Take two of these,' he said, handing out small tablets from the various jars.

'What are they?' asked Rufius, eyeing the pills warily.

'We call it *Chameleon*, it's a diluted version of *Memorix*. It gives you a temporary persona. We use them to mask our identity.' He tapped his temple with his index finger. 'Should a Sensor come sniffing, he'll think you're someone else – unless he's a good one, which is pretty unlikely around here.'

'They're other people's memories?' asked Lilly, sniffing the tablet and pulling a face. 'Who am I going to be?'

Silas shrugged. 'No idea, these are randoms, they're cheaper. Now, do you want to get in there or not?' Silas snapped, dropping two into his mouth and swallowing them dry.

Josh took one and crushed it between his teeth. The taste

wasn't unpleasant, it reminded him of the sweets his nan used to give him as a kid – like sherbet lemons.

The memories released the moment the tablet touched his tongue.

Visions of another life came flooding into his mind. It was a form of intuit, but without the actual connection to its original owner. The initial effects of the drug were amazing. If this was the lighter version of *Memorix* – Josh could see the attraction of memory trading. It was like wearing someone else's timeline, giving him a brief glimpse into their experiences. He could imagine there were more unsavoury versions to be had, especially from those locked up inside the Château.

'Who did you get?' asked Lilly, as they followed Silas towards the church.

'A banker for the Medicis,' replied Josh. 'You?'

Lilly blushed. 'A courtesan from the court of Louis XV.'

'Better than a eunuch from Imperial China,' mumbled Rufius walking past them.

Silas rapped a series of short taps on the iron-studded door, clearly in some kind of code. After a tense few minutes, the grille slid back and a deep voice said in Portuguese.

'We're closed.'

Silas stepped closer to the opening and held up a gold coin. 'Ah, but opportunity knocks only once.' He rolled it over the backs of his knuckles like a magician and it disappeared.

A pair of blue eyes glared through the aperture. 'What do you want?'

'To work less and earn more,' replied Silas, 'and to die in the arms of a beautiful woman.'

Josh wasn't sure if Silas was being flippant or it was some kind of password. Sabien didn't seem that impressed, he glanced at Rufius, who simply shrugged in response.

Suddenly, Josh felt the feather-like touch of the doorman's mind. He was an adept redactor, gently reading the false memories that *Chameleon* had deployed. By the looks on the others' faces they were clearly experiencing it too.

It took less than a minute before they heard the sound of bolts being drawn back.

They walked into the candle-lit interior of the building. The tiles of the floor were laid out in an intricate design of chequered marble, much like that of the Star Chamber. Beyond the reception area stood a beautiful courtyard garden, where a dark-skinned Arabian man sat beside a fountain, drinking tea.

'Honoured guests,' he said, getting to his feet. 'What an unexpected pleasure.'

Balthazar was dressed in the finest silks, his head wrapped in a golden turban. A scimitar hung from his waist.

'How may I be of service?' he added, bowing deeply, but keeping his eyes trained on the inspector. If he recognised Silas, he made no sign of showing it.

'Let me deal with this,' Silas whispered to Sabien as he returned the bow. 'Brother, we are here to trade.' He stood upright, holding one hand against his chest and the other gesturing in some kind of sign language.

The dealer's eyes widened slightly, his fingers moving with a subtle response. 'Indeed. Well, come take some tea and let us discuss your needs.'

They have a secret language, Josh thought, wondering exactly what passed between them. *Is he setting us up?* He felt Sabien tensing, also aware of their hand signals.

The dealer motioned to the low table, surrounded by velvet cushions.

'Blessings on you, but time is of the essence.' Silas continued. 'I have been told that you have come into possession of a certain rare artefact, one that originated from the forgotten isle.' Silas, sat down and motioned to the others to do the same. 'My friends here are very interested in obtaining it.'

Balthazar's expression changed, his genial smile falling away. 'I am afraid you are mistaken, my brother. The object of which you speak is nothing more than a myth, what on earth could make you think I would know of such a thing?'

Sabien scowled at Silas, who ignored him and laughed.

'Surely the renowned merchant of shadows has caught wind of the rumours surrounding the Atlas probe? I cannot believe that one as well-connected as you could be ignorant of such a thing! Everyone knows that the great Balthazar Al-Mansoori is the master of whispers.'

As he spoke his fingers flickered. Another conversation was being had, one that was clearly the opposite of the verbal banter.

'You honour me greatly,' replied the merchant, his hands returning the subtle gestures. 'But, the artefact you seek is indeed nothing more than a rumour, a fanciful folly dreamed up by those who imagine the world is flat, or that unicorn horn can stiffen a man's resolve.' He got to his feet. 'What I do have, is a marvellous collection of epoch orbs that I am sure your friends would cherish.'

'So you don't have the DC6?' Lilly interrupted, obviously disappointed. 'It would be about this big.' She made a shape with her hands. 'With an antennae array and a propulsion unit attached to its outer shell.'

The merchant smiled, exposing a row of bejewelled teeth. 'For a courtesan you seem to possess an incredible technical knowledge of scientific devices. Come, let me show you what I have, perhaps you will find something else that takes your fancy, my lady.' Balthazar offered her his hand.

They walked through an ornate arch guarded by two enormous Vikings with large axes strapped to their backs. 'I find the Northmen a most effective deterrent,' the merchant noted as they passed. 'They are the most terrifying warriors.'

In the room beyond was a treasure trove.

'This is my private collection,' he continued, raising his hand and sweeping it around an eclectic display of artefacts.

Lilly rushed over to a small metal cube and picked it up. 'This is the Chronohedron of Sigma? How on earth did you come by it? We've been searching for this for years.'

The merchant shrugged, rubbing his hands together. 'It would be inconsiderate of me to reveal my sources, but suffice to say that everything you see here is for sale, everything has a price.'

'But no probe?' Lilly said, studying the other items.

Balthazar shook his head, rattling the pearls that hung from his ears. 'I'm afraid not.'

'I've heard enough.' Sabien whispered to Rufius, turning to leave. 'There is sufficient contraband here to put him away for a hundred lifetimes.'

'Calm yourself man,' growled Rufius, leaning in close. 'If he realises you're Protectorate we'll not get out of here alive.'

'My friends, are you leaving so soon?' Balthazar glided towards them. 'Surely there is something that catches your eye? No one ever leaves my emporium dissatisfied. It is a matter of personal pride.'

Rufius picked up the nearest thing to hand and pretended to examine it. 'How much for this?'

The merchant flashed his glittering teeth once more. 'Ah, La Peregrina Pearl Necklace, the perfect gift for a lady. I can see you are a man of great taste. I couldn't take less than twenty escudos for it.'

'Done,' said Rufius reaching for his purse.

Balthazar looked disappointed. Silas glared at his old mentor.

'I'll give you ten,' Rufius corrected himself, taking the coins out of the leather pouch.

The merchant sneered. 'Have you come to insult me? This was once part of the Spanish crown jewels. Sixteen would be a worthy amount for such a treasure.'

Rufius clenched his jaw. 'Twelve and throw in that as well.' He pointed towards a small figurine that looked as if it had been part of an ornate chess set.

Balthazar picked up the piece. 'Fourteen and you can have the idol as a gift.'

'Done,' said Rufius.

Balthazar spat into his hand and held it out. 'It has been an honour, one hopes that you will visit my emporium again.'

'Well, that was interesting,' said Rufius, wiping his hand on his coat. 'I warned you he couldn't be trusted.'

Sabien grimaced, his eyes watching the door as he waited for Silas to appear. Lilly was chewing her lip, a grim look of determination and disappointment on her face. Josh could see how important this was to her.

'What are you going to do with those?' Josh asked, pointing at the carefully wrapped package wedged under the colonel's arm.

The watchman shrugged. 'Take them back to their rightful owners.'

Silas walked out a few moments later, a satisfied grin on his face. 'So, at least we know his price.'

'What?' snapped Lilly. 'I thought he denied any knowledge of it.'

'The subtle art of negotiation,' he said, wiggling his fingers. 'Not everything was said in words, and having members of the Order in his house is always going to make him a little nervous.'

'So the *Chameleon* was a waste of time?' said Rufius.

Silas looked at Lilly. 'It is if you're not going to play the part.'

Her cheeks flushed. 'I'm not used to playing games.'

'So what did he actually say?' asked Sabien, changing the subject.

'He's agreed to postpone the auction, if we can meet his price in the next two days.'

Lilly looked as if she was prepared to sell everything she owned. 'How much does he want?'

Silas tilted his head from side to side. 'Well, it's a little complicated. I've managed to negotiate a trade. Something Balthazar desires more than money. You should expect everything we do from now on to involve a deal. No one in my world does anything out of the goodness of their heart.'

Sabien took out the key to reattach the handcuffs.

His prisoner stepped away a little. 'I don't think they will be necessary. Where we are going that would probably get us both killed.'

'And where exactly are we going?' growled the inspector.

Silas smiled. 'We're going to steal the "Eyes of Eternity" from the Syndicate.'

45

THE PARROT

Paris, 1810

The Île de la Cité sat in the middle of the River Seine, overshadowed by the gothic towers of Notre Dame Cathedral. The only way on to the island was via a single wooden bridge, which was guarded night and day.

According to Silas, the headquarters of the Syndicate was currently located in the Conciergerie, an old palace hidden amongst the ramshackle tenement buildings on the tiny isle.

They spent the better part of the morning surveilling the area, looking for another approach, but found no other way to get onto the island without being noticed.

In 1810, this area of Paris was a slum, a maze of narrow alleys teeming with unsavoury characters. Gangs of grimy urchins prowled the streets, preying on anyone who appeared to have money. It was a desperate place, where only the toughest would survive.

'What are the Eyes of Eternity?' asked Josh, as they turned into a small passageway between two decrepit gabled buildings.

'The eyes of Baba Vanga, a seer from 1911,' answered

Rufius who was staring into one of the darkened shop windows. It appeared to be a mapmaker's shop, there were various old charts stuck to the dusty glass, obscuring the interior. 'She was quite famous in her day, able to predict future events with remarkable accuracy. Natural disasters were one of her specialties. Her eyes were preserved after her death. They are supposed to bestow her prescience on anyone that wears them.'

'Wears them?' Josh said, inwardly shivering at the idea.

'They're set into a pair of goggles, I believe.'

'Why not just talk to a seer?' asked Lilly.

'They'll be for a linear, not a member of the Order. There are numerous occult collectors who would pay a King's ransom for her eyes. Rudolf II being my most likely guess.'

Lilly eyes widened. 'Linears?'

Rufius nodded. 'This is the business of dark relics. The supply of rare or even banned artefacts, it's a very lucrative trade by all accounts.'

Josh looked along the passage. Silas and Sabien were walking on ahead surrounded by a group of children. From the fading signs of the shops hanging on the upper storeys, it was clear that this was a street of book sellers and mapmakers.

People flitted from door to door carrying bundles wrapped in brown paper. They were dressed in dark robes – travelling robes, Josh realised.

'Are those Scriptorians?'

Rufius chuckled. 'Yes, most likely from the Retrieval Department. Ones who've had their fill of running into burning buildings to rescue books. Some find it easier to employ the services of an Acquirer. There will always be someone who's willing to risk their lives for a price.'

'I never realised this was going on,' Josh said, 'how do they get away with it?'

The old man nodded towards Silas and Sabien. 'It's as old

as time itself, for every action there is an equal and opposite reaction. We try to maintain order, while the universe tends towards chaos. As long as I can remember there has always been a rogue element. When I was a boy, before the founder created the Order, we were nothing more than bands of time travellers trying to survive in the Wild West that was the past. We've come a long way since then, but some still prefer to remain *independent*.' He stressed the last word as if he meant something entirely different.

'And Silas?'

Rufius sighed. 'My biggest regret. My worst failure. I tried to make the boy something he was not. He could have joined me in the watch, but his family ruined him.'

They caught up to the other two.

'I could use a drink,' Rufius said, squinting at the signs. 'If memory serves there's a hostelry not more than thirty yards from here.'

Silas laughed. 'The Parrot? Are you sure old man? That's the grimmest drinking hole in all of Paris.'

'Perfect,' replied Rufius, patting his stomach. 'They do a passable pie too, if I'm not mistaken.'

The pub was a low-ceilinged room at the front of a three-storey house. From the street it looked like an afterthought squeezed between two larger, wood-timbered buildings. There was clearly no planning permission required in these times, the street was a hotchpotch of gabled hovels that appeared to be holding each other up like a row of old drunks.

A plank rested across a pair of brandy barrels to create a primitive bar. The man behind it was wearing a stained apron over his large stomach. His handle-bar moustache reminded

Josh of a walrus, while the fringe of grey hair around his otherwise bald head made him look like a friar.

'Monsieur Le Monde,' Rufius greeted the bartender in French. 'It's been a long time.'

The man's face lit up. 'Westinghouse, you old dog. How the devil are you?'

Rufius tilted his head from one side to the other. 'Comme ci, comme ca. Nothing that a glass of rum wouldn't resolve.'

Le Monde took them to a table at the back, away from the other customers, who looked as if they would cut your throat for speaking in the wrong accent.

The barman brought out a dark, dusty bottle and five glasses. There was little else on the menu but the pies. Rufius paid him, trying not to feel too offended when the man bit into the coins.

After he was gone, the watchman turned to Silas. 'So, I think it's time we did some straight talking, no more of this crap,' he flicked his fingers in the same way that Silas had done.

Silas's eyes widened. 'You know the silent signs?'

'Ha, you think I've been living under a rock?' Rufius picked up the rum and poured each of them a large measure.

'What did he say?' asked Sabien.

Rufius drained his glass in one go and refilled it.

'He said he has a plan. That we're all idiots and if Balthazar played his cards right he could make a tidy sum. The stuff about the Eyes of Eternity is true, for some reason the shadow merchant has fallen fowl of the Syndicate, who have it safely locked away in their vault. Apparently the merchant has promised it to a valued customer and is willing to trade one of his wives for its safe return.'

'And the Atlantis probe?'

The watchman nodded. 'It appears that he actually does have the probe, although there was something about it that wasn't clear. Perhaps Master Wormwood could fill in the gaps for us?'

Silas picked up his own glass, his hand clearly shaking. 'The probe isn't functional. He said it's broken.'

'Why would it need to be functioning?' asked Josh.

Lilly leaned forward and lowered her voice. 'Because Atlantis is in a permanent state of temporal flux, unless the device has a direct connection to the base station we won't be able to locate it – we'll be forever chasing its tail.'

'So it's useless?' said Sabien, throwing his hands up, 'this has all just been a wild goose chase?'

'Not necessarily,' replied Lilly. 'It just requires a little lateral thinking.'

'Like what?' the inspector snapped.

Lilly smiled. 'Like I may know someone who can fix it.'

'Let's eat,' said Rufius, as Le Monde appeared from the kitchen carrying a tray of steaming pies. 'I can't make sensible decisions on an empty stomach.'

The food was terrible. Josh decided it was better than going hungry. The bartender swore that it was chicken, but Rufius seemed to think that it most likely owned a tail before it went into the pot.

It transpired that Sabien was a vegetarian, which they all found a little surprising. Nineteen century French cuisine wasn't especially geared to cater to a plant-based diet, and the inspector was left with a baked potato, which Josh soon came to realise was the wiser choice.

Silas ate like a man who had lived on the street for a year, which was pretty likely from what Josh witnessed in the prison. He mopped up the gravy with a lump of stale bread and then scooped up the scraps from their bowls when they'd finished.

'I'm not proud,' he declared, the juices running down his chin. 'The Château's menu was a little limited.'

'Don't get too comfortable,' Sabien growled. 'You screw this up and you'll be back there before you know it.'

Lilly helped herself to another glass of rum. 'So, how are we going to get into the Conciergerie? There's only one bridge and it's constantly under guard.'

'I have an idea,' said Rufius, tapping the side of his head. 'A bit of lateral thinking of my own.' He winked at Lilly.

46

TIME BUOYS

Nautilus.

The temporal buoys were heavy brass spheres, reminding Caitlin of the early Russian satellites like Sputnik. They were packed with chronometric sensors and temporal gyroscopes that could monitor a radius of up to a century in either direction, transmitting variation data back to the ship via a quantum communications relay.

The buoys were sitting on a rack in the loading bay of the *Nautilus* like bombs waiting to be dropped over enemy territory.

'Fifteen minutes to destination,' her mother's voice intoned from the speaking tube. 'Opening the cargo bay doors in five.'

Caitlin went over to help her father who was preparing the first in the line.

'Eddington wants them deployed at two hundred year intervals,' he said, adjusting one of the dials. 'Can you pass me that spanner?'

Caitlin handed him the tool and he replaced the final bolts on the cover plate and tightened them.

'So they're going to emit a constant time signature?' Caitlin knew exactly how it was going to work, but enjoyed listening to him explain it in his own way – it made her feel like a child again.

Her father nodded. 'Like a metronome. Your mother has set up a receiver that can measure the signal of each one. It should tell us where the deviations are strongest and help identify the location of the anomaly.'

He got to his feet. 'Okay, let's get this beauty into position.'

There was a hoist fitted into rails on the ceiling of the bay. Caitlin helped him connect the chains to the cradle holding the buoy and then dragged it towards the circular cargo hatch. It was designed like the aperture of a camera lens so that the size of the opening could be accurately controlled, no one wanted to risk a storm-kin getting inside the ship.

'One minute until breaching commences,' remarked her mother.

Caitlin connected her safety line to the anchor point on the bulkhead and took a deep breath before donning the breathing apparatus.

She could feel her heart beat beginning to race at the thought of what could be waiting on the other side of the hatch. The last time she travelled through the Maelstrom, the *Nautilus* had broken down, leaving them at the mercy of the chaos beasts that roamed the void. Now, they were about to create a temporal breach which was the equivalent of catnip to the Djinn.

'Here we go,' said her father, his voice muffled by the oxygen mask.

The blades of the iris door rotated open and the air rushed out of the cargo bay, whipping Caitlin's hair into a frenzy. She braced herself against the pressure drop.

'Approaching eleven hundred and ten,' Her mother's

voice counted down over the wail of the wind. 'Nine, eight, seven, six, five.'

Her father pulled the buoy to the edge of the door.

'Breach established.'

The ship entered the corona of the aperture and the darkness weakened. Colour and light returned in rippling waves as if they were rising towards the surface of a deep ocean.

Caitlin caught fleeting shadows on the periphery. *Pentachions*, she thought, recognising the silhouettes of the squid-like, tentacled monsters circling just beyond the outer reaches of the widening portal.

Then, suddenly, the wind dropped and they were flying over the lush green pastures of a wide valley. She could see men and women working in the fields far below. Oxen were pulling ploughs, chased by flocks of birds eager to reap the benefits of the newly turned soil.

In the distance, a jagged range of mountains, unmistakably the Pyrenees, broke over the horizon like the edge of a forgotten world.

The pressure eased in the cargo bay, and Caitlin removed her face mask. Taking a deep breath of the cool air, a refreshing change from the recycled atmosphere inside the ship.

'France?' she asked her father.

'Gascony,' he said, taking off his own mask. 'Or Aquitaine, I can never remember the difference,' he added, pushing the brass sphere out of the door with his foot.

It hovered for a moment, the cradle still attached to the ship by chains.

'Bloody swivel pin,' Thomas said, leaning out of the door and hitting the release mechanism with the spanner. There were a series of clicks as it finally detached and the buoy separated .

They watched it drop like a cannon ball towards the

ground, until finally a small parachute deployed and two small propeller arms extended out to give it lift.

'Should be good for at least a hundred years,' her father said, pulling a lever to close the cargo bay door.

Deploying low orbit satellites over medieval France was not something Caitlin ever thought she would be doing, but these were desperate times.

'It's in position. Get us out of here,' her father said into the speaking tube.

'Roger that,' said her mother. 'Fourteenth century here we come.'

47

MONTGOLFIER

Paris 1809

The name emblazoned above the gates to the yard sounded vaguely familiar to Josh. "The Montgolfier Brothers", was written in fading gold lettering like a sign from a carnival show. Beneath it, in smaller letters, were the words "Globes Aérostatiques".

'You're not serious!' said Sabien, squinting at the signage.

'It's inspired!' exclaimed Lilly.

'What does it say?' asked Josh, his dyslexia making it impossible for his intuit to translate.

Silas laughed. 'Hot air balloon. The mad bastard's going to fly us in.'

The gates were chained with a rusting padlock. Sabien took out a leather roll of lockpicks and deftly opened it in under a minute.

'Poacher turned gamekeeper,' Rufius observed as the inspector put away his tools.

'Tricks of the trade,' Sabien replied. 'When you lie with dogs and all that...'

'Never understood that expression,' muttered Rufius.

It was late and the yard was painted silver in the moonlight. The windows of the workshop were shuttered and dark, signifying the occupants had either left for the day or were asleep. Josh heard a horse stirring inside the stables, but it settled quickly.

Walking past the discarded remnants of old gondola baskets and coils of spare rope they followed Rufius through a brick arch and into the main area.

A large balloon floated in the centre of the cobbled square, tethered to the ground by thick ropes attached to iron spikes. It was huge, over thirty feet in diameter, its surface was covered with ornately painted scenes from history, like a Grecian vase.

Rufius walked over to it and tested the lines. 'Should take the weight of all of us,' he said, looking up to the night sky. 'Assuming the wind is favourable.'

He climbed up the small ladder and hopped over the gunwale and into the basket. 'What are you all standing around for? We've less than four hours until dawn.'

There was an eerie silence as the last of the lines were released and the balloon began to rise.

Lilly slumped down inside the basket and gripped her knees tightly. 'I should have mentioned I'm not great with heights,' she said as they floated up over the buildings.

Rufius seemed blithely unaffected, adjusting the burners like an experienced aeronaut, slowing their ascent until they were hovering over the city.

It was an amazing sight; the twinkling lights of a hundred

thousand lamps spread over the dark city like a blanket of stars. Josh took a deep breath, the air was clearer up here, although he still caught a hint of coal smoke.

'Perfect! We've got a south-westerly,' Rufius observed, holding a wet finger up to the wind. 'Should take us over the isle in just over twenty minutes.'

No one else spoke, they were all too enthralled, or scared. Josh held onto the gunwale with both hands, realising that he wasn't a great fan of heights either.

'There it is,' Sabien said, ten minutes later, pointing into the distance. Josh spotted the winding silver ribbon of the Seine as it twisted through the Latin Quarter. In the middle of the river he could just make out the dark shape of an island.

'Hang on. I'm taking her down,' Rufius said, pulling on one of the ropes that hung from the side of the balloon.

Hot gas vented from an opening in the canopy and Josh felt his stomach lurch as they began to drop quickly.

Lilly made a noise like a frightened squirrel.

The roofs of the city loomed up to meet them, and Rufius frantically adjusted the burners, only just managing to raise the basket above the crumbling chimneys as they hurtled onwards towards the Île de la Cité.

'Be ready with the grappling irons,' he ordered, fighting to control their altitude.

Their speed seemed to increase as they approached. In a matter of seconds they were over the river and heading directly for the Syndicate's headquarters. Sabien and Silas stood on each side of the basket holding ropes with vicious looking hooks.

'We're only going to get one chance at this,' growled the old watchman. 'Make it count.'

As the balloon was buffeted around on the winds, he lowered them further, until the basket was scraping along the shingles of the tallest building on the island.

Sabien missed with his first attempt, but Silas's hook caught and he pulled it tight, bracing himself against the wall of the basket and quickly wrapping the rope around a cleat.

The basket tipped, throwing everyone against the side and nearly toppling Lilly out.

Sabien gathered up his hook and tossed it between two chimneys, pulling the line taut to stabilise the balloon. The basket righted itself and they found themselves floating six feet above the Conciergerie.

'All right,' said Rufius with a deep sigh of relief. 'You have one hour. Sabien, I suggest you take Josh and Silas. Lilly and I will stay here and guard the balloon. Try not to get yourself captured.'

Sabien nodded, hopping over the side of the basket and on to the sloping wooden tiles. Silas followed, as did Josh, although not with quite as much athletic grace as the inspector.

It was beginning to rain and the tiles became slippery under their feet.

The balloon ascended once more, Rufius playing out the mooring lines until they were fifty feet above the roof.

'This way,' whispered Silas, pointing towards one of the towers.

The locked door was not much of a challenge for the inspector and his interesting array of lock picks.

Once inside, they followed Silas through a labyrinth of small corridors to an old wooden staircase.

'No one uses this any more, it's not safe,' he said, testing the banister which wobbled precariously. 'Probably best if you stick to the side nearest the wall.'

The building was in a serious state of decay, the plaster was blown, coming away in places, exposing the wooden lathes beneath. It smelled of mould and stale urine, and there was a layer of dust over everything.

'What was this place?' Josh asked.

'Palais de la Cité,' Sabien said, keeping his voice low. 'Until the fourteenth century it was the residence of the Kings of France, after that it was the home of the Parlement of Paris, before the Revolution of course. Then it was a prison and a courthouse.'

'And now?'

'The Syndicate have taken it over,' Silas said quietly, raising his finger to his lips as the sound of footsteps echoed on the floor below.

Two men walked out onto the landing, one was smoking a pipe. They were speaking in French and it took Josh's mind a few seconds to reinstate the memories of the language.

'What does he want?' asked the first man.

The other spat. 'He wants you to finish the job, or he's going to have your head mounted on a stake.'

There was a sound like water pouring over the rail, and the ensuing smell told Josh that one of the men was taking a piss.

'It wasn't my fault. The bloody guard stepped in front of my shot. How was I supposed to know?'

'You know he doesn't believe in second chances.'

'The Protectorate are watching him now. There's no way I can get close enough to kill him.'

'Well it's you or him.'

Their voices trailed off and Silas gestured for them to follow him down.

At the bottom of the stairwell they could hear more chatter.

'The Hall of the Men-at-Arms,' Silas whispered, nodding towards the arched columns to their right. Beyond them, Josh caught sight of a grand dining hall, long tables crowded with a rowdy gang of cutthroats bickering over scraps of food. 'Feeding time for the animals,' Silas muttered with a smirk.

He turned towards a passageway barred by an iron grille. 'We may need your skills once more maestro.'

Sabien opened the old lock in less than a minute and they slipped through.

'They call this Rue de Paris,' Silas whispered. 'If they were going to keep the Eyes anywhere it would be down here.'

Cells lined both sides of the vaulted basement, reminding Josh more of a dungeon than a cellar.

'This is where they kept Marie Antoinette, before she was tried by the Revolutionary Council,' Sabien noted, taking off one of his gloves and touching the bare stone walls. 'A lot of people died here.'

'And we'll be among them if we don't get a shift on,' added Silas, opening one of the cell doors.

They found nothing more than rotting vegetables, barrels of rum and kegs of gunpowder.

'We're going to have to split up,' suggested Silas when they came to a junction of three passages, each lined with their own set of doors.

Sabien agreed after some persuasion, reminding his prisoner that the temporal cuffs were still functioning by pulling him back the moment he disappeared around the corner.

Josh wasn't exactly sure what they were searching for. He tried to visualise how human eyes could be fixed into a pair of goggles, but it ended up looking like something from a joke shop, so he gave up.

The cells in his section were dark, their metal bars rusted and pitted with age. He could hear rats skittering across the stone floor as he made his way, keeping one hand on the wall.

The first two were empty, excluding the cockroaches. The third contained a stack of wooden crates. Using the torch from his tachyon, he found a metal bar and prised one of them open. Gold and silver treasures glistened in the light. The larger items looked religious, as though they were stolen from a church. The cross keys insignia marking them as belonging to the Pope.

Instinctively, he touched one and felt the timeline shifting under the surface.

Suddenly, without trying, Josh found himself standing in St Peter's Basilica, in the heart of the Vatican. There were priests in scarlet robes rushing around, their faces full of concern and fear.

'The Borgia Chalice is missing!' one said to another in Italian. 'What are we to do?' The second man reminded Josh of Da Recco, the navigator.

'Who would be crazy enough to steal such a thing?'

'Lucrezia of course, who else?'

The timeline shifted, pulling him like a riptide away from the moment. He felt the continuum moving out of phase, the strands of his life unwinding. It took everything he had to bring himself back to his body.

'Okay, definitely no more weaving,' Josh whispered to himself, putting the chalice back amongst the straw.

Silas discovered the Eyes of Eternity in a small chest labelled "BV-1911".

It was a freakish thing to behold. The two white orbs swivelled in gold enclosures stitched into a leather strap.

The blue irises widened as he took it out of the box, studying him with an unblinking stare. It was slightly unnerving, looking into the disembodied eyes of a long dead seer.

He resisted the urge to put them on. He had never been one to dabble in the occult, but he could think of a few customers who would pay dearly to own them – but that wasn't part of the plan.

Instead, he placed them carefully back into their velvet-lined case.

'Silas,' hissed a deep voice from the shadows, 'how nice of you to drop by.'

Turning slowly, Silas hid the box behind his back.

A tall man with a long beard and dark, piercing eyes stepped into the room.

'Rasputin, I can explain,' Silas said, bowing his head.

The man raised his hand. 'There is no need.'

48

ALIXIA

Chapter House

There were hundreds of people lodging in the Chapter House. Alixia had somehow managed to persuade Evelyn to join the rescue mission, allowing the Hive Network to be used to bring them home.

Lyra wove her way up the staircases, between the refugees who were camped out on them. Her father had clearly been unable to keep up with the influx of arrivals.

They all looked terrified. She could feel the fear as she passed them, it was overwhelming her senses. Lyra drove her fingernails into her palms, using the pain to block them out.

Her mother was in the roof garden, which had been transformed into a hospital ward, the rare orchids and ancient palms replaced by iron bedsteads and IV drips.

Alixia was tending to a patient, dressed in a starched nurse's uniform.

'Lyra, where have you been?' she snapped, adjusting the pillow to make the man more comfortable.

Lyra could tell from her tone that her answer would have to be a good one. It was clear that her mother was stressed.

'I went to see Kaori about the Nazgûl.'

Alixia's eyes narrowed. 'I thought the founder had forbidden all travel to the Frontier. It's too dangerous.'

'I know mother, but this was important. I think we may have discovered something about them that can help.'

Her mother tutted, crossing her arms. 'We need your help here young woman! We're running out of space and your father and your brothers are trying their best to keep up with the demand.'

Lyra folded her arms. 'I am helping. I think I've found where they come from.'

'And where is that exactly?'

'There's a place, inside the Shadow Realm. I call it Barad-dûr. Whatever is causing all of this, I think it is linked. The wraith was human once, it showed me things. Terrible things.'

Tears rolled down Lyra cheeks.

Alixia took a moment, her expression softening as she realised what Lyra was planning to do next.

'You're going there aren't you?'

Lyra nodded. 'I have to mama. It's the only way to know.'

Alixia opened her arms as Lyra approached. 'My brave girl,' she whispered, as they embraced, kissing her forehead and stroking her hair. 'You must do what you think is right.'

49

EYES OF ETERNITY

Conciergerie, Paris, 1810.

Rufius and Lilly were standing between two burly guards when Silas followed Rasputin into the Grand Chamber. The flaking walls were decorated with tapestries and gilt-framed paintings from various grand houses, as if someone were trying to restore it to the former glory of a royal palace.

'Westinghouse,' said the leader of the Syndicate in a thick Russian accent, walking up to the old watchman. 'It has been quite some time since we last met.'

'Since you tried to have me killed,' Rufius corrected him.

Rasputin shrugged. 'You were interfering in my affairs, the fate of an entire nation was at stake.'

'One that you had no right to meddle with. You started a revolution! Ended a dynastic line that had reigned for over three centuries.'

Rasputin shook his head. 'No, I merely ensured that the right path was taken. Is that not what your precious Copernicans would say?'

'They spend an infinite amount of time calculating the right course of action. You merely decided it on a whim. The consequences of your decisions are still affecting the continuum even now.'

The Russian simply shrugged. 'What can I say. Business is good.'

A set of ornate doors opened, Sabien and Josh were marched into the room.

'Ah, the party is complete.' Rasputin clapped his hands together. 'Now we can begin.'

He walked over to a throne-like chair positioned on a dais in the middle of the chamber. Sitting down, he crossed his legs, exposing a flash of the purple silk lining of the long cassock.

'Silas tells me that you are on a mission.' He motioned to his guards to bring the prisoners closer.

Sabien's hands were bound tightly behind his back, and there was a bruise under one eye. Josh noticed that Rufius was sporting a nasty red welt across his cheek too.

'We were sent to find an artefact,' Sabien growled. 'You are impeding the lawful execution of that order.'

Rasputin picked up the box and took out the Eyes of Eternity. 'This is my property. What you are doing would be seen as stealing in the eyes of the law. No pun intended.'

Sabien considered reminding the man that possession of goods, most likely stolen ones, was not the same as ownership, but decided against it.

Rasputin strapped the goggles to his head. 'What I fail to understand is why you would need these. What possible use could the Order have for them. You have an entire guild full of seers at your disposal. Do you not? Why risk coming into my domain for such an arcane trinket?'

'It is part of an ongoing investigation,' replied Sabien, failing to hide his dislike for the man. If this was the leader of the Dark Guild, then Josh guessed he was public enemy number one in the Protectorate's book.

Rasputin held up his hands in front of his face. The pale orbs tracked his hands as if they were his own eyes.

'Interesting,' he said. 'I forgot what Baba Vanga was capable of. So you're looking for the lost island?'

Rufius tensed, his arms straining against the cords around his wrists. 'That's none of your damned business,' he snarled through gritted teeth.

'Yes we are,' gushed Lilly, ignoring the old watchman. 'We need to find it. Can you see where it is?'

'Not exactly,' Rasputin replied, moving his hands in the air as if pulling on invisible threads. 'There are too many alternates. And even if I did, why should I help you?

'Because it's the right thing to do,' replied Lilly, using her school teacher voice once more.

Rasputin's laughter filled the hall. 'Hah! Don't let this garb deceive you. It's been a long time since I believe in altruism, let alone a god. If you've spent any time with Silas you will know that everything comes at a price in our world.'

'Name it,' growled Rufius, 'and let us be done with this charade.'

Rasputin got to his feet and held up one hand. 'All in good time watchman. One must know the value of something before one can give it a price.'

There was an awkward silence as they watched the monk turn in circles around the room.

'But what has this to do with the moon?' he asked, reaching out above his head as if trying to catch it.

'The man we're looking for was a brilliant man. He placed a team on the moon a hundred years before the linears,' Lilly explained, ignoring the glares from Sabien and Rufius, who were trying to get her to keep her mouth shut.

'No, this isn't about a moon mission,' Rasputin continued, the eyes rotating wildly in their sockets. 'There's something wrong with it. The tides are changing. Seas are rising.'

He took off the goggles and stared at them in disbelief.

'There is going to be a terrible catastrophe, the moon is going to break away from its orbit.'

'There's a chance that may happen,' Lilly agreed. 'That's why we have to find Alexander or at least his research station and shut it down.'

Rasputin put the goggles back into the box. He paced around the chamber, his hands behind his back, like Professor Eddington, murmuring to himself as he walked.

'This scientist, you think he is causing this, this…' he waved his hands around as if trying to summon the right word.

'Geo-magnetic storm?' suggested Lilly. 'It's possible. The energy field his machine produced was powerful enough to move an entire island out of existence.'

'And what exactly are you planning to do when you find the lost island?'

There was a moment of silence.

'You do have a plan don't you?' he repeated, turning towards Rufius and then laughed. 'Hah! The usual Westinghouse approach, turn up and hope a solution presents itself.'

'If we don't do something we're all dead,' Rufius muttered under his breath.

Rasputin held up the box. 'My price is a simple one. I want the island.'

'You want Atlantis?' Rufius scoffed.

Rasputin nodded. 'And everything that sits upon it.'

50

PROBE

Thieves Market, Lisbon, Portugal. 1760

Balthazar inspected the goggles, carefully avoiding its gaze as he turned it over in his hands.

'I have to say, I'm impressed. I wasn't expecting you to pull it off,' he said to Silas. 'But the balloon was a work of genius.'

Silas neglected to mention that the leader of the Syndicate had actually let them go. Nor, the fact that Rasputin offered to have the Shadow Merchant tortured until he told them the location of the probe.

'The landing could have been better,' added Rufius, rubbing his jaw.

The merchant laughed, revealing a wide set of bejewelled teeth. 'I heard Napoleon was a little surprised when you dropped out of the sky into the gardens of Château Saint Cloud.'

Since they couldn't leave the conventional way from the Conciergerie without raising suspicion with the rest of the Syndicate, Rasputin gave them back the balloon, which

Rufius managed to crash land in the grounds of Napoleon's favourite château in Paris.

'So, now you have what you asked for,' said Sabien, clearly uncomfortable being surrounded by so much stolen property. 'Can we conclude this business?'

Balthazar nodded, handing the Eyes of Eternity to one of his assistants. 'Of course, follow me.'

The building was deceptively larger than it looked from the outside. They followed Balthazar down a series of narrow staircases until they came to a stone corridor. At the far end was an old metal door, its surface covered in intricate locks and dials.

'This is where I keep my most precious treasures, the rarest of collectibles. Items that were thought to have vanished forever – including the Atlantis probe.'

Josh was about to point out that he denied the probe actually existed the last time they met, but Sabien beat him to it.

'You actually said it was a myth.'

'Did I?' the merchant replied, turning certain dials on the door. 'I forget, there are so many trades, my head can't hold them all.'

Inside what must have once been the crypt of the church was a treasure trove. The shelves along each wall were stacked with antique artefacts that glinted in the torch light. In the centre was a row of stone sarcophagi inscribed with the heraldic symbols of medieval knights.

Balthazar, motioned to his servants, who lifted the heavy stone lid from one.

'This was discovered off the coast of Svalbard by a whaling boat in 1784. I recognised the marks on the casing, although as I may have mentioned, it is non-functional.'

One of his aides took a package from the coffin and placed it carefully on top of another.

Balthazar unwrapped the hessian cloth to reveal a brass sphere.

'Oh my God!' Lilly exclaimed, rushing over to it. She picked up the probe, which was not much bigger than a football and held it up for them to see.

'Is that it?' asked Rufius, clearly underwhelmed by the size.

'What did you expect?' she replied, her eyebrows knitting together into a scowl. 'This is a DC6, the most advanced temporal probe that was ever made. It has more than three hundred internal functions and can send data over thousands of years. Actually, that's a good point, where are the antennae?'

She put the probe down and started to search inside the sarcophagus. 'They would have been about eight inches in length and telescopic.'

Balthazar shrugged his shoulders and raised his hands. 'As I said before, the thing is broken, but it is yours if you still want it.'

'Oh I want it,' said Lilly, picking up an ornately decorated space helmet. 'And this too. Where on earth did you find this?'

'That thing? Have it. There hasn't been a lot of interest in space memorabilia since the moon landings.'

'What are we going to do with it?' Rufius asked, running his hand over the smooth surface. There were a series of numbers stamped into the metal and a symbol that Lilly insisted was the insignia of Atlas Station. 'There's no timeline that I can see and without the connection to the base station it's just a hunk of metal.'

'There is someone who may be able to help,' said Lilly,

staring at the probe. 'One of the original members of the moon mission. She was their chief engineer, Eira Winterbourne. If anyone would know how to get this working it would be her.'

'And where exactly would we find this Winterbourne?' asked Sabien.

'After the moon, the team was disbanded, Eira went to study super-massive black holes. She's the resident astronomer on the Paranal Observatory in the Atacama Desert, Chile.'

'When?'

'1472.'

'That may be a little tricky to reach.' Rufius picked up the probe and looked around for a suitable box to put it in. 'Joshua, contact Evelyn and see where the nearest Hive node is. I'm guessing there isn't much in the way of traffic back to that time.'

51

ORBITS

Map Room, Copernican Hall.

Professor Eddington stood in the centre of a large model of the solar system watching the various planets orbit around him as if he were the sun. With a flick of his hand he paused the planetary motion and stepped away, leaving a glowing sphere in his place and walked between Mars and Jupiter.

'This is the standard ecliptic plane of the Earth around Sol.'

A holographic line appeared, tracing a path around him and back to the small blue sphere. 'As you will see when we overlay the latest predicted trajectory, we are currently deviating from this path by at least two point four per cent.'

Another line appeared, this time in red, showing the Earth moving a few degrees off course and closer to the fiery orb.

'And how would this course change affect the climate?' asked the founder.

'There would be a rise in temperature, which would cause glaciers to melt, raising sea levels and flooding most of the planet. Without land to absorb some of the sun's heat, temperatures would continue to rise, boosted further still by the rising levels of the carbon dioxide and vapours that the oceans released into the air. All life as we know it would be lost.'

The founder considered the facts, watching the small grey globe spinning erratically around the blue planet. 'The axial tilt will be affected too?'

'Indeed it will. We may find that seasons are no longer consistent.'

'Have you spoke to Newton about this?'

Eddington nodded. 'And Galileo. They both concur, this new trajectory will cause an extinction level event unless we can correct the moon's orbit.'

It was clear from the founder's sanguine expression that he understood the severity of the situation.

'How goes the triangulation? Are we closer to locating the source?'

The professor nodded to Sim who was standing at the control console. 'The first ten have been deployed. Master De Freis has been monitoring their signals.'

The solar system disappeared, replaced by a four dimensional model of the continuum.

'The buoys have been placed at two hundred year intervals across the last two millennia,' explained Sim, walking down into the holographic model. He pointed to a series of bright points in the tree-like structure. 'We are receiving telemetry from each of them. Once we have created a baseline, we should be able to determine the eras that need further investigation.'

The founder studied the model. 'Two hundred years? Can we not be more precise?'

Eddington shook his head. 'The *Nautilus* navigational systems are being adversely affected by the gravitational waves. Her ability to deploy accurately is becoming more difficult with every mission. Soon it will become too dangerous for her to enter the continuum at all.'

'Then we shall have to look for another way. Keep me informed of any updates,' the old man said turning to leave.

'Is there any news of Joshua Jones?' asked Sim, walking beside him.

Lord Dee twisted his head slightly, his expression inscrutable and whispered. 'Master Jones is currently missing in action, as are Rufius Westinghouse and Inspector Sabien. One assumes they are still investigating the revelations of Silas Wormwood, but who can say?'

Sim couldn't be sure, but he could have sworn the founder winked at him as he left.

52

THE DESERT

Cerro Paranal, Atacama Desert, 1472

They had been travelling for nearly three days.

As Rufius suspected, Evelyn's network was limited, only managing to take them as far as Antofagasta, a rather unpleasant little mining town seventy miles south of Mount Cerro Paranal.

They took it in turns to carry the probe, which was heavier than it looked. It was hard going, since there were no horses or mules, and the llama Rufius bought from one of the locals ran away on the first night.

They marched slowly across the arid terrain. Its barren landscape was a mixture of sand and rock, like something from the surface of Mars. The silence was profound, broken only by the occasional gust of wind. The Atacama was one of the driest places on Earth and the temperature at midday could reach forty degrees — and there was little in the way of shade.

'Wish we still had that damn balloon,' said Rufius, mopping his brow with a handkerchief. 'I can cope with just about anything apart from heat.'

'We should make camp soon,' advised Sabien, shading his eyes as he looked up at the sun's position.

Josh shrugged off the backpack containing the probe and stretched his back. His shirt was soaked with sweat, so he took it off and tied it around his head to make a sun hat.

'So, what did the Inca do for sunglasses?' he asked, unscrewing the cap on the waterskin and taking a long drink.

'They didn't,' said Lilly, sitting down on a nearby rock. 'But the Chinese used lenses made from smoky quartz as far back as the twelfth century, and there is evidence that the Inuit would fashion snowglasses out of walrus tusks.'

Josh tried not to think about the Arctic, the water was warm and tasted of leather. An ice-cold drink was exactly what he wanted right now.

At night the temperature in the desert would plummet to near-zero, and there was little in the way of stuff to burn. He'd come to the conclusion that this place was trying to kill them.

'What on earth made her want to set up down here?'

Lilly looked up at the bright blue sky. 'It has the clearest view of the universe. In the twentieth century they will build some of the largest astronomical telescopes on the top of the mountain. I guess Professor Winterbourne thought it the best place to set up her observatory. '

'I bet she doesn't get a lot of visitors.'

'I believe that may be the most significant reason of all.'

They sheltered beneath a rocky outcrop, too tired to talk, and dozed through most of the afternoon.

Silas talked in his sleep, nothing that Josh could make out but it sounded as if he was pleading, like a small child to a parent.

Sabien stood in the shadows staring at the mountain. He was the only other Protectorate officer Josh had met, excluding Dalton and his crazy mother. The colonel seemed to have a mutual respect for the policeman, it was hard to believe there was actually someone that the old man considered to be an equal.

Rufius was using the rucksack of the probe as a pillow, snoring loudly and swatting away the small biting flies in his sleep.

Lilly spent most of the time tinkering with the probe, her eyes wide and full of amazement as if it were the Crown Jewels.

Josh wondered what Caitlin and Zack were doing right now. It felt like months since he'd seen them. Taking out his almanac, he flicked through the pages of old mission briefs until he found the photograph he'd taken from his locker. Caitlin knew some clever way to store videos on paper, which involved a certain kind of camera and a special type of chronologically-treated ink.

As he watched the two of them playing in their garden on a beautiful, sunny day, Josh wished he could step back into that moment.

He turned the photo over, on the other side was a picture of Caitlin with Zack on the day he was born. They were propped up on pillows in Catherine the Great's bed. She hated the way she looked, saying it was like she'd been dragged through a hedge backwards, but Josh insisted on keeping it.

It was the proudest day of his life, and the saddest too, knowing how much his mother would have loved to have met her grandson.

They were safe on the Nautilus, he reminded himself, trying not to imagine the chaos they were flying through. It was reassuring to know that if the universe was really on the verge of collapse, his family were on the only ship that could survive it.

Although, he wasn't sure what kind of life Zack would have. That was the problem about becoming a parent, dealing with the unknown.

All you can do is hope for the best. His mother used to say. *But prepare for the worst.*

'Is that your kid?' Silas asked, pointing at the picture.

Josh hadn't heard him stir, but tried not to show his surprise.

'Yes,' he said, like any proud dad. 'Zachary. He's nearly two now.'

Silas sat down beside him, rubbing his eyes as if still half-asleep. 'I always wondered what it would be like to have kids.'

Josh laughed. 'Well, you don't get a lot of sleep for starters.'

'Yes, my mother used to say we came alive at night.'

'Do you have brothers and sisters?'

Silas nodded, holding up the fingers of one hand. 'Five, although there were rumours that there maybe more. My father was something of a charmer.'

'And were they all — '

'Criminals? Indeed we were,' he said proudly. 'The Worm-woods controlled most of the fifteenth century and were making in-roads into the sixteenth. That was until dad got it into his head to diversify into Russian royalty. I think he fancied his chances with Catherine the Great to be honest.'

Josh knew very little about the Romanovs, other than the fact they were killed during the early days of the revolution.

'I was only twelve when they went after the Tzar. They left me with aunty Mary, said it was too dangerous.' He picked up a small rock and tossed it at a lizard that was scuttling across the dry sand. 'She wasn't really my aunt, turns out she was a nark, an undercover crow.'

'And you ended up with him?' Josh said, nodding towards the sleeping watchman.

'Aye, that I did. Stupid old sod thought he could put me on the straight and narrow.'

'I don't know. He's not that bad. He's saved my arse more than once.'

'Oh, don't get me wrong. There's no one I would rather have by my side in a fight, but once you let him down, there's no coming back.'

Silas looked thoughtfully at the old man for the longest time. 'Anyways, time to get moving. If we hoof it we should be able to make the mountain before the cold chills our bones. I don't know about you, but I'm not a fan of the great outdoors.'

53

HERMIT

Paranal Observatory, Chile. 1472

The climb up the mountain took the rest of the afternoon and into the evening. The air was thinner at eight and a half thousand feet above sea level, and they were all finding it hard going by the time they reached the summit.

The observatory consisted of four massive brass satellite dishes, each one with its parabolic bowl pointing up into a different part of the starry sky.

Nestling amongst them was a small stone fortress. The battlements were strung with lines of rope on which someone's washing was drying in the breeze.

The view was breathtaking, Josh had never seen the universe laid out in quite so much detail. They all took a moment to acclimatise, breathing deeply as they stared openmouthed into the vast celestial canvas above them.

The stars shimmered against the dark blue curtain. The Milky Way stretched across the sky like a luminous river, its dense clusters of stars and nebulae clearly visible to the naked eye.

'How many are there?' Silas wondered aloud.

'About four and a half thousand with the naked eye,' said Lilly.

'A hundred billion in our galaxy,' Josh added, remembering one of the random facts from his mother's quiz shows.

Lilly look impressed.

'And there are two trillion galaxies, so two hundred billion trillion or to put it another way – a sextillion,' she continued, clearly not wanting to be outdone.

'More than there are grains of sand,' added Rufius.

There was a neatly-kept kitchen garden laid out around the tiny castle. Its raised beds were sustained by an intricate network of copper pipes that ran up the side of the stone wall and into a vapour trap on the roof.

'Strawberries,' observed Rufius, picking one of the red fruits and popping it into his mouth. 'Delicious.'

A sound like a feral dog came from somewhere inside the building.

They all turned to see a woman appear through a door and coming running towards them. She was wearing a helmet with a torch strapped onto it and carrying a large, trumpet-shaped gun.

'Be off with you!' she screamed, in a dozen different languages.

Her hair was long and white, and her clothes were a patchwork of different materials.

Rufius raised his hands to shade his eyes from the light of her torch. 'Now hold on Professor Winterbourne, we come in peace.'

She stopped and levelled the gun at him, closing one eye as if to get a better aim.

'I'm warning you, this is a highly unreliable blunderbuss. It can take a person's arm off at sixty paces. I've filled it with my own special concoction of rock salt and lead shot. I will have no qualms about shooting the next man who touches my garden.'

Lilly stepped out from behind Rufius. Taking the probe from the rucksack on his back, she held it out for the mad woman to see. 'We've brought you this. We need your help, it seems to be malfunctioning.'

The old woman's expression changed. Lowering the gun, she removed her helmet and switched off the light. Her darkly tanned face was an older version of the woman standing beside Templeton in the photograph Lilly had shown them at the Science Museum.

She squinted at the markings on the side of the probe. 'Well now, aren't you a sight for sore eyes. Which is it a six or a seven?'

'A six, I think, although the antennae are missing.' Lilly walked towards her, and everyone relaxed a little.

Josh realised that Sabien had silently drawn a weapon. It was a pistol with some serious modifications, one that obviously could survive the temporal translation.

'A six,' the professor repeated, putting down the blunderbuss and taking the probe in both hands. 'I haven't held a six in over fifty years. Hello, my beauty, where have you been?'

She stroked the brass surface, her fingers tracing the lines of symbols. 'Hmm, lost its antennae and there's no trace of a timeline, that's not unusual. We used to find the temporal displacement would destroy any latent chronology. It was a side effect of quantum modulation.'

'Can you fix it?' asked the colonel, lowering his hands.

She tilted her head to one side. 'I might be able to, as long as you promise not to eat any more of my strawberries.'

He nodded. 'My apologies. We've been travelling for three days to find you. I don't suppose you have anything decent to drink?'

Eira laughed. 'Now that I can help you with.' She turned

back towards the castle. 'And I might just have a pot of Caldillo de Congrio if you fancy a bite to eat.'

After three days of rations, the soup was delicious. It was an interesting vegetable stew of sorts, with a subtle hint of fish, although Josh could find no evidence of any meat, which seemed to please Sabien, who devoured it.

The castle had its own water supply, which was sweet and cold, and very welcome after the brackish taint of the water skins.

The thick walls kept the chill of the evening at bay. Eira opened the door of the stove and the room warmed quickly.

Sitting around the large wooden table, watching their group slowly unwind after the gruelling journey, Josh wondered how long the eccentric old professor had lived here alone.

The circular room was like something from a planetarium, the walls were covered in star maps and astrological charts.

'I've been studying black holes for the last decade,' she said, as if answering Josh's unspoken question. 'My array can detect the microwave signatures of super massive black holes. I've discovered fifty-three in the last ten years. Alexander theorised that if one studied the gravitational field dynamics at the event horizon one would discover a whole new field of temporal mechanics.'

'What was he like?' asked Lilly, putting down her spoon and leaning forward on her elbows.

Eira looked wistfully off into the distance, her eyes glazing over. 'We first crossed paths at university. He was the most intense tutor I had ever studied under. I thought he was going to throw me off of the course.'

She gathered up the empty bowls before Silas had a chance to lick them and put them in the sink.

'He was years ahead of his time. A true genius, well at

least at the beginning. His work on quantum tunnelling was inspired, we used to joke that his future self must have come back to show him the way.'

'This was at the Temporal Institute? Where he formed the Chronometric Society,' added Lilly.

'Yes,' Eira said, holding up her right hand to show the faculty ring. 'Exploramus Heri, Formamus Cras.'

'Explore the past, shape the future,' translated Lilly, holding up her own.

Eira looked impressed. 'What did you study?'

Lilly blushed. 'You, mostly. Or rather the work of the Society.'

'We have our own course now? Wow, that does make me feel old.'

'Your theories changed our understanding of time.'

The professor smiled. 'And we had the best kind of parties. You could get drunk fifteen times in one night and still not have a hangover in the morning. We were some of the brightest in our fields. And he was like a god.'

'So what went wrong?' asked Rufius.

'Alexander became obsessed with spacetime. He developed a dynamic reference framework, one that could calculate the relativistic adjustments of the spatial and temporal coordinates needed to put a man on the moon. He convinced the university to start the research division, and of course we all joined up without a second thought.'

'He put someone on the moon?' said Silas, much to Lilly's disappointment, it was clear he hadn't been paying attention at her briefing.

'Three of us, in fact. It was the most amazing moment in the history of the Temporal Institute,' her expression saddened. 'And its greatest failure.'

'They all died,' explained Lilly.

'Tabitha, Jacob and Nathaniel. They were my best friends. It was the worst possible outcome. The Institute shut the project down and we went our separate ways. I never saw Alexander again.'

'But you know how to fix this?' asked Rufius, pointing at the probe.

Eira laughed, picking up the device. 'I bloody hope so, it's based on my design.'

The upper floor of the tower was a workshop of sorts. An assortment of strange-looking tools hung from rafters and blueprints lined the walls. There was a row of half-finished clockwork machines sitting on a long wooden workbench.

Eira placed the probe on a metal stand and began to search through a toolbox until she found a pair of multi-lensed spectacles which she balanced on the end of her nose.

'Most of the issues we experienced with the early DC6s were to do with the power source. I was forever having to replace them, something about their sensor arrays would chew through the battery in no time.'

She picked up a tiny screwdriver and began to loosen one of the panels.

'They were supposed to be able to survive for hundreds of years, replenishing themselves using a form of graviton recovery. But I lost count of the number of these that vanished without trace.'

'What does it do?'

She took out the first of the screws and placed it carefully on the table.

'We would send them into deep time. Millions of years into the past, to test our calculations. We used to call it target practice. Trying to hit a planet that's travelling through time and space is quite a complex process.'

'How do we know this one belongs to Atlas Station?' asked Sabien.

Eira tapped on the mark on the side of the casing. 'The insignia. The badge for the mission.'

Josh hadn't paid it much attention until she pointed it out. Etched into the brass was a roundel with the usual NASA-like motifs of planets and stars, as well as a circle with a cross through its centre.

'What's that?' he asked.

'That's the symbol for Earth, and here,' she tapped on another glyph which had a circle with an arrow coming out of it. 'This is Mars.'

'Mars?' exclaimed Rufius.

She continued to remove the brass screws. 'I only found out later that Alexander was working in secret. He'd set up the Atlas Station as a cover, the temporal observatory was actually a reboot of the moon project, except this time he was trying to reach the red planet.'

'Why?'

Eira looked up from her work, her eyes magnified by the powerful lenses.

'Because he believed there was once a great civilisation on it. He wanted to go back to a time when Mars would have supported life.'

'That must have been billions of years ago,' said Lilly.

'Four and a half billion to be precise. The late Noachian Period.'

Eira lifted the panel away, exposing an intricate clockwork mechanism. She adjusted the lenses on her headset and picked up a pair of long thin pliers.

'The annoying thing about the power cell was that the most efficient place to put it was in the central core. It was easier to replace the whole unit than take it apart. In those days we had the luxury of near infinite funding to be so extravagant.'

There was a clicking sound as she manipulated the tools. The others gathered behind her to get a closer look.

'You're in my light,' she growled at Rufius, who quickly stepped back.

She switched on a small head torch and peered into the unit.

'There you are,' she whispered. Pulling out a tiny metal power cell. 'The flux capacitor was a beautiful piece of miniaturisation, even if I do say so myself. It will take a few hours to recharge it, my only source of electricity is the wind turbine on the roof and it's been playing up lately.'

54

SHADOW REALM

Shadow Realm

'Where exactly are we going?' asked Kaori, as they walked through a dark forest. The air was heavy and smelled of rotten wood and beetles.

'Barad-dûr,' said Lyra, marching on in front. 'This is the quickest way. Although the last time I was here the trees weren't so grumpy? They keep moving the path.'

'Grumpy? So this is Mirkwood?'

'It has had many names,' added Kelly, looking nervously over his shoulder 'I think the sooner we're clear of it the better.'

They followed the path for what felt like a day. The Grand Seer muttered under his breath as they walked, jumping at the slightest sound and making runic gestures at shadows.

'Be not afeard; the isle is full of noises, Sounds and sweet airs that give delight and hurt not.'

Finally they reached the edge of the forest.

•   •   •

Ahead of them, beyond a low plain of grassland, rose a range of high peaks. Kaori was beginning to see why Lyra chose Middle Earth for a reference.

'The castle lies on the other side of the mountains.'

'Ered Lithui, the Ash Mountains,' whispered Kaori under her breath.

Kelly peered into the distance. 'That is quite a distance, are you quite sure this is the way?'

Lyra sighed. 'I saw what I saw. Devlin showed me the place.'

'I have no doubt,' said the Grand Seer stretching his back. 'But these old bones have long since lost their youthful stride. I merely seek a quicker route and a perhaps a few moments of rest.' He broke off a twig from a low hanging branch and began to draw a circle in the hard ground.

Kaori sat down on a nearby log and took out her canteen.

The water was tainted and warm, but it cleared the dust from her throat. The Grand Seer removed something from his bag and handed it to Lyra, who went around the circle placing various items at strategic points.

Now they were clear of the ominous gloom of the forest, Kaori felt her mood lift a little. There was a stillness about the realm that she hadn't appreciated before. Flowers grew amongst the meadow grasses around them, and the sky to the west had a glimmer of blue about it.

Lyra and Kelly finished the circle and waved her over.

'What is it?' Kaori asked, looking down at the intricate markings on the ground.

'A portal of sorts,' the Grand Seer said, taking out a small bottle and pouring its contents onto the ground. 'Abandon is not the only one with knowledge of the old ways.'

The liquid bubbled as it soaked into the earth. The glyphs around the circle began to glow as a dark hole expanded from the centre of the damp patch.

'The fabric of this realm is as thin as tissue paper, held together with nothing more than thistledown and cobwebs.'

55

OBSERVATORY

Paranal Observatory, Chile. 1472

They watched the moon rise over the desert from the roof of the castle. The silence was so deep and profound that Josh could hear rock cracking as it cooled. There was a gentle wind, like a whisper, scented with the promise of rain, but it never came.

The satellite dishes turned silver in the moonlight.

'What do you pick up on those?' Josh asked Eira while she adjusted the mast of the wind turbine.

'They're receiving radio waves from distant stars; super-novas and all manner of celestial events. I've been scanning the sky for the last twenty years, building up a map of the background noise, finding the holes.'

'Black holes?'

She nodded. 'They're the most interesting of all. Alexander was convinced that they could teach us how to manipulate spacetime in ways that would allow us to travel beyond our universe.'

'Like a warp drive?'

Eira looked confused. 'How do you know about warp? It

was only ever discussed as a theoretical possibility. No one outside of the Institute knew about it.'

Josh didn't have the heart to tell her about Star Trek. 'I don't know, I guess I read about it somewhere. I'm from the present.'

She tutted and scowled like an old school teacher. 'Well I suppose someone has to be. Did you witness the moon landings?'

Josh laughed. 'No. I wasn't even born then. The present has moved on a bit since that happened. In fact they've pretty much given up on space travel.'

Eira sighed, taking off her hat and scratching her head. 'Yes, I tend to forget that time marches on. I've been so caught up in my work sometimes I can't remember what day it is. One day is much like another here.'

'Not much in the way of wind?' observed Rufius looking off towards the Atlas mountains.

'It's called Puelche, it'll come.'

'How long before we have enough charge?' Josh asked, watched the blades of the windmill turning slowly.

Eira picked up the battery and held it next to her ear. 'Another couple of hours should do it. In the meantime, I suggest we all get some rest.' She settled down into an old chair and pulled her hat down over her face.

Rufius glanced at Sabien, who also clearly thought the woman was mad.

Silas and Lilly were playing cards at the table when they came down two hours later.

'That's not fair! You're cheating,' she said, putting down her hand.

'How else am I supposed to win?' he said, revealing a royal flush.

'Skill, luck, chance? All the normal ways,' Lilly said, folding her arms and pouting like a small child.

'That's not how I was taught to play,' he said, leaning back in his chair. 'My old man said it was only the stupid and the simple that played by the rules.'

'That'll be why he's locked up in the Château for all time,' Lilly growled, 'not exactly the best role model was he?'

Silas's expression darkened. 'No. I don't suppose he was.'

'Right you two,' barked Eira, 'come and help me get this back in. Lilly your hands will be steadier than mine, and I've a feeling your eyes are sharper than a fox's young man.'

It took the pair less than ten minutes to reinsert the battery.

Once it was in place, Eira reattached the panel and moved a series of switches until the probe began to hum.

'There you are,' she said with a smile, her eyes gleaming. 'Now, let's see where you've been.'

The probe's memory bank contained an activity log, one that could be downloaded into an almanac via a thin cable. Josh had no idea that almanacs even came with ports, but there it was, hidden in the spine of Rufius's journal.

'They got rid of it in the Mark III,' explained the old watchman, seeing the confusion on Josh's face. 'Some pen pusher decided it wasn't necessary.'

The data streamed on to the blank pages, starting as rows of numbers in thin columns, but as the almanac recognised the format it transformed into charts and chronologies.

'She's definitely seen some unusual events,' Rufius observed. 'I don't recognise half of these timelines.'

Eira huffed. 'Give it here.'

She snatched the book from him, putting on a pair of spectacles that were dangling from a chain around her neck.

'Hmm. Much as I hate to admit it, you're right. These don't resemble anything from our continuum.'

'Which means what exactly?' asked Silas, hovering behind them trying to get a better look.

'That it's been elsewhere,' the old woman snapped. 'Obviously affected by Alexander's experiment.'

'So how do we use it to find Atlantis?' asked Sabien.

The professor took off her glasses and held up the still animating pages of Rufius's almanac. 'There's an origin code,' she tapped on a point in the chart. 'If I feed it back into its navigational matrix, it should initiate a recall subroutine and send the probe back to home, wherever that is. All you need to do is follow it.'

She pulled the lead out of the almanac and plugged in a small keypad, then proceeded to key in the coordinates.

Lilly watched in awe, her eyes wide like a child opening her first Christmas present. 'Follow it how?'

Rufius placed his hand on the side of the sphere. 'Old-fashioned, analog way seems best to me.'

They all followed suit. Feeling the temporal fields of the probe increasing.

'Hold on,' said Eira, finishing the sequence. 'This might get a little rough.'

56

TSUNAMI

Aleutian Islands, Alaska. 2021

Caitlin climbed out onto the deck of the *Nautilus's* conning tower. It was bitterly cold, ice coated the metal rungs of the ladder, stinging her hands. She pulled on a pair of gloves that her mother insisted she take.

They were just above the fiftieth parallel, in an area within the Alaskan Arctic boundary. The Aleutian Islands formed part of a volcanic archipelago that stretched from Alaska to the Kamchatka Peninsula in Russia, creating a natural border between the Bering Sea and the Pacific Ocean.

Taking out a pair of high-powered Antiquarian binoculars, Caitlin looked southward towards the last known location of the tsunami. Ominous storm clouds were gathering on the horizon like the ash clouds from a massive volcanic eruption.

The heads-up display on the lenses told her the wave was still more than fifty miles away, and travelling at over five hundred miles per hour. She could just make out the white peaks of its crests, it looked more like a mountain range thundering towards her.

'How high is it now?' her mother's voice asked through the tinny speaker built into the side of the tower.

Caitlin adjusted the focus on the lenses, allowing the readings to calibrate.

'Over one hundred and fifty feet,' she replied into the speaking tube.

Twice as high as the one in Mexico, she thought, *and three times the one before that in Greenland.*

'They're getting stronger,' her mother noted, obviously coming to the same conclusion.

Fortunately the Aleutian Islands were mostly uninhabited. The previous disasters they visited resulted in thousands of casualties, wiping out hundreds of homes and farms in the fourteenth and fifteenth centuries.

'We've got less than six minutes until it makes landfall,' she advised her mother.

'Time you came back down. I need to prep the ship for submersion.'

One of the benefits of the *Nautilus* was that it was built to be as airtight as a submarine. There were pockets of atmosphere in the Maelstrom, bubbles of time with breathable air, but it was still a rare commodity. The ship's air filtration was a little Heath Robinson, which meant that it began to smell of burnt toast after a few days of recycling. But, having a submersible came in rather useful when you were surveying the tidal effects of the moon shifting orbit.

After successfully deploying the temporal buoys, Professor Eddington asked her parents to monitor the effects of the gravitational instability at key points along the continuum.

Caitlin tagged along. Josh was still away on a mission that no one seemed to have any idea about, including Sim, who was struggling with the data from the triangulation buoys.

It was five days now since she last heard from Josh, and she would have been worried if it wasn't for the fact that she knew he was with Rufius.

She considered bringing Zack along for the ride, but after the argument with Josh, Caitlin felt the need to prove she was still useful. Zack seemed happy enough with Alixia and auntie Lyra, who was teaching him the basics of becoming a seer.

A real bond was forming between the two of them. Her step-sister's abilities meant she could communicate with him in ways that no one else could. He had only mastered the basics of 'Mama' and 'Papa', but Lyra was having much deeper conversations with him that went beyond speech.

'It's not words,' Lyra explained to her, 'more like feelings and emotions. He's a very powerful seer,' she added. 'I can help him learn to harness his gift, before it becomes uncontrollable.'

Caitlin grudgingly agreed, she was needed elsewhere.

From the data the Copernicans were able to gather, the moon's orbit was changing the shape of the oceans and causing massive fluctuations in the tides. It bore all of the characteristics of an earthquake or a landslide causing tsunamis, or as the Japanese would call them, 'harbour waves'.

Caitlin slid down the ladder onto the bridge. 'Okay,' she said, throwing the lever that closed the hatch, 'she's sealed.'

Her mother pulled back on the steering column, and Caitlin felt the ship pitch as it turned into the oncoming wave.

'Aren't we going to leave?' she asked, assuming that they would simply open a breach back into the Maelstrom.

'Not enough time. Better to dive under it. I need to take some measurements anyway. Strap yourself in.'

57

ATLANTIS

Atlantis

There was a strange sensation running through Josh's body when he came to.

It was nothing like the nauseating disorientation he suffered when he first travelled with the colonel. This was different, it felt like every cell in his body was vibrating. His nerves tingled with pins and needles, reminding him of the electric shock he received once while attempting to fix his mum's TV.

'It'll pass,' reassured Eira, somewhere off in the darkness. 'It's the after effect of the gravitational fields we passed through.'

Josh opened his eyes. Blinking to clear his vision, he found he was standing in what appeared to be a storage facility, the walls were lined with racks of probes.

Rufius was wandering around in his usual impatient way, examining various pieces of equipment while Eira was helping Lilly to her feet.

Silas and Sabien were nowhere to be seen.

'Where are the others?' Josh asked, getting to his feet.

'Silas disappeared the moment we arrived,' Rufius replied. 'Sabien's gone off in search of him. Apparently the handcuffs don't work here.'

'Are we actually on Atlantis?'

'Atlas Station,' Eira corrected him. 'Atlantis was Plato's invention.'

The probe hovered in the air in front of her, a single blue light blinking intermittently like a cyclopean eye. She tapped one of its buttons. 'Good boy, well done. Off you pop.'

It drifted away and into an empty slot on one of the shelves.

'Atlas Station,' murmured Lilly, her eyes wide like a kid in a toy shop.

'Don't get too excited,' said Eira, wiping her finger through the dust on one of the probes. 'By the look of this place, no one has been down here for some time.'

Josh walked over to join Rufius.

'So what's the plan?'

The colonel scratched his beard. 'Find whoever's running this place and convince them to switch off whatever is creating the anomaly.'

'There should be an internal comms system,' said Eira going towards a set of large metal shutters that formed one of the walls. She pushed a button on the controls and a set of motors kicked in above them, rolling the shutters slowly upward.

The world beyond it was not quite what Josh expected.

Ice and snow covered the entire island.

They were standing in a cave hollowed out of the side of a mountain. The shallow basin below them was ringed by a range of high peaks. It was like looking down into the crater of a dormant volcano.

In the centre of the hollow stood what appeared to be a

lighthouse surrounded by smaller buildings. A strange red light flickered in the lantern room as if the bulb was failing.

Rufius and Josh came to join her. 'Is that it?' the old watchman asked.

Eira took out a tiny telescope from inside her jacket and surveyed the scene. 'Part of it. Knowing Alexander most of the lab will be underground.'

'Isn't it supposed to be Mediterranean?' he continued, his breath turning into clouds of white smoke as he blew on his hands.

'Originally, yes, but the climate seems to have been seriously affected. I expected unusual weather, but this looks like they've been trapped in an ice age.'

Taking out his tachyon, Rufius tapped on the dials. 'Hmm, not going to get a lot out of that, it still thinks we're in 1427.'

Sabien returned a few minutes later with a very sorry-looking Silas, who was now handcuffed to his captor.

'There's an extensive cave system back there, filled with all manner of devices.'

'Deep time monitoring equipment no doubt. Alexander would have built the exploration base a safe distance from the main station. Just in case –'

Rufius laughed. 'Just in case they brought back something nasty. A wise man indeed.'

'Like what? Where was he sending them?' asked Josh.

The watchman held up his almanac. 'According to the logs from the probe; various parts of the outer solar system, circa two billion years ago.'

Josh once travelled six hundred million years into the past using Solomon's ring. It took him back further than any other member of the Order. What he found was nothing more than an icy wasteland. He couldn't imagine what it would be like two billion years ago.

'Was there really life back then?'

The colonel shrugged, looking around the room. 'Who

knows? But if there was, you certainly wouldn't want to bring it back to the ranch. I'm assuming there are some thermal sensors that we've probably set off just by being here.'

Eira put down her telescope. 'That's actually a good point. They should have kicked in by now. We're effectively a foreign contaminant in terms of a quarantine protocol. Something's not right. We should probably get moving before the security system comes out of hibernation.'

Sabien found a path cut into the rock leading down from the cave towards the base.

Once they reached ground level, it was slow going. The snow was deep, and without the right equipment they struggled to make any headway. None of them were wearing warm enough clothes, and their travel robes did little to hold out the cold.

There was an eerie silence to the island. There were no birds, no signs of life of any kind. It was as if they were archaeologists opening a tomb that had lain undiscovered for thousands of years.

Josh could still remember the first time it snowed on the Bevin Estate. Being so close to London meant that it was a rare event for it to settle for more than a few hours.

He went out early, before his mother woke, borrowing her woolly hat and coat because he didn't have anything thick enough.

The whole of the estate was smothered in six inches of pure white. It was magical, as if he had walked into Narnia. Taking those first few steps onto the virgin snow was like treading on the surface of an alien planet, or Antarctica, his were the first tracks and he loved it.

Snow muffled the sound of the city, making everything

more surreal: cars looked more like sleeping polar bears, the bare branches of the trees were frosted with stalactites and the playground equipment transformed into ice-sculptures. For the first twenty minutes, Josh had it all to himself – it was heaven to an eight-year-old.

Then Lenin and his gang turned up and started a snowball fight that resulted in Josh getting a black eye.

It took over an hour to reach the first of the buildings, which were built in concentric rings around the tower. As they approached, the tall structure began to look more like the barrel of an enormous cannon than a lighthouse.

They were losing daylight and the temperature was dropping rapidly. Winds were stirring up a blizzard making it difficult to see further than a few metres. Rufius rammed his shoulder into one of the nearest doors which gave way on the second attempt and they all piled inside.

The hut was like something out of the Second World War, with a semi-circular roof made from corrugated iron sheets. There were old storage lockers and metal-framed beds along each side, all of them stripped of sheets and mattresses.

A stove sat in the centre, surrounded by metal chairs.

'Nissen hut,' said Rufius, going over to the stove and poking around in the firebox. 'Whoever was here last, burned everything they could find.' He added, pulling out what was left of an almanac.

Sabien took off one of his gloves and ran his fingers over the cold metal of a bedstead. 'There's no time signature.'

'Hasn't been one on anything I've tried since we got here,' Rufius agreed.

'This doesn't make sense,' said Eira, rubbing her hands together. 'It's hardly warmer in here. They would have only used these while the base was being constructed.'

'I don't care,' said Silas shivering, his lips turning blue.

'Can we please just find something to burn before we all freeze to death?'

Eira walked to the far end of the hut and opened the door into another similar dormitory.

'If these are living quarters, where is the lab?' she muttered to herself. 'What were you thinking Alexander. It wasn't this cold when you started.'

In the third hut they found a canteen, its windows were broken and the howling gale was piling drifts of snow up against the tables. Silas went over to one of the hobs and tried to light the burners, but there was no gas.

Sabien turned to Rufius. 'If we don't find shelter soon we're going to have to abort.'

'What exactly does that involve?' Rufius said. 'Because as far as I can see there's no going back the way we came.'

The inspector nodded grimly.

'What about the lighthouse?' asked Josh, trying to control his shivering.

'It would be madness to go out in the storm. We'll have to stay here and try to keep warm til morning,' replied Rufius.

'We won't last that long,' complained Silas.

Eira appeared from a storage cupboard, she was talking to herself. 'It was always a game with you wasn't it? I should have guessed.'

She was holding something in one hand that Josh couldn't quite make out until she got closer. Then he realised it was a set of keys.

'Did you find something?' asked Silas.

The old woman held up one of the keys. 'I told you, this isn't right. I'm not sure what's happened here. The Alexander I knew wouldn't slum it in a bunch of old Nissen Huts. Follow me.'

They traipsed into the storage cupboard, where the long empty shelves made Silas groan.

'This isn't a storage room,' she said, putting the key into a slot in the back wall. 'It's an elevator.'

'Where did you find the keys?' Sabien asked as the room slowly descended.

She laughed jangling them on her finger. 'We used to play a game, back at the Institute, with displacement keys. The campus was spread over a large area, so we created temporal shortcuts to get us from one end to the other. Over time it became something of a competitive sport. Seeing who could build the most interest route by connecting the various parts together. The winner got to keep the keys.'

She pointed to a small silver trophy that sat on one of the shelves. 'The Templeton cup, we always kept the keys in it. It's nice to see he kept up the tradition.'

At the bottom of the deep shaft the elevator ground to a halt.

The temperature changed dramatically on the way down. All of them began to relax as the shivering abated.

Stepping into a large, hollowed-out cavern, Josh was immediately struck by the scale of the operation. It was a vast space, filled with massive machinery, something like a turbine hall from a power station.

Before them stood four enormous generators, each one the height of a double decker bus. Inside their gantries were large silver cylinders encased in coils of copper and connected to pipes that ran across the floor and up the walls.

A row of control consoles sat in front of them, panels of dials and switches blinked automatically with no sign of an operator.

'Gravimetric field generators,' Eira explained, 'although I've never seen ones at this scale.'

The equipment hummed like a hive of bees, and there was a strange smell in the air, it was full of ozone, the fresh scent after a thunder storm. It made the hairs on the back of Josh's neck stand up.

'Can we just shut them down?' asked Rufius, going over to one of the consoles.

Eira joined him, wiping the dust from some of the screens. 'Hmm, I've not worked with this system, it's far more complicated than the one we used for the moon. I think it's best if we find Alexander, or at least one of his engineers. If you don't shut this down in the right sequence it could blow us all into the next dimension.'

58

VOLCANOS

Sumbawa, Dutch East Indies. 1815.

Mount Tambora dominated the northern end of the island of Sumbawa, in what would one day become Indonesia. It was a stratovolcano formed by active subduction zones that were shifting the tectonic plates far below the ocean floor.

The plume of smoke issuing from its caldera was over a mile high when the *Nautilus* arrived.

'She's going to blow,' said Caitlin's father, checking the time on his tachyon. 'We've got less than ten minutes.'

'That'll have to do,' her mother replied, piloting the ship over the smouldering mountain and began the descent into the caldera.

'The Copernicans are estimating a death toll of over seventy thousand,' he added, reading the latest report from his almanac. 'They predict over one hundred cubic kilometres of pyroclastic rock is going to be ejected in this next eruption – at least half of the mountain.'

'No pressure then,' said her mother through gritted teeth. 'Is the bomb ready?'

'Good to go,' Caitlin replied through the speaking tube.

She was in the cargo bay, watching the Antiquarian Ordinance team make the final adjustments to the device.

It was a time-bomb, which was originally Sim's idea, who was deeply disappointed when he wasn't allowed to accompany them.

His suggestion was to detonate the weapon as close to the eruption as possible, sending the event back ten thousand years to a time when it would have less impact on the population.

After the Aleutian Islands, the problems with the moon's erratic orbit escalated. It was affecting more than just the tides now. The Earth's tectonic plates were shifting at an accelerated rate, causing massive disruption to the lithosphere and the magma beneath.

The timebomb would save the inhabitants of the island and those affected by the tsunami that would follow in its wake.

'Temperature at one thousand celsius and rising,' intoned her father, watching the dials rising on the console.

'Heat shields holding,' replied Juliana, imaging how hot the outer hull of the ship would be as it descended the five mile vent towards the boiling magma chamber.

'Two minutes to deployment,' she warned her daughter.

'Roger that,' came the reply.

'Twelve hundred degrees, and I'm showing pyroclastic activity. She's close.'

'Okay,' said Juliana, wiping the sweat from her brow. 'I think we're as good as we're going to get.' She flicked the switches on the main console. 'Let's drop this baby and get the hell out of here.'

· · ·

The Antiquarian Ordnance team stepped away from the bomb as the outer casing sealed itself shut. The shell was designed to withstand the fierce temperatures long enough to penetrate the magma.

They loaded it into the torpedo tube and nodded to Caitlin.

Her thumb hovered over the launch button waiting for her mother's command. She was sweating profusely, the heat was intense, and she tried not to imagine what it would be like if the cargo bay doors failed.

'Fire!' came her mother's order.

59

THE MAP

Atlas Station.

Lilly found a blueprint of the base pinned to the wall of an office marked 'Generation Supervisor.' It had long since been abandoned, the carpet was covered in a thick layer of dust and the contents of the manager's desk were scattered over the floor as if someone has been searching for something in a hurry.

She took a deep, calming breath, still coming to terms with the fact that she was actually standing in the sub-basement of Atlas Station.

Lilly spent most of her adult life dreaming about this moment, never for one second believing it would ever become a reality. Although, she had to admit, it was a little disappointing to find that something had obviously gone very wrong.

Rufius suggested they split up and look for a map. Eira and the others were searching the adjoining rooms, all except for

Silas, who was chained to a table that was bolted to the floor in the central hall.

He looked completely unfazed by the restraints when Lilly returned with the plans. She wondered what it would be like to be so nonchalant about the Protectorate, to actively choose to live outside of the Order and their rules. Her parents always taught her to respect and obey the law, warning her that if she didn't, they would come without warning and arrest her in the middle of the night. As a child, she lived in fear of the "Crows", her nightmares filled with dark, faceless officers appearing from her wardrobe and taking her away.

She spread the plans across the table and carefully weighed down the curling edges with old coffee cups and ash trays.

'You're a curator right?' said Silas, shifting his weight on the metal chair. 'I'm guessing you haven't travelled much.'

'I did my gap year,' Lilly replied. 'Visited a few interesting places.'

He smiled, holding up a hand and began counting on his fingers. 'Let me guess. You started with the Paris in the twenties, then back to Renaissance Florence, followed by Ancient Rome and then partied at Alexander the Great's funeral, maybe stopped off in the Wild West?'

She sneered. 'Actually I started with the Tang Dynasty, followed by the Edo period in Japan, Islamic Golden Age, and ended up in pre-Columbian America.'

'Silas knows all about the Aztec,' said Sabien, coming to stand beside him. 'Especially the arrival of Cortés.'

Silas shrugged. 'I told you it was a holiday.' He held up his manacled wrists. 'Can we take these off now?'

•　•　•

While the inspector unlocked his chains, the others returned carrying various bits of equipment. Lilly tried not to show how pleased she was to be the only one who found a map.

'You found it!' exclaimed Eira, studying the blueprint.

From the layout of the installation it was clear the turbine hall acted as a central hub with the other sections branching off like the arms of a snowflake.

'We need to find Mission Control,' Eira said, putting on yet another pair of glasses. 'If he's anywhere, he'll be there.'

It was a sprawling industrial complex, built on a number of levels. They appeared to be in one of the lower sections.

Generally, Josh had always had a good memory for maps. The patterns stuck in his head in ways that numbers and letters never did. He could look at a chart once and memorise it instantly. But this one was different, the repetitive nature of the structure made it hard to find any usable landmarks.

'There,' said Lilly, finally locating an area marked with the legend "MCC" — 'Mission Control Centre.'

'What is that?' asked Rufius, pointing at another section, two floors above it, which appeared to be a series of concentric rings.

Eira squinted at the map. 'That looks like a Temporal Conduit.'

'In layman's terms?'

'A time tunnel. It's what Alexander built to take us to the moon. Although ours was significantly smaller than that one.'

The watchman scratched his beard. 'I think we should split into two groups. Sabien, Josh and I will take the tunnel. Eira and Lilly, you go to Mission Control.'

'What about me?' asked Silas.

'Right now you're a liability, and having you manacled to him is a burden. Inspector, I suggest you find a suitable place to confine him and join us. The priority now is to shutdown this facility.'

The Protectorate officer shook his head. 'He stays with me.'

Rufius shrugged. 'Your choice.'

Following the map, Lilly led them out of the far side of the turbine hall and along a passage that ended at a set of heavy pressure doors. It took three of them to open it manually, revealing a tunnel wide enough to drive a truck down.

The curved walls were smooth, broken only by a network of pipes that ran along the ceiling. Everything was painted in a dull grey, reminding Josh of a Russian nuclear bunker.

They walked in silence, listening for any sound of occupation. There was nothing but the distant thrum of machinery. Every few minutes the lights would flicker, throwing them into darkness for a second. Eira produced a small torch from one of her many pockets and strode on ahead, walking remarkably quickly for a woman of her age.

'It's too quiet,' Rufius muttered under his breath. 'Feels more like a tomb.'

'How many people were stationed here?' asked Sabien, his voice echoing down the tunnel.

Eira slowed her pace, allowing them to catch up to her. 'The moon mission had over a hundred staff. By the size of this place I would say double that at least. But it would have been designed to run autonomously for centuries if left unmanned. Alexander was always fascinated by NASA redundancy systems. After the disaster with the moon, he wouldn't take any risks.'

She stopped, putting her hands on her hips. 'To be honest, I'm not sure we're going to find anybody. This place looks like it was abandoned half a century ago.' Pointing to a set of stairs. 'Well, this is where we part company. Avoid using the lifts, the power seems to be rather unreliable.'

The woman carried on down the corridor, with Lilly quickening her pace to keep up.

Rufius turned to Sabien. 'I've a bad feeling about this. I'd rather you had both hands if we run into trouble,' he said, looking at Silas. 'This is not the time for your games. If we don't fix this, the Earth could crash into the Sun. Do you think you could stop thinking about yourself for a few hours?'

Silas shrugged. 'For a price.'

Sabien's jaw clenched. 'And what would that be?'

'If I help you. You release my parents.'

The inspector shook his head. 'They were responsible for one of the worst crimes of the Nineteenth Century.'

'Well it won't matter if the Earth is vaporised will it?' Silas replied. 'I'm stuck on this island too, it's not like I can get very far is it.'

Josh could see from the inspector's expression that he was considering various scenarios, trying to figure out what the risks were. Finally, Sabien shook his head. 'I'm not authorised to offer you a deal.'

Rufius snorted. 'Well I bloody can. If we manage to get out of this alive. I will help you with the appeal. I can't make any promises, but I think your assistance in this matter may go a long way with the founder.'

'Fair enough,' said Silas, holding out his manacled hand for Rufius to shake. 'It's a deal.'

The watchman shook it and nodded to Sabien to release him, which the officer grudgingly did.

'Joshua, I assume you know where we need to go?'

Josh closed his eyes, conjuring up the image of the map in his mind. 'Four floors up.'

60

BARAD-DÛR

Barad-dûr, Shadow Realm.

The Dark Tower rose above them like a black obelisk, piercing the heavy storm clouds with its broken spire.

Kelly's spell brought them closer than he anticipated, but there were no guards on the battlements, no one to raise the alarm.

They walked through a narrow defile in the rock, the grey shale on the path making it slow going as they climbed towards the entrance.

'What is this place?' asked Kaori, picking up a lump of rock and weighing it in her hand. 'I mean, not the Tolkien version, but actually how was this place created.'

The Grand Seer shrugged, his cloak of feathers rustling. 'There are many mysteries that the past has chosen to overlook.'

'I think it's like an attic in an old mansion,' Lyra began, 'full of things that time has forgotten.'

Kaori looked up at the tower, she could feel Ophelia stirring inside her, sensing the danger ahead. 'Except this doesn't resemble anything from our world.'

'From another version of the continuum perhaps?' mused Kelly.

The doctor didn't seem convinced. 'These wraiths are like nothing we've encountered before. They manifest properties that shouldn't be physically possible, breaking some of the fundamental laws of the universe, it's as if they're from another plane.'

'Well, wherever they're from, this is the place Devlin showed me,' Lyra said, pointing up at the towering black fortress.

Kaori threw the rock away. 'Okay. Shields up!'

The outline of her ghast shimmered into place as she walked away. The others followed, switching on the devices clipped to their belts.

The entrance to the tower was nowhere to be seen. At the base, the walls were sheer and solid with no sign of a doorway. While Kelly paced back and forth, muttering various incantations to himself, Lyra stood still staring at the dark stone as if willing it to open.

'It doesn't like strangers,' she whispered when Kaori came to join her. 'The door is hiding.'

Kaori took a vial out of her jacket, it was a sample of the wraith that she extracted during one of her experiments. 'I thought we might need this,' she said, holding it out to Lyra.

The seer nodded and took the glass tube. 'It might be enough,' she added, breaking the seal and pulling out the stopper.

Tendrils of smoke wove out of the vial and hovered for a moment around Lyra's hand. The shield Kaori devised flickered as the creature probed it, shimmering like oil on water, until it gave up and flew towards the tower.

A recess formed in the stone, the impression of an arched

doorway forming as if someone were pressing a mould into clay. The stone gave way to reveal a dark corridor.

Lyra dropped the vial and clapped her hands. 'There you are!'

The Grand Seer stopped his ranting and stared into the arch. 'Be not afeard; the isle is full of noises.'

Lyra ran towards it. 'Hurry! He knows we're here.'

61

MISSION CONTROL

Atlas Station.

Mission Control was a large, semi-circular space with a bank of screens flickering on the main wall. The antiquated control desks were unmanned, their consoles abandoned as if the engineers simply walked away from their stations.

Mouldy coffee cups and half-finished cigarettes had been discarded on the desks.

'Mary Celeste,' muttered Eira, tapping on one of the keyboards. A series of commands ran across the flickering screen and then disappeared, replaced by static once more.

'What was he like?' asked Lilly, leafing through one of the command manuals.

The old woman smiled. 'Imagine the cleverest person you've ever met and multiply that by a thousand. Then subtract any form of empathy or emotion, and you've pretty much got Alexander Templeton. He was definitely on some kind of scale, Asperger's or ADHD. In another life he would have been called a Savant – no one could ever say they truly knew what was going on inside his head, but it was definitely one of the most amazing periods of my career.' Her eyes glazed over. 'The day we landed on the moon, we thought we were invincible.'

'It was an amazing achievement.'

Eira sighed deeply. 'Until it was time to leave. Somehow, we miscalculated the return trip. There was no way to bring them back. They ran out of oxygen.'

'Couldn't you go back and fix it?'

The old scientist shook her head. 'They tried, but the gravitational fields surrounding the event made the timeline too unstable. It interfered with anyone who got too close.'

Lilly had read all of the reports as part of her final dissertation. The investigation into the tragedy took over three years to complete. While Templeton was ultimately responsible for his team's safety, it was clear that there had been no negligence, nor misconduct, the committee ruled it to be 'Misadventure' and closed the case without any prosecution.

Carefully avoiding the discarded chairs and books littering the floor, Lilly walked down the steps to the front.

The large screens displayed random footage of alien structures rising from a red desert. The images were partially corrupted and jumped between different sequences, every so often interspliced with dark figures standing in front of what appeared to be a temple.

'Is that Mars?' she wondered aloud.

'Sorry, what?' Eira looked up from the console, changing to another pair of spectacles before squinting at the images. 'Ah, yes, it could well be. That appears to be downloaded data. Alexander must have fitted the DC6s with video cameras. Let's see if we can stabilise it.' She tapped on the keys of another computer.

The screens flickered and went dark.

'No, that's made it worse. Can you bring it back?' complained Lilly.

'One second,' muttered Eira, sitting down in the chair and moving the clutter to one side. 'It's been a while since I've used one of these.'

It took the old woman a few minutes and a great deal of cussing before she could bring the system back online. The displays flickered back to life and a thousand different frames played across it, too quickly for them to make sense of what they were viewing.

'Can you slow it down?' asked Lilly, coming over to stand behind her.

Eira cracked her knuckles and began to type commands into the terminal. 'If I remember correctly, Alexander favoured a low-level language for most of his control subroutines. Ones that I helped him develop.'

Lilly studied the lines of symbols that the woman was keying in. 'Is that Fortran?'

'A hybrid version of it. They eventually used it for the basis of Fortran 90'

Lilly studied the language at university. Invented in 1957 by John W. Backus and his team at IBM, its highly efficient numerical and computation capabilities were perfect for Science and Engineering projects and was one of the languages adopted by NASA during the early space missions.

Eira scrolled through lines of code making small adjustments to the programming. The feed to the main display stabilised and she sat back in her chair and folded her arms. 'There you go.'

It was Mars, there was no doubt about it. The grid of images above them showed different time-lapsed views of the red planet's history, the barren, rocky desert slowly replaced by verdant plains and towering jungles.

'How far back did it go?' asked Lilly, finding it hard to hide her astonishment.

Eira tapped the keys and scrutinising the responses on the screen in front of her. 'According to this, four and a half billion years. The Noachian Epoch.' She leaned forward as if something on the screen caught her eye. 'There's another data stream encoded in there, one second.'

She tapped another sequence into the keyboard.

The main display changed once more. It was the face of a much older Alexander Templeton, staring out from the screen. His lips were moving but no sound was coming out.

'Hold on, let me sort out the audio.'

He was holding the camera close so that his head obscured whatever was going on behind him. Lilly caught glimpses of engineers working frantically in the background.

Templeton's voice was thin and reedy. She thought there was a slight wistful tone to it, reminding Lilly of her grandfather when he would tell her a bedtime story.

'My name is Alexander Templeton, former Scientific Director of the Chronometric Institute and Project Leader of the Atlas mission. The coordinates have been entered into launch sequencer, so this should be my final entry before we attempt the displacement. I am recording this for posterity, just in case something goes wrong.'

The video image scrambled for a few seconds and the timecode jumped forward, as if Alexander slightly recorded over the previous entry.

'We stand on a precipice, on the brink of what may possibly be the most significant moment in spacetime exploration. No human has set foot on the red planet, nor will they for at least another two hundred years. But there are signs of a much older civilisation, my probes have discovered something far more ancient than anything that exists on our world. There is evidence—'

The video cut out once more, and there were strange

noises, the sound of men and women shouting as they tried to contain some kind of emergency.

Suddenly, the image returned.

'The quantum tunnel has finally stabilised. We are proceeding as planned.' He smiled. 'Forty years of work has led to this moment. Fulfilling my greatest ambition: To travel back into the distant past and stand on the living surface of another world. I cannot wait to prove to all those who doubted me, that Mars was once a beautiful, habitable world.'

The recording ended and the screen went blank.

'When did he film that?' Lilly asked, thinking how the man had aged compared to the last pictures she'd seen of him.

Eira looked distracted, as if she were still contemplating Templeton's monologue. 'That depends on what timeframe you're using. The island has been missing for over nine thousand years, but according to the internal system clock, I would say at least ten years ago.'

'So did they all go?' Lilly asked, looking at the empty seats of the command centre.

The old scientist shook her head. 'It's usually a crew of six. Chrononauts are highly trained specialists. They'll be a primary and secondary team, so twelve maximum. It sounds as though Alexander was planning to accompany them, which was his prerogative. Certainly not the entire base.'

Lilly picked up another of the manuals that sat in a pile on the desk. 'Something went wrong. There must be a log.'

62

THE TUNNEL

Atlas Station.

The time tunnel consisted of a stack of large, flat metal rings. They floated in the air above his head, forming a column rising upwards until finally disappearing through a hole in the distant roof of the cavern.

Josh guessed they were over thirty feet in diameter and made from a dull grey metal, each one hanging in the air on some invisible field. There were no signs of rivets or bolts on their surfaces, as if they had been forged from a giant mould by an ancient Norse god.

On the floor below them was a stepped circular platform with pipes running into it from all sides. As Josh climbed onto metal dais he felt the hairs on his arms rise, goosebumps puckering his skin. He looked up into the tunnel, and seeing a small red glow at the far end, realised that it must form part of what they assumed was the lighthouse.

Cautiously, he ran his hand across the underside of the lowest ring. There was no tangible timeline, or at least not a cohesive one. He could feel the echo of something ancient, like grooves etched into old rock by years of rain.

'Some form of anti-gravity system, no doubt,' observed Rufius, tapping one of the rings with his knuckle. It rang like a bell, shifted slightly before returning to its original position. 'Impressive piece of engineering.'

The rings were positioned in the centre of the chamber looking more like the launch tube for a ballistic missile than a temporal portal. Around the walls were cabinets of switchgear and enormous crackling capacitors, the kind that would have looked more at home in Tesla's workshop in Wardenclyffe.

There was an unusual energy field emanating from them. The air tasted odd, as if it were charged with something stranger than electricity.

At the far end of the cavern was a bank of consoles, their screens displaying a constant flow of data. Inspector Sabien stood at one of them, studying the scrolling code, his face a mask of concentration.

'There's a pattern,' he said, when Rufius came to join him. 'It's repeating every five hundred lines or so.'

'What is it?'

Sabien shook his head. 'No idea, could be Templeton's lottery numbers for all I know.'

Rufius scratched his beard, looking around the empty chamber. 'Still no sign of any crew–'

'You have to see this,' interrupted Silas, calling out from a side door.

The interior of the vault was dark and it took Josh's eyes a second to acclimatise to the low lighting.

Silas was standing over a glass, coffin-like capsule, its internal illumination lighting up the grim expression on his face.

'What did you do?' snapped Sabien, marching over to him.

'Nothing,' Silas replied, holding up his hands in mock surrender. 'It must have a proximity sensor.'

Sabien grunted and looked down into the compartment. The body stored within it was pale and thin. Wearing a thin white shift, the arms were crossed over their chest like an Egyptian mummy. Tubes ran into a mask that obscured its face.

'Stasis pod,' he muttered, studying the readouts flickering across the glass door. 'It's the same pattern as the console.'

'There are more,' said Josh, walking further into the vault and triggering a cascade of other illuminated capsules.

In total they found pods containing over fifty members of the crew. Each one in a seemingly catatonic state.

Searching the other sections, they discovered two more storage areas with similar arrays of pods. Over a hundred and fifty men and women were being kept in suspended animation.

Eira and Lilly appeared a few minutes later, carrying a stack of books.

'They're here,' Rufius said. 'He's put them all into stasis.'

The old woman shook her head, taking one of the books from Lilly and opening it. 'Not stasis. Transferred consciousness.'

She laid the book on the nearest desk and stood back.

A holographic image of Templeton's head appeared floating just above the page.

Josh had never seen anything like it.

The man's lips began to move and the Director's voice came into his head.

'Direct neural feed,' explained Lilly, catching his look of bewilderment. 'It was one of his side projects.'

· · ·

I have long suspected that there would be a limitation to how far a human body can travel through time. The continued exposure of gravimetric forces during temporal displacement can be extremely detrimental to our physiology, especially over such an extended period.

My research has proven there to be a finite limit to our ability to cross vast distances of time and space; somewhere in the region of seven hundred and fifty million years to be precise. The mind however, that is an infinitely more resilient piece of apparatus.

By detaching the consciousness from its physical shell, I have been able to travel across the known universe and beyond.

I have walked on distant planets.

Watched nameless stars form and seen them die–

The image flickered as Eira skipped a few pages. 'His mind wanders for a few minutes,' she explained. 'This is the most interesting part.'

I have discovered something wonderful on the red planet, something that will change our understanding of this universe. There are remnants of a great civilisation, one that left this mortal coil many billions of years ago.

We now prepare for the greatest experiment of all. The entire team will move to Mars, automatons have been sent ahead. Their mechanical bodies will become our hosts, our avatars, while we build a gateway. Once that has been established I will be able to open a Rosen Bridge between our two worlds.

The recording ended.

'That was his last entry,' Eira said, closing the book.

'He's insane,' said Sabien.

'Not necessarily,' the old woman muttered, studying the data scrolling across one of the screens.

'You're telling me it's possible to separate a consciousness from a body and project it a billion years into the past?'

'Alexander was a brilliant man who surrounded himself with geniuses. There is no telling what they were capable of.'

'My orders were to shut this place down!' insisted Sabien. 'The fate of the Earth depends on it.'

She ignored his outburst and calmly walked over to the raised platform and looked up into the column of rings. 'Well, we're going to need their help to decommission it. The question is how do we bring them back?'

'Where is the mission team? Surely someone should have been left behind to man the station, a skeleton crew of some kind.' said Rufius.

Eira stood on tip toes to reach up and touch one of the rings. 'There's obviously been another incident. Which would explain why the station has re-entered the continuum. It's trying to return to the original mission'

'This is getting us nowhere,' said Sabien. 'Why can't we just pull the plug?'

Eira scowled, putting her hands on her hips. 'Beneath our feet is an extremely powerful graviton generator, so powerful that it's affecting the orbit of the moon. Can you imagine what would happen if we triggered a gravitational collapse. Forget a few high tides. The geo-magnetic forces could turn Earth into a black hole.'

'We could go up and get the others back,' suggested Josh.

'To Mars?' Rufius said, unable to keep the disbelief out of his voice.

The old woman eyes twinkled as she considered the idea. 'Why not old man? One more adventure before you hang up your boots?'

'Because the last mission, if I recall correctly, ended in the deaths of the entire team.'

Eira's expression hardened, her lips drawn into a thin white line. 'You don't have to remind me, I was there. This would be different. They were physically deployed.'

Josh stepped forward. 'I'll go,' he said before Rufius had a chance to reply.

'I'll handle this,' growled the old man.

Silas was thumbing through one of the manuals that Lilly brought back. 'It says here that there should be a fail-safe, like a dead-man's handle.'

Sabien snatched the book from him.

Eira nodded. 'Alexander would have thought of every eventuality. If the control crew have been incapacitated the system should initiate a recall and returned the away team.'

Sabien studied the document. 'There's a six-hour reset. Which means someone is still down here.'

'Inspector, I suggest you and Silas look for the rest of the crew,' Eira said. 'Lilly I will need you to prep the pods and run the launch sequence.'

The capsule was cool and quiet once the lid closed. Josh took a deep breath, telling himself everything would be fine, but wondering what Caitlin would say if she knew what he was about to do. Probably something along the lines of: "Mars! Are you out of your mind?"

Lilly's eyes narrowed as she concentrated on the initiation sequence, tapping various symbols on the control panel. She smiled weakly when she realised Josh was watching her.

He felt the mask slide into place, the electrodes deploying like a crown over his forehead. 'It's going to feel a little strange,' she tried to reassure him through the intercom.

Can't be any stranger than having the consciousness of another person living in your head, thought Josh as something sharp pricked the back of his neck.

63

TRIANGULATION

Founder's Study.

'The triangulation buoys have located the island, my Lord,' said Professor Eddington, walking into the Lord Dee's study without knocking. Sim trailed in behind looking rather sheepish at the lack of decorum.

'Excellent!' the founder said, putting down the book he was reading. 'Where is it?'

'Not in one single period, but rotating through a series of seemingly random points in the continuum.'

The founder's brows arched, taking off his spectacles. 'Seemingly? That is not a word that I hear a Copernican professor use very often.'

'Master De Freis believes he has discovered a pattern,' Eddington said, stepping aside and nodding to his assistant. 'If you would care to explain.'

Sim cleared his throat and smiled awkwardly. 'Well, I've been analysing the data, and as the professor rightly states: it appears that the island is moving erratically, shifting through time at various unrelated points. Which I have plotted out.'

Taking out his almanac, he laid it on the founder's desk

and opened it on a double page spread of over a hundred random points, each one carefully annotated.

'I see what you mean,' said the founder, balancing his glasses on the end of his nose. 'So have you created an algorithm to predict its next location?'

Sim nodded, the founder was quite possibly the only man with an IQ greater than that of Professor Eddington.

'It doesn't follow any of the usual stochastic differentials, so I applied a semimartingale, and there it was.'

He tapped on the page and a series of equations replaced the timeline.

'Ah, I see,' said the founder.

'The intervals are following the Fibonacci Sequence,' added Eddington proudly. 'It was quite an inspired discovery.'

Sim tried not to blush, but failed.

'Indeed it is. So, Master De Freis, where can we expect to find Atlantis next?'

The actuary tapped on the page enlarging the map of the North Sea. 'Off the coast of Norway in 6225 BCE. I believe it will trigger the Storregga event, a paleotsunami that obliterated Doggerland and a quarter of the Mesolithic population of Britain.'

64

MARS

Mars. 4.5 billion years ago.

It felt as if he were waking from a deep, dreamless sleep. His body was numb, and then as Josh came to, he realised that he could feel nothing at all.

'Connection established,' said a woman's soft voice inside his head.

A series of lights flashed before his eyes, followed by a sequence of flickering symbols as data flowed through a sea of absolute darkness.

'Initiating visual stream,' the voice assured him.

Shapes formed. Blurred and monochrome at first, they shifted slightly, their edges sharpening as the resolution increased.

'Synaptic integration in three, two, one…'

Suddenly, he was standing inside a large hangar lined with rows of mechanical spacesuits. It looked like something from a Jules Verne novel, the cumbersome Victorian robots were hanging from rails as if on a production line. The jointed limbs of their brass exoskeletons reminding Josh that these were the automatons that Templeton mentioned in his log.

And two of them were walking towards him.

The glass domes of their helmets were glowing with an eery green luminescence, and as they drew near, Josh could make out the ghostly faces of Rufius and Eira.

Their movements were unnatural, walking erratically, like marionettes on strings.

'This will take some getting used to,' said the colonel through an internal speaker. His holographic head floating disjointedly inside the helmet.

Josh looked down at his hands, the brass fingers responding to his flexing as if they were his own. He lifted them to his face, marvelling at the intricate metal gearing.

'How?'

'Biometric feedback,' Eira explained. The unit is wired to your neural cortex, everything should react as if it were your own. It's in real-time, there's no latency which is incredible when you think our bodies are billions of years in the future. A marvellous piece of temporal engineering.'

'It tends to work better when you don't think about it,' added the colonel.

Josh tried moving his feet. The boots felt heavy as if walking through treacle. He shuffled forward and lost balance, the avatar lurched and stumbled.

Rufius caught him before he fell. 'Easy boy, you're trying too hard. Just relax.'

He took a deep breath. Or rather he didn't, there was no need. Panic began to set in. *I'm not here.* He reminded himself. *I'm safe in a pod, this is just a dream.*

The next few steps were easier, until he managed to walk to the far end of the hangar.

'Good!' said Eira, 'I think we're ready.'

After a few attempts, she managed to open the bay doors, the rusted gears complaining from years of neglect. Beyond the metal hatch lay a deep valley of lush green vegetation.

'How far have we gone back?' asked Josh.

'Four and a half billion years,' answered Rufius, who still couldn't believe it himself from the tone of his voice. 'I never thought I'd be standing on Mars.'

Josh was finding it hard to reconcile the jungle before him with the pictures of the barren, red desert that NASA's Curiosity rover captured back in his time. Grainy images of what looked like Nevada did nothing to inspire the general public, except for the conspiracy theorists who spent most of their time trying to find evidence of Martian civilisation and water erosion.

'Have you found any sign of the others?' asked the colonel.

'These units have an internal power source that should last the best part of twenty-four hours,' said Eira. 'So their range is limited, they will have to recharge. I'm guessing Alexander has built a number of these facilities.'

She tapped a dial on the forearm of her suit and a small, three dimensional map appeared in one corner of her helmet.

'Yes. According to this, there is network of them, hold on —' she paused, squinting at something on the screen. 'They are obviously equipped with tracking devices, I can see a cluster of avatars over a hundred miles away to the South.'

Josh did the same, bringing up a heads-up display of the terrain around him. A finely detailed map, like the ones the Copernicans would draw in his almanac, rotated on the screen, showing him there were bases at key points along a route through the terrain that led to a cluster of red dots.

'There's over a hundred of them,' whispered Josh.

'Then I suggest we get a move on,' declared Rufius, striding out into the jungle.

They left the facility, which Eira explained, was essentially a manufacturing plant transported through time in pieces and assembled by remotely controlled drones. Once operational, the factory would construct avatars using locally sourced materials.

To Josh it looked more like someone had built a Jenga tower out of shipping containers.

'The automatons were something that Alexander started experimenting with on the moon mission. But back in those days, they were just autonomous cargo lifters, nothing as sophisticated as this.' She wiggled her fingers in front of his helmet.

Fortunately, something had already carved a path through the jungle, making it easier to follow the trail to the next base. Not that it was any effort. Riding along in the head of a military-grade, all-terrain android was like playing a video game, only with incredibly realistic graphics and haptic feedback.

The path became a series of switchbacks taking them down the side of the valley. At the bottom they found a clear, blue river snaking its way towards the South.

'Let's follow the water,' Eira suggested, her body half-submerged in the stream. Small fish swam around her suit, their bodies glinting with speckles of gold in the sunlight.

Josh looked up towards the sun. He knew it took nearly five minutes longer for its light to reach Mars compared to Earth, but it looked pretty much the same, although the colour of the sky wasn't quite right.

They moved at speed, the stabilisers of the suits seemingly able to cope with the roughest ground. Josh's display told him they were approaching close to thirty miles per hour.

None of the other stations showed any sign of habitation. In less than three hours they reached the final base.

'What the devil is that?' Josh heard Rufius say as he rounded a bend in the river.

This was no manufacturing plant. As Josh caught up with the others he saw the towering blocks of stone carved out of the valley walls. A monumental fortress rose above them, ancient and weather-beaten, it looked like the stronghold of a Martian King.

65

SHADOW REALM

Barad-dûr, Shadow Realm.

The interior of the tower was a vast necropolis. Dark avenues of crypt-like buildings appeared to stretch for miles in every direction.

'A city of the dead?' wondered Kelly, studying the monumental architecture. He reached inside his cloak and pulled out a scrying orb which began to glow with a baleful light.

'No,' replied Lyra, shuddering as she touched the cold stone, 'more like a prison.'

Kaori took a device from her backpack and scanned the area. 'The environmental readings are weird,' she said, frowning at the screen. 'I'm picking up high levels of graviton radiation ahead of us. There must be some kind of breach.'

'Nothing but dust and ashes,' murmured the Grand Seer, putting the orb inside his cloak. 'The Old King has claimed them all.'

'Where are the Nazgûl?' Kaori wondered, looking behind her. 'Can you sense them?' she asked Lyra.

Lyra closed her eyes and tilted her head back. 'No. They're not here. Or at least not close enough for me to feel them.'

Kaori put the scanner away and took out a stubby-looking pistol.

'Okay, let's keep moving. Lyra let me know the moment you sense anything.'

They both nodded and followed the diminutive doctor who was now fully encased in a dragon-like armoured carapace.

66

THE TELL

Atlas Station.

Silas watched closely as Lilly checked the life signs on the capsules. He was fascinated by the concentration on her face. Like a schoolgirl studying a mathematical formula, her eyebrows formed a v-shape and her lips whispered silent equations under her breath.

'Do you ever wonder what it would be like to go up there?' he asked, casually looking around for something to pick the lock. Sabien had chained him to one of the larger ventilation pipes while he went off searching the other rooms for any sign of survivors.

'Hmm?' she said, only half-listening. 'Of course! I've spent my life studying this solar system. It's the first thing I think about when I wake up.'

'So why don't you go?' He nodded to an empty compartment. 'You could show me how to set it up.'

He caught the flicker of desire in her eyes, nothing more than a momentary hesitation before she replied. His father used to call it the 'tell', once you saw it, you knew there was a chance to turn them.

She glanced over at the pod. 'Er no. I have to stay here. They might need me.'

Silas found a small piece of wire behind one of the consoles and dragged it closer with his foot.

'The Inspector's here. We'll keep an eye on things. I'm guessing most of it is automated anyway.'

'It is.'

'When are you going to get another chance like this?' he asked, bending down to pick up the wire while she tried to focus on her work. 'You could just pop up there and back in no time. Just to have a look.'

'No, I can't. They're depending on me,' she said, shaking her head.

Sabien's return was signalled by the activating of pods at the far end of the vault.

'Shite,' Silas cursed under his breath, quickly placing the wire into his mouth and pushing it down between his teeth and the inside of his cheek.

'Is he causing you trouble Ma'am?' asked the inspector.

'No,' replied Lilly, avoiding his gaze. 'He's been fine.'

Silas smiled inwardly. The fact she hadn't mentioned their discussion meant she was still interested. They shared a secret now, one that he could use to his advantage. If he could just lose the crow for long enough.

'Any luck?' Silas asked, while Sabien leaned over him to check his handcuffs.

'Not yet,' he growled. 'But if there's anyone left here I'll find them.'

'Perhaps they're on a different level?' suggested Lilly, much to Silas's amazement.

'That was one of the reasons I came back.' Sabien stepped back and turned towards her. 'I wanted to make sure you were okay before searching the other floors. It will be quicker if I do it alone. Are you sure you don't want me take him with me?'

'No,' she shook her head, 'he's fine.'

Sabien turned his steely glare on Silas once more. 'No trouble, you hear me? I can be back here in seconds.' He walked back to Lilly. 'One wrong move and you call out for me okay.'

'Yes, of course.'

With that the officer marched out of the door and was gone.

'Right then,' said Silas, rubbing his hands together and leaving the cuffs behind. 'Are we doing this or what?'

67

MARTIANS

Mars

The Martian fortress was an imposing structure. Cut into the cliff face, its sides smooth like a granite monolith, it rose up from the valley floor to tower over them.

A staircase had been carved into the grey-blue stone, with broad steps leading up to a tall, arched gateway. Traces of gold still remained amongst the surface details of the weather-worn facade, eroded by countless millennia of storms.

As Josh climbed towards it, he tried to picture how majestic it would have looked in its heyday and what kind of people would have passed through its gates.

Reaching the arch, which he estimated was over twelve feet high, he wondered if it was an indication of the size of the race that built it. His mind began to play tricks on him as they passed beneath the gatehouse, imagining black-eyed, grey-skinned Martians lurking in the shadows.

'Can this suit detect life signs? Like thermal imaging?'

'I should think so, just ask it,' replied Eira, marching on into the courtyard beyond.

'Ask the suit?'

'It's more than just a mechanical exoskeleton. It's got an AI. In fact if I'm not mistaken, Alexander used my voice. Although I was much younger then.'

Josh wondered how you were supposed to address a mechanical host.

'Er, hello, suit?'

Eira laughed. 'You don't need to use your voice. Just think it. You're neurologically linked remember.'

Suit?

'Yes Joshua. How may I be of assistance?' came the reply in a young woman's voice. It could have been Eira, but it was hard to tell.

What should I call you?

'My designation is 29-1009-XAL. But you may call me XAL.'

XAL can you switch on thermal imaging please?

'With pleasure.'

The video feed changed to show a thermal scan of the area directly in front of him. The two other robots were red figures in an otherwise pale blue environment.

No aliens. He thought.

'No other life forms detected,' XAL agreed. 'Would you like me to monitor for them?'

You can do that?

'Yes, I am aware that humans prefer the visible light spectrum. I can monitor the rest of the electromagnetic bands for signs of other entities and alert you.'

Great thanks.

His vision returned to normal and he accelerated his pace to catch up to the others.

What Josh had assumed was a courtyard was actually a grand entrance hall. A long avenue stretched out before them, lined on both sides with stone totems. The monoliths were carved with symbols of a language he'd never seen.

'Do you recognise the glyphs?' Rufius asked Eira over the radio.

'Never seen anything like it,' she replied. 'Neither has the suit. In fact it seems to have no data on this building at all. Which seems strange considering these suits are networked, so anything one learns, the others share in the knowledge.'

The floor sloped gradually upwards towards another set of massive doors, far taller than the last and Josh realised their size was more an indication of status rather than the height of the race that built them.

Rufius's host looked back down the slope. His hands on his hips. 'Where exactly does it say the other units should be?'

'Right here,' replied Eira, examining the map once more.

'Excuse me Joshua, but I am picking up emissions in the higher EM spectrum. Would you like to see it?' asked the suit on his personal channel.

Yes.

Images of ghostly creatures replaced his normal vision. They were too far away to make out their form, but they were somewhere behind the door that Eira was trying to open.

'I'm seeing signs of life inside,' said Joshua over the main channel. 'At least ten creatures. I can't make out what they are.'

Eira's avatar turned towards him. 'Can you ask your suit to share the feed?'

Josh instructed the suit.

'Okay, I'm not sure what they are either, but they're not human or avatar. Rufius have you figured out the weapons capability of your bot?'

Rufius's avatar lifted one arm and it reconfigured itself into a heavy calibre rifle.

'I'll take that as a yes.'

'What happens if our suits get damaged while we're controlling them?' asked Josh. Watching his own arm rebuild itself into a weapon.

'You'll return to the pod. Unless someone cuts the connection.'

'And then what?'

She paused for slightly too long. 'No one actually knows. I guess your memory engrams would be stored in the droid until it could be reconnected. This technology was only a prototype when I left Alexander's team.'

68

SILAS REVEALED

Atlas Station.

Silas helped Lilly into the pod and closed the lid.

'Are you sure you want to do this?' he asked, knowing full well that she was desperate to see Mars.

Lilly nodded, closing her eyes as the pod's neural interface slid over the top of her head.

He went through the initiation sequence exactly as she had shown him. It was a simple series of commands. The first three were biometric, allowing the pod to take over the management of her body, monitoring her life support while the stasis field kicked in.

The next four were part of the connection to the quantum tunnel and the last two would transport her consciousness to Mars.

Silas stopped on step seven, his finger hovering over the penultimate icon.

He took a step back from the pod. Her face was still, peaceful and serene. 'Apologies Sleeping Beauty, but I can't have you going up there and telling them you've left me all on my lonesome down here. Can I?'

Pausing for a moment, he looked around the chamber for any sign of the inspector. 'Now, the next question is, where's that damned crow?'

He rubbed his wrists subconsciously. 'And how long before he comes back.'

Sabien was three floors below on a mezzanine overlooking the turbine hall. This level appeared to be the crew quarters. The small cabins on each side of the corridor were all the same: two bunks, two lockers and a table with two stools. Some of the occupants had decorated them with photographs from home, or childish drawings of family.

All of them were empty. As a crime scene it was hard to read. There were no obvious signs of struggle; clothes were neatly stacked in their lockers, bed sheets folded back ready for inspection.

At the end of the passage was a pair of double doors, the sign above them read "Culina Perpetua", Latin for the "Perpetual Kitchen".

Pushing them open, he walked into a large refectory with rows of steel tables bolted to the floor.

His experienced eyes scanned the room, noting the discarded plates and cutlery scattered across the tabletops; the angle of the chairs where they had been pushed back, as if someone rose in a hurry. Whatever disrupted their usual routine, this was where the crew had been, at a meeting perhaps, or whilst eating together.

Sabien took off one of his gloves and swept his fingers along the surface of the nearest bench – there was no chronology. Just as Eira had warned, the fields emanating from the generators were interfering with his abilities.

For the first time, he could pick up a fork with his bare hands and not experience the lives of every diner that had ever used it.

Having spent most of his life trying to shut out the noise, the silence was an amazing relief.

Virtually no one chose to become a temporal detective. The Protectorate had the lowest intake of all the guilds in the Order; mainly because their job was to investigate the worst events imaginable.

Exploring the timelines of a crime scene could be seen as a curse. Reliving the last moments of the victim's life over and over again, observing every last detail, would drive the sanest man to madness – and there were many who couldn't handle it, the average length of duty in homicide was five years.

Sabien was in his twentieth – he was good at it.

Entering the kitchen, there was clear evidence of recent activity. Discarded tin cans lay empty on the floor, their jagged lids crudely opened with signs they had been eaten from directly.

In a storage room, hidden away behind a rack of shelves, the inspector found the remains of a makeshift bed. Someone had obviously been sleeping here, at least until the food ran out.

Putting his gloves back on, he knelt down and searched the stained blankets. There were scraps of paper hidden under the sheets, each with a hastily scribbled symbol that looked vaguely familiar.

Astrological symbols.

The rest of the storeroom was empty, a stark reminder to Sabien of his own meagre food supplies. But his stomach was accustomed to surviving on rations – it was just part of the job.

Silas strolled along the line of stasis pods, ignoring the illuminated displays as they flickered to life on the glass canopies. He wasn't interested in them, they were serving their own endless sentence by choice.

The capsule he was looking for would be different, probably hidden, or at least made to look as if it were offline.

Just like Lilly, he studied Templeton for years. The man was a genius, of that there was no doubt. A brilliant obsessive who would stop at nothing to achieve his goals. Silas had a lot of respect for him, if it wasn't for the fact that his inventions were currently holding his parents in cryostasis, he probably would have even admired him.

Silas spent years planning for this moment. It began as nothing more than a dream, a childish fantasy of rescuing his parents from purgatory. The Château was impregnable thanks in part to Templeton's ingenuity, and with him missing there was no way to learn his secrets, or to find a back door into his system.

Not until the probe came up for sale.

Silas knew it was his only chance, but he would need help. He couldn't launch an expedition of this magnitude without the resources of the Order.

Getting caught was easy, convincing them to help him find Atlantis was more of a challenge.

And now, somewhere in this chamber was the man who held the key to it all.

In the next section, Silas finally found a defective capsule. Its glass canopy covered in symbols glowed red within warning triangles.

Ignoring them, he followed the opening procedures that Lilly had taught him.

As the seal broke, there was a deep, mournful groan. Silas felt his heart begin to race, he always assumed they would all be dead. Swallowing hard, he braced himself as the lid slowly raised.

The body inside was emaciated, skin stretched over bone like an unwrapped Egyptian mummy. This was all that remained of Alexander Templeton.

All except for the key that hung around his neck.

Silas held his breath as he leaned over the body to remove it.

The metal was cold in his hand, but he could feel its power flowing beneath the surface.

'Now let's see what we can do with this,' he muttered to himself.

Sabien found the survivor in one of the other storerooms. The man was in a terrible state, his clothes torn and soiled, scrawling on the walls with the end of a teaspoon.

'He's coming back for us,' he repeated under his breath. 'They didn't believe me, but I know it.'

His arms were covered in unfamiliar symbols. Hundreds of tiny characters carved into intricate lines, sometimes he had written over his own work.

'Who?' the detective asked, crouching down to meet the man's eyes.

They were wild, the kind of insane stare that Sabien had seen more than once in Bedlam.

'Prospero,' the survivor replied, tapping on an outline of a man in long robes. 'The Old King comes for us all.'

The man was making no sense, he had obviously spent far too long on his own.

'What is your name?'

'Caliban,' he replied with a manic chuckle. 'Or is it Ariel?'

Sabien was beginning to lose his patience. 'Where are the others?'

He shook his head, his matted hair covering part of his face. 'All lost! To prayers, to prayers! All lost!'

There was little he could do for the wretch, who crawled

into a dark corner and continued quoting Shakespeare to himself.

69

THE TOMB OF THE MARTIAN KING

Mars

The seals around the door cracked and the granite surface rapidly retreated away from them in a cloud of dust.

'What did you do?' said Rufius.

'Wasn't me,' said Eira. 'There must be some kind of sensor.'

They moved forward as one, following the door as it slid backwards along a tunnel. The sound of grinding rock put Josh's teeth on edge, as did the visual of the ghostly creatures that were waiting at the end of the corridor.

Do you recognise them? he asked the suit.

'No Joshua, their energy patterns are not stored within my database.'

Then he remembered what Eira said about the suits sharing information.

Are there more of you here?

'Yes, there are other avatars within this facility.'

Can you ask them?

'They are currently offline.'

Josh wondered if the suit was capable of lying, or at least

holding back some of the facts. He couldn't be sure why he didn't trust it, he heard somewhere that robots weren't supposed to have the capacity to lie.

Suddenly, the block dropped into a hole in the floor, creating a resounding boom that echoed around the atrium beyond.

'Well there goes the element of surprise,' said Rufius, cocking his rifle and moving out to the right. 'Spread out.'

Josh shifted to the opposite side, leaving Eira in the centre.

The chamber was vast, its walls sloped inwards, decorated with panels of scenes from an ancient battle. Thin shafts of sunlight streamed through slits high in the distant ceiling. They fell onto a monumental sculpture of an austere-looking figure in long, flowing robes. It was carved from the same gold-seamed stone as the gatehouse, dominating the centre of the mausoleum – like the tomb of a long dead king.

The monument was over a hundred feet tall, built in stepped sections like a ziggurat. The features of the central figure were elongated, its face was humanoid but distorted, as if it had been squashed in a vice. The head was fringed with a mane of what appeared to be snakes and the hands held some kind of orb which glowed weakly.

Surrounding the tomb, kneeling as if in prayer, were the avatars of the missing crew. Their domed helmets were dark, the power units were obviously dead. Whatever Templeton's team had discovered here, they had obviously never left.

Drifting around the head of the sculpture were ethereal spectres, skeins of darkness circled the rock like storm birds caught in a whirlwind. They reminded Josh slightly of the Nazgûl they encountered in the Shadow Realm.

'Wraiths,' whispered Rufius, shouldering his rifle and aiming it at them.

'Hold your fire man. They're not attacking,' whispered Eira. 'They're waiting.'

Between the feet of the stone king was an entrance, where rubble lay strewn across the ground, the remnants of a sealed door.

Rufius pointed his gun towards it. 'I say we take cover in there,' he said, picking his way between the kneeling suits.

Josh and Eira followed.

A narrow passage sloped down into the interior of the tomb. Josh noticed scratches on the walls where previous visitors had scored the granite as they passed.

The lights from his suit flickered into life as the passage darkened, revealing walls covered in hieroglyphs, but not the Egyptian kind, these looked more like numbers to Josh. Every ten feet or so, the faces of terrifying monsters were carved in bas-relief, like gargoyles leering out from the dark.

The tomb itself was a cube-shaped room made from a black stone that absorbed the light. It looked vaguely familiar, and it took a moment for Josh to remember why. This was the tomb he saw on the battlefield at Mons, the one linked to the marks on the bodies of the zombie army.

In the centre of the space was a stone sarcophagus, the lid of which had been removed, laying cracked in pieces on the floor.

Eira stood motionless, staring into the coffin. She muttered to herself. 'My god.'

'What is it?' asked the colonel, coming to join her.

70

PRISON BREAK

Château D'If

Silas appeared in the control room of the prison and sank to his knees.

Templeton's key was the only vestige that could bring him directly into the operational heart of the Château, but it took all of his energy and skill to navigate through the distorted timelines.

The Copernicans were not wrong about the effects of the gravitational flux. There were moments when Silas thought he would be stranded in the past. It was only the years of time-running that kept him from appearing in some random part of the Pliocene.

The room was empty, as he knew it would be.

One of the other reasons for getting caught was so that he could glean enough information from the guards' schedules to know when they would be busy elsewhere. It took nearly a year, but it was worth it.

•   •   •

Getting to his feet, he went over to the main console. The control desk was unsurprisingly basic. The prison's temporal shielding was one of the first of Templeton's inventions to ever be used outside of a lab, and had to be operated by a low-grade Protectorate guard with the mental capacity of a ten-year old.

Crude cathode-ray screens flickered with instructions in green text. There were a series of dials and analog meters built into the long metal desk which looked as if it was modelled on a system from a Russian nuclear reactor.

Silas sat down at one of the terminals and flexed his fingers. The characters on the keyboard were worn and dirty, and there was food trapped under the space bar.

'Filthy philistines,' he said, taking Templeton's key from around his neck and sliding it into the empty slot in the main console.

A bank of illuminated buttons immediately sprang to life, ones that looked as if they hadn't been touched in years. There were words stencilled onto them, but the faded lettering made it impossible to read.

The flickering screen displayed a series of sub-routines and then cleared down to a simple command prompt.

SUDO :>

Silas typed in the first of the three commands he'd gleaned from a guard.

INITIATE LD SEQ T0019A

And hit the return key.

Two intricate clockwork spindles clicked and whirred into action behind him. A stack of paper cards shuffled through them as the program was loaded. The screen went blank for a few seconds before a stream of data began scrolling down the screen.

One of the reasons Silas despised the Order was their insistence on categorising their members, forcing them to choose the guild they should join based on their abilities.

For many it was a simple choice, but it never suited his particular set of skills.

He was born with an eclectic range of abilities, part seer, part redactor and capable of shifting through the most meagre of timelines at high speed.

Growing up, his parents recognised what he was capable of, using it to line their own pockets. Silas had never been happier than he was back then; his family were the only ones who ever really understood him. 'My little canary,' his mother used to call him.

But once they were captured and he was made a ward of the court, Silas became something of an enigma, a square peg. Never comfortable taking orders or abiding by the strict rules of the Order – he constantly failed to meet everyone's expectations.

They'd all underestimated him, and now he was going to show them what he was capable of.

He was going to set them free.

First, there was the minor problem of learning how the prison worked, which was difficult since it was one of the most closely guarded secrets in the Protectorate.

No one ever managed to escape the Château and live to tell the tale.

Which meant getting caught.

Getting nicked was something Silas spent most of his adult life avoiding. After all, his reputation was at stake. So it had to look good, make sure they sent the best of the Crows to track him down, and then lead them a merry dance.

Having won numerous trophies for his time-running it was a piece of cake. Slipping between eras in seconds took a lot of practice, and he still held the record for the century run: ten decades in less than four minutes. No one could catch him, not if he didn't want them to.

Sabien was the perfect stooge for his grand plan.

Once in custody, it was only a matter of time before they would throw him in the same prison as his family, just out of spite – especially if he kept his mouth shut.

The ability to read minds was commonly known as 'redacting' within the Order. Naturally, most redactors worked for either the Protectorate or the Syndicate. Both sides valued the psychic abilities and paid handsomely.

Most needed to make physical contact with an individual to enter their consciousness, but Silas could do it from a distance.

Not only could he sense other people's thoughts from a few yards away, but he could also influence their actions. To him their minds were like clockwork machines, he could see the internal gearing and adjust them.

It didn't work on everyone, of course. Rufius was far too irascible and stuck in his ways, but the guards at the prison were easy pickings, and it only took a few weeks to find the right man.

The one responsible for the shield command protocols.

Silas typed in the second command:
INIT SAFETY SHUTDOWN
The system responded:
> INSERT KEYS

* * *

Unfortunately, a few weeks in the Château had cost him over a year in real time.

But it was worth it.

Although having the command sequence was only half of the problem. It wasn't possible to switch off the fields without the failsafe keys, which were held by three separate guards.

Silas couldn't control all three men at once.

He needed the master key, and the only one in existence belonged to its creator, Alexander Templeton.

Which meant finding Atlantis.

Silas turned the Templeton key anticlockwise.

A light appeared beneath a red button labelled SHUTDOWN.

Hitting the button triggered a series of silent alarms, which he cancelled with the third code, typing in a command override. Anyone looking at the monitoring systems would think it was a test.

Smiling to himself, Silas flicked a switch and sat back in the chair. The old screens switched to a camera feed, showing various views of the prison complex.

It was chaos.

The cell doors along the corridors swung open like a stack of dominoes. Guards were running to and fro in a state of total confusion.

There were over three hundred prisoners in the facility and fewer than thirty guards. Stasis containment was an easy thing to maintain, there was no one to feed or take to the exercise yard and therefore it only required a skeleton crew to run.

Prisoners began to appear from the cells, scratching and yawning as if having woken from a good night's sleep.

Their jailers ran for their lives.

Silas found the intercom and switched it on to the speaker. The sound of hundreds of men and women tasting freedom for the first time in centuries was intense. He tried not to think about what they would do to the guards.

Switching through the views, he found the camera nearest to his parents' cell.

His father appeared first, stretching his heavily tattooed arms over his head like a wrestler about to enter the ring.

He was a brute of a man, over six foot five with a large barrel of a chest. He looked every inch the strongman from a circus – exactly as Silas remembered him.

His mother came out a few seconds later, still wearing the Russian ballgown she'd stolen from one of the Romanov Tsarinas.

'Ello! Who do we have ere then?' his father bellowed, as Silas walked down the corridor towards them. 'Why Queenie, my dear, I do believe it's none other than our youngest, come to rescue us.'

His mother squinted at him, she was always too vain to admit she needed glasses. 'Silas? My darling, is that you?'

Silas weaved between the other prisoners who were jostling each other as they made their way to the exits. Silas's parents took their time. His father was never one for queuing.

'Is this your doing by any chance?' his father asked, twisting the end of his handle bar moustache. 'You come to break us out of this place, have you boy?'

'My 'aven't you grown,' said his mother. 'Look at 'im, George, he's the spit of your Frederick.'

Silas had rehearsed their reunion some many different ways in his head.

When he was a child, his favourite version involved them gathering him up and running off to the cabin. He had only been there once, and he wasn't sure where it was, only that it was near a lake and they had spent a long hot summer there, 'laying low' as his mother used to call it.

'Yes,' Silas said his voice reverting back to its native patter. 'Listen Pa, we haven't got long. I need to get you out of here sharpish, before the screws raise the alarm.'

His father nodded, slapping him on the shoulder. 'Lead on my boy. We're in your capable hands.'

71

ABANDON

Mars

The body lying in the sarcophagus was over twelve feet long.

Dressed in ornate battle armour, its skeletal fingers gripped a vicious-looking longsword. The tarnished metal of the breastplate was inscribed with a heraldic crest that reminded Josh of a medieval knight. Its face was hidden behind a golden mask that matched the features on the monumental sculpture.

'The tomb of a Martian warrior king,' said Rufius, gazing at the body, 'not something I ever thought I would find myself standing inside.'

'An entirely alien race,' said Eira. 'Alexander was right all along.'

Rufius walked around the sarcophagus. 'So where is he?'

The walls were carved with intricate ideograms and hieroglyphics which glowed slightly in the semi-darkness. As Josh examined it, the suit spoke up: 'It appears that you are trying to ascertain the meaning of the pictograms. Would you like me to decipher it?'

Yes.

A thin line of laser light shone out from the side of Josh's helmet and scanned the script.

'It may take some time,' the suit reported. 'There are over five hundred thousand semiotic symbols in my database, but no definite correlation, I will resort to pattern matching.'

Josh turned back towards Rufius and Eira. 'My suit says it's going to try and translate the text.'

'Good,' said the old watchman, turning around slowly, studying the rest of the room. 'Now, unless my eyes deceive me, this feels like too large a structure for such a small tomb.'

Eira tutted. 'I think you'll find the Pyramids of Giza were built to similar proportions. The size of the monument is directly related to the status of the Pharaoh.'

Rufius examined the walls more carefully, his metal fingers tapping on various sections of the stone.

'They also built false chambers, to deter grave robbers.'

He stopped at one of the gargoyles, which Josh thought bore a striking resemblance to a monad.

'If you wanted to hide something, you'd put it behind the thing that no one would want to go near, wouldn't you?' the watchman continued, putting his hand inside the gaping mouth of the monster.

They all heard an audible click.

The surface of the opposite wall began to shimmer like melting wax.

'I'm registering unusual electromagnetic fluctuations,' noted Josh's suit. 'Would you like to see?'

Yes.

It switched his vision to thermal, showing a swirling miasma of lines moving across the walls. They were like spirals of rippling energy radiating out from the centre.

'There's a breach,' whispered Josh, pointing towards the centre of the anomaly, 'something's coming.'

They all took a step back as the solid block of stone simply disappeared.

A long, dark corridor stretched out before them.

'Well now,' gloated Rufius, aiming the torch on his rifle along the passageway, 'seems there *is* more to this place than meets the eye.'

'Lucky guess,' muttered Eira.

On each side of the passage were crypt-like tombs, their entrances barred with metal grilles. Josh could hear the slithering of things inside, but decided it was wiser not to ask the suit to switch back to thermal.

'Looks more like a necropolis,' observed the old watchman, keeping his rifle trained on the openings.

Josh realised the grilles were cemented into the rock like security bars on a window.

'I have completed the translation,' said the suit on Josh's personal channel. 'Would you like me to summarise?'

Yes.

'This was the tomb of Mal-Shajan the Martyr, the warrior king of the Q'tharian, who valiantly gave his life to defeat the Defilers of Draaxon. His body was enshrined here with those that he defeated, as was the ritual Q'tharian way, so they may serve as his acolytes in the next life.'

Josh stopped in his tracks. 'I think we need to get out of here.'

'Why?'

'It's not a cemetery, it's a prison.' He told the suit to share the translation with the others.

'Defilers?' asked Eira.

'Whatever they were. I'm guessing they're not quite as dead as their captors thought they were,' added Rufius, testing the bars of a nearby crypt. The iron grille was rusted through and came away easily in his hands.

The floor began to shake, like the tremors before an earthquake. A deep, low sound filled the air like the grinding of rocks.

Suddenly, a shimmering mirror-field flickered to life at the far end of the passageway.

'We should leave,' repeated Josh.

As the field stabilised they could see Lyra, Doctor Shika and the Grand Seer standing on the other side.

'Westinghouse, is that you?' asked the doctor, who was shrouded by a ghostly outline of a dragon-like creature.

'It is Kaori, where are you?'

'In the Shadow realm, where are you?'

'Mars. Four and a half billion years ago.'

The doctor squinted at them. 'What are you wearing?'

Eira interrupted. 'There's no time to explain. You need to close down this portal. Do you have a disrupter?'

Kaori nodded. 'Yes, but shouldn't you join us first?'

'We can't, just collapse the breach. I have a feeling it will get his attention.'

The doctor nodded and took off her backpack.

Lyra walked up to the portal. 'Josh, Sim has worked out the location of the Island, they will be there soon. He's with Caitlin on the *Nautilus*.'

'Thanks,' Josh replied. 'Are they okay?'

'They are safe for now, but Professor Eddington says there is little time left. You have to find Templeton.'

'Oh, I think this should do the trick,' said Eira, watching Kaori setting up the disrupter. 'Shutting down his secret tunnel should get his attention.'

'Okay, stand back,' said Doctor Shika, unwinding a cable.

Lyra waved goodbye and stepped away to join the others.

The surface of the portal rippled, bulging outward towards them as if something had exploded on the other side of it. The colour changed to a midnight blue, and Josh thought he could see stars inside it.

'So what happens now?' asked Rufius.

'We wait,' Eira snapped, turning back and walking towards the tomb.

'Where are you going?'

'To get the sword, I have a feeling we might need it.'

72

HEARTBREAK

Conciergerie, Paris, 1810.

The reception his parents received as they entered the Conciergerie was reminiscent of a victorious general returning home from the war.

Everyone rose to greet them, clapping and cheering as they strode triumphantly through the corridors towards the Great Hall.

Someone gave his father a cigar and a glass of rum. He slugged the liquor back in one gulp and threw the glass into a fireplace. Placing the cigar between his teeth he went into the crowd, shaking hands with old friends and slapping well-wishers on the back.

Silas trailed along behind, glowing with pride, knowing that he played his part in restoring them to their former glory. The old crew were back together, and everyone seemed to be over the moon about it.

Entering the Hall, they found Rasputin waiting for them. The Russian monk rose from his throne, lifting his hands in welcome. 'Well, this is a great day!' he declared, his voice quieting the room. 'The return of Slippery Jack, no less.'

His father bowed his head. 'Much obliged my liege. I knew you wouldn't let me rot in there.'

'Not I, Jack, this was all young Silas's doing,' the leader of the Syndicate said, his dark eyes turning to Silas. 'Come forward my artful dodger, and take your rightful place beside your father. You have done well.'

'Didn't he just?' agreed his father, wrapping his arm around his son's shoulders. 'Proper chip off the old block.'

Silas felt the colour rising in his cheeks.

Rasputin sat back down on his throne and motioned him to approach. 'So tell me the tale. Did you find the lost island?'

'I did, my Lord.'

'And what did you discover? Has the disaster been averted?'

Silas shook his head. 'The station was abandoned, the scientists have all fled. I left Westinghouse and the others trying to find someone who could shutdown the generator.'

Rasputin was clearly troubled by the news, his thick eyebrows knitting together into a scowl. 'Catastrophes are generally not good for business.'

'Which is why I kept this.' Silas held up Templeton's key. 'The Order would give anything for it,' he added, seeing the greed rekindle in their leader's eyes.

'They would indeed,' interrupted his father, snatching the key from him. 'We could ask for the Crown Jewels or the San José Galleon.'

'Indeed we could, George,' said Rasputin, walking down the steps and putting his arm around the shoulders of his father. 'I think we should discuss this over dinner.'

'Good idea, I've a fancy for a suckling pig.'

'And some rum,' added Silas's mother, licking her lips.

• • •

The meal was extravagant, greater even than the banquet that Moctezuma had given in Tenochtitlán.

Laden with platters of honey-glazed pig, pheasant and racks of beef, the long dining tables stretched between the arched columns of the Hall of the Men-at-Arms.

From the royal insignia etched into the handles of the silver spoons, it appeared the entire spread was stolen from the Palace of Versailles, which in truth, it probably had been.

By the looks of the guests, the entire upper echelon of the Syndicate were sitting down to eat. Representatives from every one of the Dark Guild's most influential families had been invited.

Silas recognised a few of the Dons, but his father knew them all. One by one they each paid tribute to him, like an undefeated gladiator, his old man was showered with gifts.

But somehow, amongst the celebrations and the reminiscing, Silas got separated from his parents.

Treated as honoured guests, they sat on each side of Rasputin at the head of the table. While Silas was seated further down, sitting between a surly-looking pirate with terrible halitosis and a woman who was supposedly the courtesan to Louis IX.

He told himself it would be fine. This was their first night of freedom after all, it was only normal for them to want to party with their old friends. They would call him up to join the discussion once the meal was over.

But the invitation never came.

After two hours of waiting, bored to death by the courtesan's recollections of the King's terrible bedroom habits, Rasputin stood up and escorted his parents into his private apartments.

Silas watched them leave, unsure of whether he should follow.

This was not quite how he imagined it would go; they were supposed to be working this together.

When he was younger, he always did exactly as he was told. He could still feel the sting of his father's hand from the times when he didn't. Everything revolved around the "business", there was never any time for school or games. Silas learned many useful things from his parents, but it was Rufius that taught him how to read and write.

'Nothing good ever came out of a book,' his mother used to say. 'Less you could sell it.'

Looking back, she wasn't much of a mother either, more interested in the inside of a wine bottle than ensuring her children were fed and clothed.

They were a legendary couple of outlaws whose kids were an unexpected byproduct of their debauched lifestyle. Children were nothing more than another mouth to feed. If you couldn't earn your keep by the time you were six, she'd threaten to sell you to the Barbary Slavers.

Not that she ever did.

Silas had five brothers and a sister. The eldest two died and one ran away, leaving the remaining four to become part of the Wormwood franchise, "The Firm", as his dad liked to call it.

73

ABANDON

Mars

Abandon was waiting for them in the outer chamber of the tomb, his eyes burning with fire. Wraiths swarmed around him like a cloak of shadows.

'Who dares to enter my domain?' His voice echoed off the walls, amplified a hundredfold.

Mal-Shajan's sword glowed in Eira's hand, reacting to the proximity of the wraiths, who shied away from its presence.

'And you've desecrated the tomb!' he screamed at her.

'Alexander?' said Eira, walking towards the Old King. 'Is that really you?'

The fire in the man's eyes dimmed slightly.

His expression changed, his brows furrowing as he studied the mechanical automaton striding towards him.

Josh and Rufius shouldered their weapons, watching on in amazement as she ignored the cloud of malevolent creatures surrounding him.

'It's me Eira.'

A flicker of recognition passed over his face. 'Eira?' he repeated in a whisper.

'What happened to you?' she asked, putting her hand out towards him.

He stepped back.

'Don't judge me woman!' He raised his staff and slammed it down on the stone floor. 'You have no idea of what I have become.'

'Where have you been?'

His eyes darkened until they were black pools.

'I have been to the edge of the universe. Walked the paths of eternity. I have seen things that you wouldn't believe.'

'Your machine is destroying the planet.'

He shrugged, his mouth twisting into a grin. 'There are so many more to choose from.'

'I need you to tell me how to shut down the graviton generator.'

He shook his head. 'NO!'

The wraiths swarmed around him, creating a wall between them.

'You should not be here! This is a place of the damned. You must leave!'

The pitch of his voice was different, more human, and for a moment, Josh thought he saw the man in the photograph.

Abandon let out a mournful groan and struck out at Eira with his staff. She parried his blow with the sword. Arcs of lightning flared out from the blade, scattering the wraiths and lighting up the entire chamber. The discharge of the weapon shook the ground beneath their feet. The tremors increased and the servos in Josh's suit began to complain as it tried to keep him upright.

Lumps of masonry fell from the ceiling as the supporting columns crumbled.

'We need to go!' said Rufius over the radio. 'He's going to bring the whole place down.'

'How do we disconnect?' asked Josh.

'Just ask the suit,' shouted Eira, the light in her helmet dimming.

The feeling slowly returned to Josh's fingers, it felt like pins and needles after sleeping on your arm.

Opening his eyes, he watched the symbols on the inside of the capsule scrolling over the glass, going through the final stages of decompression.

As the last of them faded, the canopy seal hissed and opened.

'Welcome back boy,' said Rufius, helping him out of the pod. 'How's the head?'

'I'm okay,' replied Josh, looking around the chamber. 'Where is she?'

'She's gone looking for Lilly. There's no sign of her or the other two. I'm assuming that they've found something interesting.'

Josh rubbed his eyes, it felt like he'd just woken from the craziest dream. 'Did we just meet –'

'Templeton? Yes, I believe we did. There's no time for explanations, we need to find his capsule. Eira believes that if we can revive him we might still have a chance of shutting this thing down.'

74

SURVIVOR

Atlas Station, Atlantis.

'Where did you find him?' asked Eira, kneeling down beside the survivor.

'He was holed up in one of the storage cupboards,' replied Sabien, looking behind them. 'Where's Lilly?'

'We were about to ask you the same question,' said Rufius.

'She was keeping an eye on Silas.' Sabien's expression hardened. 'See if you can get any sense out of him,' he said, leaving them and disappearing into one of the chambers.

'What's your name?' Eira said, putting her hand on the man's shoulder, which was shaking uncontrollably.

'Ed-Ed-Edward, Edward Miller,' he replied through chattering teeth.

She smiled. 'Nice to meet you Edward. My name is Eira Winterbourne.'

His eyes went wide. 'Winterbourne? Professor Winterbourne?'

Eira nodded. 'One and the same. Now, can you tell me, are you alone, where are the other members of your crew?'

'Dead,' he said, shrinking away from her touch. 'They took them.'

'They?' asked Josh.

The man pointed up into the column of rings above their heads.

'From Mars?' asked Eira, glancing up at the dark tube.

The colour drained from the engineer's already pale face. 'The ghosts. We should never have opened the tomb.'

'What happened?'

The man put his hands over his ears and began rocking back and forth. 'They're all gone. All gone. I heard them screaming.'

Eira took a deep breath and tried changing the subject.

'Edward, look at me, you're okay. What's your position here? What did you do?'

Edward's expression changed, becoming more rational once more. 'Senior T-T-Technician, on the q-q-quantum fusion reactor.'

'Good,' she said, nodding at Rufius's sudden look of interest. 'So you know how to shut the system down?'

He shook his head violently like a petulant child. 'No, no, no, no, can't be done without the master key.'

'Templeton's key?' asked Rufius.

Edward nodded.

'And can you tell me where the Director's capsule is?'

'N-n-no, No, No. It's broken.'

She took a deep breath. 'You mean it's defective?'

'Broken,' he repeated, begin to rock once more. 'They're all broken.'

Rufius took Eira to one side. 'This is getting us nowhere. Do you think he knows how to switch this infernal machine off?'

She watched the man crawl under the nearest desk. 'He's suffering from some form of post traumatic stress. I don't think he's going to be any use to us.'

The watchman grunted. 'We've got to find a way to bring Templeton back.'

'If he's right, and the capsule is broken then it may well be too late.'

Sabien returned a few minutes later with a bewildered looking Lilly in tow.

'He's gone,' he said through tight lips. 'Escaped. Left her locked in a pod.'

'He can't have gone far,' Rufius reminded him. 'We're all trapped here until we find a way to switch that off.'

The inspector didn't seem convinced. 'He's a time runner, one of the best. He'll have found a way off this rock.'

'What did you find up there?' Lilly asked.

Eira sighed, sitting down on a chair, her eyes filled with tears. 'It's worse than I imagined. They were excavating an ancient tomb. I think Alexander became infected by whatever was sealed inside.'

'He's Abandon,' added Josh, 'or at least part of him is. The texts in the crypt spoke of defeating some ancient evil. They sealed it away with the king who died defending them.'

'Alexander was obsessed with finding a Martian civilisation,' Eira continued, oblivious of the others. 'All those years searching for a way to reach back far enough into the past and what does he have to show for it?'

'And what about the crew?' asked Lilly.

Rufius shook his head. 'The suits were all empty. There was no sign of any survivors.'

Lilly gasped, looking back towards the stasis chambers. 'So they're all gone?'

The old woman stood up and wiped her cheeks with her

sleeve. 'All except Alexander and whatever those creatures are that he's tamed.'

Suddenly the background hum of the machinery changed pitch, the rings of the tunnel above their heads began to glow and vibrate.

'No, No, No,' screamed Edward, getting to his feet and waving his hands around. 'We have to leave! The ghosts are coming.'

Rufius grabbed him by the shoulders. 'Can't you stop them?'

Edward shook his head. 'Not without the key.'

With that, the man turned on his heels and ran towards the nearest exit.

'Leave him,' Eira said, staring up into the tunnel. 'As I suspected, Alexander is coming back to protect his experiment.'

'Maybe we should go?' said Josh. 'Find this key?'

Before anyone had a chance to respond, a thin ray of light shone down from the column and the rings descended onto the raised platform.

Sabien took out his guns and cocked them, as did Rufius. Eira went to one of the consoles and checked the data.

Everyone held their breath.

75

TIME RUNNER

Conciergerie, Paris, 1810.

Silas wandered aimlessly around the headquarters of the Syndicate for the rest of the evening. The conference between Rasputin, his parents and the leaders of the various families continued behind closed doors.

For a while, he tried to 'listen', but there was something or someone blocking his psychic abilities, which was no surprise to Silas as Rasputin had many talented redactors at his disposal.

Without Templeton's key his leverage was lost. His one bargaining chip was gone and it was starting to make him nervous. Years of surviving on his own taught him one thing above all others: you always needed to keep an ace up your sleeve, and Silas just handed over his most valuable asset to his parents.

All the years of planning, the time he spent in prison, the effort that went into rescuing them and he gave away his advantage in less than a minute. All Silas managed to achieve was to release some of the most dangerous criminals in history, the majority of whom seemed to have returned to the Conciergerie to celebrate their freedom.

The building was in a continuous state of debauchery. Drunken gangs roamed the corridors as parties moved from room to room. Old scores were being settled in various ways, some good-humoured while others more deadly.

Silas stepped over yet another body, unsure as to whether it was just sleeping off the drink or dead.

It was anarchy and the only ones who could stop it were too busy planning how to hold the continuum to ransom.

His gut instinct was telling him to leave. Any hopes of a family reunion had vanished, overshadowed by the opportunity to fleece the Oblivion Order.

Silas was beginning to realise the cherished memories of his parents were nothing more than pipe dreams, a fantasy created by a boy who had lost everything.

All those years holding on to the idea of bringing the "Firm" back together, that somehow they would be just like before – it was all a lie, there was nothing for him here.

They didn't care about him any more than a farmer cared for his dog.

The only person who had ever helped him was currently trapped on Mars.

Rufius was the closest thing Silas had ever known to a real father—he could see that clearly now. The mad old bugger had been the only one willing to take him in when the Protectorate was ready to send him off to the redactors.

Those first few weeks must have been a nightmare for the watchman. Silas tried to run away on at least five different occasions. Once making it all the way back to the Middle Ages.

He could still see the look on Rufius's face when he found himself in the court of Alfred the Great.

Silas loved time running, he was very good at it.

Thankfully, his mentor recognised his talent early on, encouraging his apprentice to enter the trials for the guild tournament. The Order held a competition every year, a kind of temporal Olympics, and each guild would send a squad of their best chronothetes to take part.

There were various activities, from relic relays to deep-time diving, each event designed to test the individual to the best of their abilities. The Draconians would always win the martial competitions, and generally the Scriptorians came last in everything, but they didn't seem to mind.

The Watchmen's division was officially attached to the Copernican Guild and since hardly any of their actuaries were physically fit enough to compete, there were always opportunities to take part for anyone who volunteered.

And time running was quite a specialist activity.

The course was different every year, and usually involved at least ten different time periods. It was a mixture of a marathon and an orienteering race, one where you had to find the right waymarkers in each era to move on to the next stage.

For a kid with nothing else to lose, it was as if all his Christmases had come at once. Not that Silas ever experienced an actual Christmas, but learning to navigate complex temporal paths at speed gave him a satisfying sense of achievement. Solving the puzzles kept his overactive mind in check.

Rufius became his coach, getting up in the early hours every day to work with him before school.

He could still see the old watchman standing on the top of Scafell Pike with a stopwatch. Waiting in the pouring rain for Silas to return with the objects he had hidden in various locations the night before.

For four years in a row, Silas won every race.

No one could touch him.

Then, on his sixteenth birthday, everything changed.

The apprenticeship came to an end. Silas was now of an age when he could choose which direction his career within the Order could take.

Racing had been the most important thing in his life until then.

He assumed the natural thing to do would be to join the Watch, but Rufius refused to take him on.

'It's not a job for the young,' he said. 'You should join the Protectorate or the Draconians.'

Disappointed by the rejection, Silas left.

He couldn't understand why Rufius would even suggest joining the Crows, the mortal enemies of his family, nor did he have any real desire to fight the creatures of the Maelstrom.

So he chose neither.

On the day he passed out of the academy, he took a position with the Copernicans and within a year, was assigned to another watchman by the name of Gideon Ravenscroft, a drunken, lazy fool who was more than happy to take on an eager young pup.

Rufius objected, but was overruled. No one joined the Watch out of choice, to have such a young volunteer was something of a novelty.

As the old man would find out much later, Silas influenced his career within the guild, using his redactive skills to 'push' the minds of the relevant people to progress his rise through the ranks.

And then there was the incident in Dallas.

· · ·

'Wormwood?' asked a passing guard.

Silas snapped out of his reverie. 'Yes?'

'They're asking for you. Upstairs.' The man jerked his thumb in the air.

76

DR BROCA

Conciergerie, Paris.

Silas walked into Rasputin's office, which was once part of the Royal apartments of King Philip IV.

'Come in,' the leader of the Syndicate welcomed him in a gruff Russian accent.

His father was standing by one of the tall windows, smoking a cigar while his mother was reclining on a chaise longue. There was another man that Silas didn't recognise loitering at the other end of the room.

'We've been discussing the opportunity,' Rasputin continued. 'There are a few more details I need while I consider my options. Please take a seat.'

Silas sat beside his mother, who was three sheets to the wind by the smell of her breath. She was wearing a ridiculous wig and her make up was applied too thickly, which he'd never noticed before, and it made her look like a dockside tart.

Rasputin picked up Templeton's key. 'It strikes us that there may be something far more valuable than using this as a bargaining chip.'

Silas scoffed. 'Like what? We're talking about the fate of the planet.'

His father blew out a large smoke ring and turned towards him.

'And who told you that boy?' he snapped. 'One of them clackers I bet.'

'You saw it,' Silas said, 'In the Eyes of Eternity.'

The monk shrugged. 'One of many possible outcomes.'

'Don't believe them Coppernickers,' slurred his mother, taking another slug of rum. 'Bunch of stuck up bean counters.'

Silas couldn't quite believe what he was hearing.

'But they'll give you whatever you want for it.'

Rasputin held up the key letting it glint in the light of the candles. 'Ah! But imagine what the man behind all this has stored in his head. The brain of such a genius would be worth a fortune on the memory market. His intellect is far too valuable to leave to rot in a jar.'

Trading in memories never appealed to Silas, they tended to involve too much hassle – the extractions generally got messy. But, Rasputin was right, the mind of the man would have a wealth of knowledge, including how to shutdown his gravitational engines.

'They'll pay a pretty penny for his head,' his mother said, rubbing her fingers together. 'Bloody do-gooders.'

His father put the cigar between his teeth and crouched down in front of Silas. 'We're sending you back in boy.'

'Back to Atlantis?' Silas asked.

'Where else?' He cuffed him hard around the head. Making Silas's ears ring. 'Although you'll be accompanied.' His father nodded to the man at the other end of the room. 'Just to make sure you stick to the plan.'

'I've never taken a brain,' muttered Silas under his breath, shuddering at the thought of cutting open someone's skull. 'What if I mess it up?'

Rasputin handed him Templeton's key. 'Leave that to our friend Dr Broca. All you need to do right now is get him onto the island.'

77

NAUTILUS

North Sea. 6225 BC

The *Nautilus* shuddered as Juliana fought to control the ship. 'She's taking a hell of a beating,' she said through gritted teeth, pulling hard on the wheel. 'Are you sure this is the right place?'

Sim checked his almanac. 'According to my calculations, the island will appear in less than ten minutes.'

They were in a holding position over the North Sea, a hundred kilometres west of the Norwegian coast.

'How much longer?' demanded Grandmaster Derado over the intercom. He was waiting with a squadron of Dreadnoughts in the forward cargo bay, which was taking the majority of the punishment.

'Ten minutes,' Juliana replied into the speaking tube. 'Although I'm not sure she'll be able to take much more than five.'

'We'll be ready.'

. . .

Caitlin slid down the ladder from the conning tower accompanied by a shower of seawater. 'It's getting pretty choppy out there, feels like a storm's coming,' she said, taking off her sou'wester.

'That correlates with what's been reported at other sightings. The localised gravitational fields disrupt the weather system,' said Sim.

'That and the extreme fluctuations in the magnetosphere,' added Caitlin's mother as the ship bucked once more.

'I've got something,' her father said, his face lit up by the green glow of the radar screen. 'Dead ahead.'

'It's coming!' squealed Lyra, staring out of the observation window.

Sim and Caitlin rushed to join her as the sea spiralled upwards into a column of water.

The sky darkened and thunder clouds gathered over the swirling vortex, which grew until it towered over the ship.

'Brace yourselves,' warned Juliana, pulling up on the controls. The ship lifted clear of the surface and into the air.

The prow of the *Nautilus* plunged into the swirling grey wall. The hull moaned like a wounded whale under the crushing force of the swell. Rivets shot out from the bulkheads, allowing jets of water to spray through the newly formed holes.

'Thomas! Equalise the pressure!' ordered Caitlin's mother. 'Quickly!'

Like a climber on a sheer cliff face, her father moved carefully from one hand hold to the next along the wall until he reached a series of valve wheels. He began to crank them open and they felt the air pressure increase, stopping the leaks in seconds.

Everyone relaxed a little, yawning to unblock their ears.

'She's not built for this kind of punishment,' muttered Juliana, stroking the controls. 'Are you old girl?'

'We need to gain altitude quickly,' said Sim, consulting his almanac. 'According to my research, the island is ringed by mountains that rise nearly two kilometres above sea level.'

'Now you tell me,' cursed Juliana, pushing her feet hard down on the dive plane pedals.

The deck pitched violently, throwing them backwards. Lyra and Caitlin only just caught Sim before he fell.

'I can't control it. I'm going to have to shut down the engines,' Caitlin's mother shouted over the noise. 'We're in the hands of the gods now.' She took her hands away from the wheel and the shaking reduced as the ship turned into the winding torrent of water.

Caught in the vortex, the sound of the turbines was replaced by an eerie silence. The internal lights flickered and died, as if something was draining the ship of its power. They got slowly to their feet, and came to stand by the window.

'I can see something,' said Lyra after a few minutes. She pointed at a spot in the swirling grey water.

Sim squinted in the general direction. 'I can't see anything.'

'Not with your eyes, silly.'

'I think she's right,' said Caitlin's father, putting his hand on the glass. 'There, that looks like a mountain.'

The colour of the wall was changing, the grey replaced by hues of white and green, like watching the creation of a pastel painting, the image seemed to sharpen until they broke through the wall and found themselves in clean air.

The island was a ring of jagged peaks encircling an icy

plain, like the caldera of an ancient volcano. At its centre, a solitary structure towered above concentric rings of buildings, reminding Sim of the Draconian lighthouse.

Although this was different, instead of a glowing light in the lantern room, a shaft of intense energy was being channeled out into the stratosphere.

'What is that?' asked Caitlin.

'Axis Mundi,' said Lyra. 'The navel of the cosmos.'

'The gravitational anomaly, to be more precise,' corrected Sim.

Julianna sat back in her seat and grabbed the steering wheel. 'He's right, I need to put her down as soon as possible, the gravitational flux is off the scale.' She turned to the speaking tube and spoke into it. 'Derado, prepare your men for a hard landing.'

THE RETURN

Atlas Station, Atlantis.

The rings floated back up into the tunnel.

Abandon stood on the platform, surrounded by a squad of exosuits, their helmets filled with the dark, smoky tendrils of his wraiths.

'You dare to enter my realm!' he bellowed, his voice echoing across the chamber.

His guards, who were already configured for combat, raised their weapons and fired.

Rufius dropped to one knee and took careful aim at the first, putting a bullet through the glass dome which had no real effect.

'Aim for their power cores,' shouted Eira from behind the console.

Sabien ducked and rolled, coming up behind another desk. His shot hit the next wraith squarely in the chest and the lights on his suit dimmed and went out.

'Nice shot,' noted Rufius, moving out of the line of fire and taking cover behind a column of pipes. 'Josh take Lilly, see if you can find Templeton's pod.'

Josh nodded, grabbed Lilly and dragged her into the nearest side chamber.

Two more wraiths fell to Sabien's next volley.

Abandon roared, driving his staff down onto the platform and the rings descended once more.

'He's calling down more of them,' Eira said, glancing at the readouts on the console behind her.

'Can't you stop him?' shouted Rufius, taking down his first. 'I've only got five more rounds.'

'I'll try,' replied Eira, keeping low as she made her way over to another desk.

Josh and Lilly moved slowly through the first two bays, each taking a side of the chamber. The bodies inside the stasis units were gaunt and skeletal, so they checked the name tags on each of the units.

'They all look dead,' said Josh, wiping the dust from the glass door.

'It's the gravitational flux, it destabilises their stasis fields, they've continued to age.'

Josh wondered if it would even be possible to bring them back now. Who would want to return to a body that had aged so much?

As they walked into the third vault they heard voices, and Josh pulled Lilly into the shadows.

Two men were standing over a pod at the far end of the chamber.

Josh recognised Silas, but the other man was a stranger.

'You can't do that.' They heard Silas say.

The other man mumbled something unintelligible.

'No!,' replied Silas, pushing the man away from the pod.

Josh motioned to Lilly to stay still and crept towards them.

The stranger picked something up and raised it, threatening to strike Silas.

'He should know better than to trust you,' rasped the dark figure.

Silas shook his head. 'I should have known better than to trust my parents.'

Josh managed to grab the man's arm, but he was stronger than he looked and wrenched himself free from Josh's grip.

He realised the object in the man's hand was a sharp-toothed silver saw.

'Josh!' cried Silas, 'he's going to take his brain.'

The man's face was twisted with anger, his dark eyes narrowing, teeth bared like a rabid dog. He swung the saw at Josh in a scything arc, and Josh only just managed to step out of the way.

The man lost his balance and Josh landed a punch on his jaw. The stranger reeled backwards into Silas

Silas picked up something heavy and brought it down on the man's head and he crumpled to the floor like a sack of potatoes.

The rings ascended and a second wave of wraiths marched off the platform towards Rufius and Sabien.

'We could really do with some backup,' shouted the old watchman, taking down the last of the first wave with a shot.

'I'm trying!' growled Eira, hammering at the keyboard. 'He's added another level of security to it since I last used it.'

There was a noise from somewhere behind them, the

retort of automatic weapons. 'Gunsabres,' said Rufius, turning to see Derado and a squad of Draconians running into the chamber. 'About bloody time.'

'It's Templeton,' Lilly said, standing over the capsule. 'He used his wife's maiden name.' Tapping on the name tag. 'The pod has had some kind of failure, but his vitals are stable.'

'Can we wake him?' asked Josh, staring at the complex array of symbols in red triangles scrolling across the glass canopy.

'Do you know how?' replied Silas. 'Without killing him, I mean.'

Lilly shook her head and turned to leave. 'No, but Eira will.'

'Wait.' Silas held up the key. 'She'll need this to disable the generators.'

Lilly's eyes widened, taking the object in both hands as if it were some holy relic.

Josh watched her go before turning back to Silas.

'Who's he?' he asked, looking down at the unconscious man on the floor.

'Doctor Broca, he's a brain surgeon.' Silas pointed to the array of tools. A row of silver surgical instruments were neatly laid out on a cloth in front of a large glass pickling jar.

'What's he doing here?'

'The Syndicate want Templeton's mind. Or rather his memories.'

'And you brought him here?'

Silas looked down at his feet. 'I thought I was doing the right thing. I thought they would be happy that I got them out of prison.'

'Who? Your parents? How did you manage that?'

'I found out that Templeton had a master key, one that he

used for all of his inventions, a safety measure. It can shut anything down.'

Josh looked confused. 'And you decided it was better to let them out rather than save the planet?'

Silas shrugged. 'I came back didn't I?'

'You were made to.'

79

HARD LANDING

Atlas Station, Atlantis.

The *Nautilus* thundered down towards the ground. Juliana's arms ached as she strained to hold her steady, her eyes fixed on the altimeter as the numbers tumbled down towards zero.

'Thomas, I want you to restart the engines on my command.'

'Aye, captain.'

Beads of sweat rolled down her brow as she focused on the altitude. She only had one chance to get this right, the glide plane of the timeship was terrible, it wasn't built for powered flight; she was effectively flying a submarine.

'Three hundred feet,' she whispered to herself, then looked up at her husband 'Full thrust, now!'

He threw the switch. The sound of the turbines took less than a second to reach her ears, but it was the longest moment she had ever experienced.

Pulling up on the controls, she felt the ship respond. 'Come on old girl,' she murmured to herself, praying that the nose would come up.

The ground rushed up to meet them, no one spoke.

Everyone was too scared. With little in the way of landmarks once the mountains had disappeared from view, they had no idea how close they were.

The prow of the ship carved through the deep snow, ploughing a trench over half a mile long before it came to a stop.

Not the most graceful of landings, Juliana thought to herself, but they were safe. She released the cargo bay doors and watched Derado's team make for the base.

'Right,' she said, clapping her hands. 'Time for a cup of tea, I think.'

The others looked at her with expressions of disbelief.

'I think something a little stronger would be appropriate,' replied her husband, who she had never seen look quite so pale.

80

THE KEY

Atlas Station, Atlantis.

When Lilly returned to the main chamber, she found the Dreadnoughts engaged in a heavy firefight with Abandon and his wraith guards. Sabien and Rufius were pinned down behind two of the stone columns and Eira was hunched over one of the consoles. For a second, she thought the old professor was dead.

Inching along the wall, Lilly made her way slowly towards the woman.

Abandon seemed to sense that his key was nearby, his glowing eyes turning towards her.

'NO!' he bellowed, levelling his staff at where she stood. Ribbons of energy curled around its tip like a kindling fire. A red ray of light burst from it, lancing across the space between them. Lilly dived beneath it, rolling to a crouch behind a console as the beam struck the wall and burned a hole into the rock.

Abandon howled and raised his hand to a squad of his soldiers, whose exoskeletons fell to the ground, their spirits suddenly released from their suits.

Lilly froze as the nightmarish creatures raced towards her. They wore the faces of the dead crew like Halloween masks. An icy knot formed in her stomach as she realised what had happened to the missing team members.

'Lilly!' shouted Rufius, breaking her out of her reverie. 'Move!'

He was less than ten feet away, waving his hands as he ran towards her.

She felt the key warm in her hand.

Eira was calling to her too. Swallowing her fear, Lilly pushed herself away from the desk and launched herself over the console to land next to the old woman.

'Templeton's master key!' Eira said, snatching it out of her hand and ramming it into a slot on the main dashboard.

Time seemed to slow as she turned it.

The flashes of gunfire that lit up the room were like fireworks exploding in front of Lilly's eyes. Rufius disappeared under a swarm of wraiths. Their dark tendrils wrapping around his body, cloaking him in night.

The sound of the gravity engines died away like a fading siren and the lights in the time tunnel dimmed and went out.

The suits of Abandon's wraith army crumpled and fell to the floor.

He cried out as his body dissolved, turning to smoke, as did the wraiths that enveloped Rufius.

A strange silence fell over the scene, those Dreadnoughts still standing lowered their weapons and began to search the outer rooms.

'You okay?' asked Eira, getting to her feet.

Lilly nodded. 'Was that really Templeton?'

The old woman shrugged. 'It might have been once. I guess roaming through space for nine thousand years can do that to a man.'

81

REUNION

Atlas Station, Atlantis.

Grandmaster Derado appeared from inside the complex, accompanied by Rufius and Josh.

Caitlin was standing in the open cargo bay with Lyra and Sim. She rushed down the ramp and into Josh's arms.

'You took your time,' he said, kissing her neck.

'Well you can thank Sim for that, you're quite a hard man to find.'

He looked over her shoulder. 'Where's Zack?'

'He's fine. He's with Alixia.'

Josh let her go and turned back towards the base.

'You'll never guess where I've been.'

She narrowed her eyes at him and pursed her lips, studying the features of his face. 'To hell and back by the look of you.'

Josh smiled. 'Close enough.'

Inspector Sabien walked out with Silas in tow, handcuffed

together once more. The officer's jaw was clenched, striding away from the base whilst his prisoner waved at them.

'I heard he broke his folks out of prison,' said Caitlin.

'He released all of the prisoners,' Josh replied. 'Sabien isn't happy. He says there were some seriously dangerous people in there.'

'How did he manage to get away from him?'

Josh shrugged. 'I've no idea. He's a devious one, you can never really tell what he's going to do next.'

She laughed. 'Sounds like someone else I know.'

'I'm not devious'

Caitlin stroked his cheek. 'No, you're not that. Just a little unpredictable.'

82

DPR

Barad-dûr, Shadow Realm

Lyra and Kaori walked into the antechamber of the tomb, it was just as Eira described in her report, a copy of the Martian fortress in every detail. Somehow Templeton had duplicated the stronghold into the Shadow Realm.

The Xenobiology team were already setting up their equipment, high resolution scanner lasers would map every millimetre of the building, which was showing rapid signs of decay now that the power source had been shut down.

'There are other changes too,' Lyra said, holding a flower she picked from the meadow. 'The realm is changing, the paths have stopped shifting.'

'It was like a cancer,' Kaori explained, 'the gravity waves were affecting the fabric of space. I'll be surprised if the whole domain doesn't reset itself.'

Lyra looked a little sad. 'You think it'll disappear altogether?'

The doctor shrugged. 'Maybe, maybe not, my mother used to say, "Tomorrow, tomorrow's wind will blow", I guess we'll just have to wait and see.'

. . .

They walked down into the tomb, where the body of Mal-Shajan still rested in the sarcophagus.

'The Defilers of Draaxon,' Lyra read on the inscription – everyone had intuited the Q'tharian lexicon the moment it had been fully translated. The entire Order had become a little obsessed with all things Martian.

'Were they from Mars?' she asked.

'No, I don't think either species originated from the red planet,' Kaori said, putting on a pair of latex gloves and starting to examine the dead warrior. 'This looks more like an armoured spacesuit, and that sword is made from metals that shouldn't exist.'

'That explains it,' said Lyra, placing the flower on his chest.

'Explains what?'

'The other timeline in Devlin's wraith.'

'Officially we're calling them *Aetherbane*, they've been given their own taxonomy now.'

Lyra pouted. 'I like Nazgûl better.'

Kaori was working on loosening the helmet of the king. 'Anyway, what about the other timeline?'

'It was old. Stretching back further than anything I've ever sensed. It went back into the deep past. Exactly how old is the universe?'

'About thirteen and a half billion years.' She inserted a screwdriver under the side of one of the masks panels.

'Not as much as that,' Lyra replied, frowning. 'Maybe half.'

'You're saying they're six billion years old?'

There was a hiss as the seal broke on the mask and Kaori lifted the plate away.

The grey skin of the face underneath took their breath away.

'I think they both were,' whispered Lyra.

83

THE MOON

Sea of Tranquility, Moon. 6225 BC

'She's listing a little to starboard,' noted Eira. 'Bring her up six degrees.'

'Aye, aye,' replied Juliana, adjusting one of the levers.

The *Nautilus* drifted silently across the pale, cratered surface of the moon. Stirring the dust into eddies, it towed the cargo towards the temporary base established by Lilly and a team of Antiquarians.

Eira's plan was to use one of the ship's spare gravitational engines as a stabiliser to bring the rocky satellite back into line.

The old professor took less than a week to calculate the adjustments required to put the moon back into a correct orbit. Even Professor Eddington was amazed at the speed at which she found a suitable solution.

He stood at the observation window, with the founder.

'I've never understood Templeton's fascination with the outer planets,' the professor admitted, watching the barren landscape roll out beneath them.

The founder sighed. 'We have much still to learn about the

worlds beyond our own, their history leaves many unanswered questions.'

The ship slowed as it approached the dark side.

'Switching to night mode,' declared Juliana over the tannoy system. The lamps dimmed on the observation deck and running lights illuminated the outside view.

'Have you made any progress on the mission logs?' asked the founder.

Eddington nodded. 'Yes, my Lord, it appears that Templeton discovered an ancient civilisation known as the Q'tharians. A race who established an outpost on Mars over four billion years ago. The tomb was both a mausoleum and a prison. It appears that Templeton discovered the remnants of a demonic horde known as Defilers of Draaxon. They were cognivores who devoured the disconnected consciousnesses of his entire team. The Xenobiologysts have classified them as a type four malevolent species, and named them *Aetherbanes*.'

'Hell is empty, and all the devils are here,' the old man quoted.

'Indeed they are,' agreed the professor.

The founder sighed. 'Well, Alexander certainly was an ambitious man.'

'I think he's reach exceeded his grasp.'

'It is a lesson to us all.'

'Our latest predictions show there is a ninety-four per cent probability the linears will attempt a mission to the red planet by 2030. Should we intervene?'

The founder shook his head. 'I doubt there will be much evidence left of the Q'tharians by then. I think we can safely assume that their existence will remain a secret.'

84

———

EPILOGUE

Protectorate HQ

Sabien sat at his desk, browsing through the list of escaped prisoners in his almanac. Some of their names were struck through, indicating they were already safely back in custody. Either because they were too stupid to realise they were carrying a tracking device embedded in their arms when they first arrived at the Château, or because of Silas.

His sentence had been commuted on the understanding that he would help hunt down every convict he inadvertently released.

The inspector was reluctant at first, but he had to admit, the Protectorate had never met a better seeker. Silas's abilities to find a trail were verging on supernatural. He excelled at the chase, even when they covered their tracks so well that even Sabien couldn't follow.

There were already noises being made on the seventy-seventh floor about offering Wormwood a warrant, especially after he assisted in storming the Syndicate headquarters.

• • •

Silas acted as a guide on the raid. His parents were still sleeping off a drunken party when Sabien and a Protectorate team descended on the Conciergerie from the airship.

Over two hundred members of the Dark Guild were apprehended that day including their leader, Rasputin.

Silas was present when they brought the captives into custody. He watched his mother and father being processed through one-way glass.

'They're not who I thought they were,' Silas answered when one of the other officers asked what made him give them up. 'I remembered them differently.'

But Sabien was not completely convinced of the man's rehabilitation. He was a born survivor, doing whatever it took to get by.

At the bottom of the page he reached the most wanted man on the list: L'Oscurità, "the Darkness", still remained at large. One of the deadliest assassins in history had disappeared from time. No one could find him – not even Silas.

Sabien would not rest until he was caught.

85

MISSION LOGS OF MARS

The following is a transcript from the Mars Mission log of the Chronometric Institute

MISSION LOG:
Scientific Director Templeton
Atlas Station

Mission Day 35:

Finally, we have received data from one of the probes. We now have a reference point in time to target the tunnel and commence to the second phase of the project.

Mission Day 60:

The initial tests of the displacement array have proved we can successfully deploy the equipment to the target era. Miller has confirmed that the telemetry from the autonomous unit was received and the base factory construction programme could commence.

. . .

Mission Day 75:

Recently, the quantum tunnel has shown signs of instability, similar to those issues we encountered during the latter stages of the moon deployment. Fluctuations in the earth's magnetosphere require constant adjustment. The engineering team are working on enhancing the gravitational dampening to compensate. Work continues on the Mars base. The manufacture of twenty autonomous units per week now looks realistic. The quality of the raw materials for the production has proved to be higher than originally expected.

Mission Day 88:

The results from the initial samples collected from the local fauna show that Mars could indeed support life four billion years ago. The atmosphere is a rich mixture of Carbon Dioxide, Water Vapour and Hydrogen – not viable for humans.

Mission Day 94:

Further issues with the stability of the tunnel have continued to frustrate the project. It seems unlikely that we will be able to deploy a team directly onto the surface, but Miller has been working on a remote connection that would allow us to 'virtually' experience the Martian world.

Mission Day 100:

I have long suspected that there would be a limit to how far a human body can travel through time. The continued exposure of gravimetric forces during temporal displacement can be extremely detrimental to our physiology, especially over such an extended period. My research has proven there to be a finite limit to our ability to cross vast distances through time and space; somewhere in the region of a seven hundred and fifty million years to be precise. The mind however, that is an infinitely more resilient piece of apparatus. By detaching the consciousness from its physical shell, I have been able to travel across the known universe and beyond. I have walked on distant planets. Watched nameless stars form and seen them die.

Mission Day 129:

Initial tests of the virtual remote viewing have proved successful. Miller has fashioned a headset connected directly to the video feed from the autonomous units. I have seen the planet as it once was, a rich and verdant land. We are accelerating the autonomous manufacture, Miller and Kellerman are currently working on a neural link that will allow us to connect directly with the cybernetic feeds from the robots.

Mission Day 150:

The gravitational fluctuations are becoming increasingly difficult to control. I have instructed engineering to run an analysis of the cause. They are confident that it can be controlled. Miller and Kellerman demonstrated the prototype of the neural links, much like a stasis pod, it utilises the data stream of the tunnel to provide a near simultaneous experience.

Mission Day 155:

The first of the test neural deployments has been completed. It was a great success. Miller is the first human consciousness to stand on the surface of Mars. He is complaining of headaches and nightmares. Doctor Tennison has prescribed a sedative and the medical team are making a number of adjustments to the equipment.

I have approved the production of twelve units and begun the selection process for the first and second away teams.

Mission Day 175:

Miller is not well. Tennison has had to sedate him. He's delusional, complaining of seeing nightmarish creatures.

The doctor has concerns that it may be as a result of the neural link, but none of the other members of the away teams have reported any issues during their training. I have decided to continue on that basis.

Mission Day 200:

The first team of six have completed their first mission to Mars. We now preparing to explore the area around the main base. Drone reconnaissance has shown there to be a number of key sites that exhibit unnatural geological structures.

Mission Day 202:

Miller has disappeared. I have instructed security to lockdown the base until he is discovered.

Mission Day 205:

The second away team has discovered what appears to be a monumental structure five miles from the main base and are planning to set up an excavation camp.

Engineering has presented a series of modifications to the gravity generators that should stabilise the fluctuation issue.

• • •

Mission Day 220:

Miller has still not been found.

Mission Day 222:

Exciting news: The away team have discovered signs of a previous civilisation. The structure appears to be a tomb. I have ordered the first team to join them and have begun production of more avatars. The crew are very excited at this discovery, as am I. There is irrefutable evidence of an ancient Martian culture.

Mission Day 224:

The team have made significant progress with the excavation. I now think it is time for me to take charge personally.

Mission day 226:

The tomb has been opened. We are still working on translating the hieroglyphics, but it is clear that this was once the tomb of a great king.

Mission Day 230:

I have discovered something wonderful on the red planet, something that will change our understanding of this universe. There are remnants of a great civilisation, one that left this plane many billions of years ago.

Mission Day 238:

The upgrades to the generator have been completed and are scheduled to come online in the next few hours.

. . .

Mission Day 239:

There have been significant complications with the upgrade to the generators. The entire base is now under threat. We have lost contact with the outside world. All communications are down. Engineering believes we may have actually left the continuum. The temperature outside has plummeted, leading me to believe we may have relocated to the Cryogenian.

Mission Day 240:

The generators are no longer responding to our commands. Engineering have lost control. An evacuation is now our only hope. My plan is to put everyone into stasis and relocate to Mars.

Mission Day 260:

This is Edward Miller, sole survivor of the Atlas project. There is something terrible on Mars. Something that should never have been set free. Alexander has taken them all there to die.

The Defilers are coming for us all.

LOG ENDS.

Other books in the Infinity Engines universe.

The Infinity Engines

1. Anachronist

2. Maelstrom

3. Eschaton

4. Aeons

5. Tesseract

6. Contagion

7. Tempest

Infinity Engines Origins

Chimæra

Changeling

Infinity Engines Missions

1776

1888

Victoria Rex

BONUS BOOK

If you would like to be kept up to date on future stories and learn more about the world of The Infinity Engines plus get a FREE ebook, please join my mailing list here:

books.infinityengines.com/VictoriaRex

ACKNOWLEDGEMENTS

This series would not exist without the tireless support of my family. I am forever grateful for their patience.

To the usual suspects: Karen, Simon, Dee and the beta readers team, who helped to find the snags, plot holes and typos, my thanks to you all.

And to you my dear reader, I hope you enjoyed the book, please feel free to join my community and let me know what you thought of it. And on that note, if you would be so kind as to leave a review on Amazon that would be most appreciated.

Cheers,
Andy x

ABOUT THE AUTHOR

For more information about The Infinity Engines series and other Here Be Dragons books please visit:
www.infinityengines.com

www.ingramcontent.com/pod-product-compliance
Lightning Source LLC
Chambersburg PA
CBHW030920120726
47906CB00002B/414